Unhidden

THE GATEKEEPER CHRONICLES
Book One

DINA M. GIVEN

UNHIDDEN
The Gatekeeper Chronicles, Book #1
by Dina M. Given

Publisher: Team D Enterprises, LLC

ISBN: 0692342087 (ISBN13: 9780692342084)

Cover Design by Hang Le (www.byhangle.com)

Editing by C&D Editing (www.cdediting.weebly.com)

Copyediting by SJS Editorial Design
(www.facebook.com/SJSEditorialDesign)

Formatting by Wicked Book Covers
(www.wickedbookcovers.com)

Illustrations by Celia Connaire, Black-Haired Demon
Illustration (www.blackhaireddemon.com)

To my loving husband and two children who didn't complain too much when I came home from my day job just to start working my night job writing this book. Juggling is tough, and I couldn't have done without their support. I love you guys!

Chapter One

COLD MARBLE PRESSED against my face, numbing my cheek. My stomach roiled from the spinning of the room, threatening to release my dinner. I took a deep, ragged breath and tried to keep the dizziness under control. A voice in my head screamed at me to get up and defend myself, but my body wouldn't obey. With a herculean effort, I pulled my legs under me in an effort to rise.

I felt the vibration in the floor before I heard the heavy thud of footsteps. The bastard was back for more. *It must be my lucky day.* A vice clamped around my ankles, and I slid along the smooth stone floors of the mansion. Crystal chandeliers and Renaissance paintings streaked across my vision as I was pulled through an open doorway.

I twisted and flailed, scrabbling to clutch the doorframe to stop my relentless slide into the darkened room. I tried to make it a rule to never be forced into a room when I didn't know what lay within.

I managed a weak handhold on the doorframe, but with a sharp tug, my captor caused me to easily lose my grip. He—because only a man could own hands that large and strong—"accidentally" slammed me into a coffee table before coming to a stop without releasing me.

The concussive grenade that was triggered when I had been finishing my sweep of the last room in the mansion had left my temples throbbing, preventing me from lifting my head to get a good look at my captor. I needed to pull myself together if I was going to fight my way out of here.

Swallowing hard, I took a silent inventory of my injuries: a few bruises, no broken bones, no bleeding. Sweet. This was going to be easier than I'd thought.

Compartmentalizing the pain—a trick I had learned years ago in the Special Forces—I readied myself to twist sharply to the side in an effort to release my ankles and make a run for it. Then another set of bear paws clamped down hard around my wrists, pulling them over my head. *Crap!* This would make escape a bit more difficult, although not necessarily impossible. I simply had to be patient enough to wait for an opening, and patience was not one of my virtues.

"I know you are thinking about trying to escape, Miss Hayes. I would advise you against it," said a smooth, male voice. He spoke very proper Queen's English, as if he came from old money and would never dream of using a contraction. It made me think of those period British romance movies like *Sense and Sensibility*. I pictured him wearing a Victorian tailcoat and ascot, with a smarmy-looking mustache adorning his face.

I managed to lift my head a few centimeters off the hardwood floor. With my feet and the person holding them hidden in deep shadows, it was impossible to make out anything more than a crouched, hulking figure.

The English man was sitting in a cozy-looking, red leather armchair. A colorful Tiffany lamp cast a dim glow that didn't extend very far into the room, and a thick folder sat next to it on the table.

When the Brit leaned forward, the scant light illuminating his features, I recognized him at once.

"Mr. Darko, I must say, it's quite a surprise to see you here." My visions of Hugh Grant disappeared, replaced by the sight of the father who had hired me to find and recover his little girl, Sarah.

Vincent Darko wasn't wearing coat tails, but his well-tailored gray suit probably cost more than my Ducati. He wasn't unattractive, yet I wouldn't describe him as handsome. He was slim, almost slight, with an effeminate air about him. Maybe it was the way he crossed his legs at the knees or the way his hands hung a little limp at the wrists. Coupled with that egotistical over-confidence, he had the air of a man trying to prove he was no longer the little kid who could be bullied on the playground.

"Did you grow a set of balls and choose to find your daughter on your own?"

He chuckled deeply in response, though the amusement never reached his eyes. "I'm glad to see that, even in your current predicament, you haven't lost your usual charm."

"Oh, I've been in worse situations." I managed a small shrug, which also served to test the grip of my captor who had my wrists. It was solid, but he clenched tighter for a moment when I moved, telling me he was somewhat relaxed and not holding me as tightly as he could have been. "So, what brings you to the Mexican jungle? Wait, let me guess. Your daughter never was kidnapped, was she?" I made a show of eyeing him up and down. "I actually have a hard time believing any woman would have sex with you, so I'm willing to bet Sarah doesn't even exist, does she?"

"Oh, but that's where you are wrong. Come!" he called, like he was commanding an unruly puppy.

The child who emerged from the shadows was a scrawny, bedraggled little thing. Her emaciated frame gave her the appearance of a six-year-old, not the ten-year-old that Darko had claimed her to be. Tear tracks stained her grimy cheeks, and she was hunched over, hugging herself, her matted hair falling into her face.

I ground my teeth together as I looked upon her. A fury rose up through my gut and threatened to explode, but it would have been impotent in my current situation. I choked it back down, holding it in reserve for the right time.

"I did need sufficient motivation to get you here, after all, and most humans seem to have a soft spot for these little creatures," Darko said.

Humans? His odd word use put a chill on my fury. What was that supposed to mean?

Not only was Darko a jackass, he may also be a little crazy. In my experience, crazy was dangerous because of its unpredictability. I needed to break the hold on my wrists and ankles, overpower the guards, grab the girl, and make my way out while avoiding pursuit and capture. That was a tall order, even for me.

I did have accomplices outside of the building; however, Darko would have known I hadn't come alone. He knew I had assembled a small team for this mission. His men were likely scouting the surrounding jungle, looking for Jason and Daniel right now. I assumed they hadn't been found yet; otherwise, Darko would use them as hostages against me to more easily get whatever he wanted. If Jason and Daniel hadn't been compromised, they would come for me when our pre-arranged twenty minutes was up and I didn't show. So, at most, I only had to stall for about another eight minutes.

I forcibly relaxed my body. I needed my captors as loose and off-guard as possible. "Besides my obviously sparkling personality, why else would you want to bring me here?"

"Possibly for nothing." He paused, a small smile tugging at one corner of his mouth. "And possibly for everything." He reached for the folder and slowly opened it without taking his eyes from me. The cover of the folder was labeled TOP SECRET: DESERT FIRE. That didn't ring any bells for me, and I knew about most of the top-secret military operations conducted in the last century. Darko lowered his gaze to the top sheet of paper and began reading. "Emma Hayes, female, brown hair, green eyes, five-foot-four, birth date unknown." He paused dramatically on that last statement. "How is it that your birth date is unknown?" he asked with false curiosity.

"I know what my birth date is. But don't you know it's rude to ask a woman her age?"

He ignored me and continued, "You were in a car accident at the age of sixteen that killed your parents and put you in a coma for one year. Upon awakening, you exhibited severe memory loss. After rehabilitation, you went into the foster system." He looked up at me, clucking his tongue. "That must be quite disconcerting."

"I appreciate your heartfelt concern, but that was a long time ago, and I turned out just fine." I tried to sound flippant, ignoring the sudden and familiar tightness in my chest.

"That remains to be seen. So, tell me, how does a young woman such as yourself join the military, get accepted into the Army Special Forces' Delta Force unit, and then become a mercenary for hire?"

"Why don't you free my hands and I'll show you?"

"I am certain you are quite impressive."

"I assure you, I am. Thanks for the trip down memory lane, but I could have told you all of that back in New York, without being restrained."

"What I need from you isn't in New York. As for being restrained, I doubt you would have come willingly if you knew what I had planned for you."

"Why don't you enlighten me?"

"Oh, but I rather like surprises." He steepled his fingers under his chin and stared hard at me, as if trying to discover my secrets by sight alone. "You were a very difficult woman to find, Miss Hayes. Even after all this effort, I am still unconvinced you are the one we have been looking for. However, my employer is quite adamant that you are. No matter. We shall find out soon enough." He looked past me to the goon who was holding my wrists and nodded.

It was time for me to go, or I may not get another chance. I grabbed onto my captor's large wrists. Using him for leverage,

I jerked my knees up, breaking the hold on my ankles. Before anyone could react, my legs went up and over my head, wrapping around the neck of the one holding my wrists. I squeezed my thighs, trying to pop his head like a grape.

Men usually panicked at the asphyxiation and started clawing at my legs to loosen them. This one didn't seem affected by my squeeze play at all; however, he didn't like me wrapped around his neck. Clamping his ham hands around my thighs, he pried them apart much more easily than should have been possible.

Placing my palms on the floor, I pulled my knees into my chest and donkey-kicked him in the gut. A deep rumble rose from the shadows, guttural and hungry. I imagined it was what a giant prehistoric bear would have sounded like.

I landed on my feet, spinning into a roundhouse kick. Making contact with my captor's thick skull, I knocked him to the floor, silencing his growl.

I leapt away and found the wall with my back so I could scan the entire room. Darko still sat in his chair, looking very focused yet also entirely too unconcerned at the activity around him.

Oozing out of the darkness, the brute that had been holding my ankles revealed himself ... and he wasn't human.

I froze, dumbfounded by what I was looking at. The creature stood about six and a half feet tall, all sinuous muscles. He had a humanoid shape with arms, legs, torso, and head, all where they were supposed to be, though that was where the similarities ended. He was completely hairless with arms that hung to his knees, ending in large, clawed hands. His knee joints were bent the wrong way, and a long, black tongue snaked out from a lipless, gaping maw.

My addled brain screamed, *Weapon. Find a fucking weapon!*

Military training kicking in, I compartmentalized what I was seeing for processing at a later time, focusing only on survival. I grabbed for the radio in my vest pocket and realized it was missing. They must have taken it off me when they had dragged me into the room. My head had been so fuzzy at the time I hadn't even noticed. Okay, so I was on my own. It certainly wasn't the first time.

Instead of running for the door, as I was sure they expected, I leapt toward Darko and grabbed the Tiffany lamp off the table at his side. Swinging it like a bat, the cord unplugged from the wall, plunging the room into complete darkness. My senses went on high alert, straining to hear the sounds of movement coming closer. All was silent.

I held the lamp in my right hand and felt for the table with my left. I found it quickly and followed it around to the back of Darko's chair in an effort to put a barrier between the creature and me.

I knew I was at a serious disadvantage on all fronts. This thing was clearly bigger, badder, and stronger than I was, and at the moment, I had nothing to fight it with other than an expensive, decorative lamp. I didn't even know the layout of the room. I could easily run into unseen obstacles. I needed something to give me an advantage.

Suddenly, that bear-like growl caught my attention. Then I heard shuffling and rustling noises coming from the far corner of the room. I could only guess it was my second captor, the one I had sent sprawling with a roundhouse kick.

If I had thought one monster was going to be difficult to beat, two of them were going to be virtually impossible. My only chance was to make it back into the hallway and to my gun, where it probably still lay after they had knocked it from my hands.

I could feel them circling me, readying an attack from either side. I heard the groan of floorboards getting too close.

"Are you just about ready to concede, Miss Hayes?" Darko's smooth voice oozed out of the darkness, causing me to flinch. I was glad no one had seen that. "Or would you like to play the odds, which I can assure you are not in your favor?"

Unwilling to admit defeat, I realized I still had my night vision goggles propped on top of my head. I reached up and slowly eased them over my eyes. "Actually, Darko, I don't like to gamble, so I think I'm going to change the game." Even as I adjusted to the contrasting black and white images, I sensed the first creature more than saw it.

I swung the lamp at where I judged its head to be, but it lifted an arm to block the attack, and I ended up hitting its forearm instead. The glass lampshade shattered into thousands of colorful shards. Darko raised his arms over his head to try to protect himself from the raining glass, yet he remained seated in his leather chair, like a king on his throne.

Using the distraction, I leaned over the back of the chair and wrapped the electrical cord around Darko's neck. Holding the chord and using the back of the chair as leverage, I vaulted myself up and over, landing gracefully to face Darko.

His hands flew to his neck, trying to loosen the cord, but I leaned back, tightening the noose, not giving him a chance to get his fingers underneath it. He wheezed and gurgled, trying to suck in a breath, as I lifted him from his seat by pulling roughly on the cord. I twisted him so his back was to my front, using him as a hostage and human shield. Then I backed toward the door that led to the hallway … and to my gun.

The two creatures were following, but cautiously, staying back a few feet without making any sudden moves. Rumbling growls sounded deep in their chests.

"Hey, kid," I called to the child who still stood hunched in on herself, trying to stay out of the way of the fighting. Her head snapped up at the sound of my voice, but I couldn't see the expression on her face through the goggles. "Do you know how to find your way out of the building?" When she gave a small nod, I continued, "Don't stop running until you are through the front gate. I have friends out there who will help you. Go!" At that, she darted through the door and down the hall in the direction I had come from. I knew Jason would see her in his sniper riflescope and clear a path for her through the gate if she was pursued.

"Call off your goons, Darko, or I'm going to squeeze the life out of you and enjoy doing it." I tightened the noose, emphasizing my point.

He responded with another gurgle, so I loosened up on the cord just enough to allow him to speak. He gasped for air and hoarsely said, "You're doing well, Miss Hayes, but you will not succeed in escaping."

I jerked the cord tight again, continuing to back toward the dimly lit corridor. My head spun to the left and right, eyes darting around for my weapon. As my hands grew clammy at the thought of being defenseless, I finally saw it about fifty feet down the hall to my left.

That's when someone flipped on the lights. White light burned into my retinas. A spotlight flared behind my closed lids, shards of pain driving into my eyeballs. With my hands on Darko's leash, I was unable to remove the night vision goggles.

Darko suddenly dropped to the floor and twisted, pulling the cord from my hands and rolling away from me. The two creatures were on me instantly. One backhanded me across the face, knocking my goggles off and sending me careening down the hallway. The wall rushed up to stop my slide, stinging my back. I could feel my face swelling up, and I wiped a trickle of blood off my cheek. Luckily, I landed that much closer to my weapon.

Before I could measure my next move, the creature dove at me. When I rolled to the side, it missed crushing my chest with its bulk, but it landed on my left shoulder, dislocating it. Lightning pain shot through my arm, and I let out a sharp cry.

Claws, teeth, and a slavering black tongue rose over me as I lay prone on the floor. It could have easily ripped my throat out or killed me in a dozen hideous ways. It seemed to realize this, too. Its jaw cracked and popped, unhinging so wide it could make a meal of my head in one bite. Hot, putrid saliva dripped onto my face, leaking into my open wound and searing it like acid. I hissed at the sensation and turned away; however, I couldn't escape its fetid breath.

It leaned in, eager and hungry, while I was frozen. I would meet death in the jaws of an inhuman beast. It would drink my blood, feast on my organs, and gnaw on my bones for dessert.

Darko's hoarse voice called from down the hall. "Don't kill her! We need her."

The thing paused and let out a high-pitched wail of anger at being deprived of its dinner. The sound shattered my fear.

I threw up a knee, violently slamming it in the creature's crotch. Thankfully, it was humanoid enough, that it had the same effect as any other male. He howled and rolled off me into the fetal position. I immediately scrambled backward, sliding along the marble floor. My left arm, screaming in pain, remained limp at my side.

With my right arm, I reached over my head to grab the gun. As my fingers wrapped around the grip, the familiar feeling was like coming home again.

I pointed the Glock down the length of my body, and without a moment's hesitation, I pulled the trigger in three quick, precise squeezes. The head of the creature I had nut-cracked exploded in a spray of blood and gore.

Shifting the gun's sight, I found the second creature barreling down the hall toward me. The first three shots hit him square in the chest, yet he hardly slowed. I lifted the gun slightly, took a deep breath and held it, then squeezed the trigger, putting a round straight through its eye and into its brain. That time, it stumbled yet still kept coming. I put four more rounds into its head, not missing a shot, before it finally crashed to the floor only inches shy of my feet.

Darko merely stood there, a sly half-smile tugging at the corner of his mouth while I unsteadily got to my feet, pushing myself up with my gun hand. Despite the fact that Darko carried no weapon I could see, for a moment, I considered shooting him. He had set me up, kidnapped an innocent girl, and commanded those creatures. Even though he had stopped them from killing me, I was sure he wouldn't hesitate if he got what he wanted from me.

With him only a few yards away, I had a clear shot. I pointed my weapon at him, and for the first time today, he reacted. The blood drained from his face, his eyes darting around, seeking escape. He quickly came to the same conclusion I had—there was no escape for him.

My finger tightened on the trigger, but before I could get off the shot, a large animal bounded from the shadows behind him. It leapt past Darko, springing at me on all fours. I didn't have much time to take it in, but it looked like a cross between a bear and a crocodile. It was the size of a bear with dry, scaly skin, and a mouth full of sharp teeth. Two tusks extended from the roof of its mouth, past its jaw. It bellowed like a foghorn as it charged.

I discharged the shots meant for Darko at this new monster; however, they bounced off its tough hide like harmless insects.

Turning, I sprinted for the exit and all but flew down the stairs, taking three and four at a time. The beast slid past the stairs, slamming into a wall as it tried to slow its momentum, buying me a few seconds.

I hit the foyer and flew through the open front door. I could only pray Jason still had his sniper rifle at the ready and was looking through his scope at that moment.

The beast charged through the front doors behind me, gaining quickly now that it had more room to maneuver. I didn't hear the crack of rifle shots, thanks to Jason's silencer, but the beast crashed to the ground like a fallen tree. It slid several feet from momentum, coming to a stop directly behind my fleeing form. I hadn't realized how close it had been. Only a few seconds more, and I would have been a goner.

I slowed and stopped, turning toward where I knew Jason was hiding in the trees, giving a small wave of thanks. Barely sparing a glance at the creature, not wanting to acknowledge its existence in my world, I staggered to the gate, my chest heaving under the exertion of that sprint.

A small figure stepped out of the shadows directly in front of me, moving with uncertainty. My gun was up in an instant. Seeing the little girl, I jerked the barrel away from her and re-holstered the gun.

"Hey, sweetie. Why didn't you run out of here like I told you to?" She simply dipped her head, averting her eyes. I kneeled in front of her and tried to sound reassuring. "You don't have anything to worry about now. You're safe, and I'm going to get you out of here."

As she slowly lifted her head, I looked into her serious face yet didn't find the eyes of a child—not a human child, at least. Her pupils shifted into cat-like slits. Gone was the terrified little girl, and in her place was a cold, calculating creature. I registered momentary shock, but that was about all the time I had to react.

She struck as fast as a viper. I felt a piercing sting in my neck before it began to numb, the sensation radiating out from the wound and spreading throughout my body as her venom pumped quickly through my bloodstream. My body instantly went slack, and I toppled onto my side.

Anger overwhelmed the fear. I sure as hell wasn't going to go down without taking Darko with me. Although it took considerable will to move my quickly numbing fingers, I fumbled clumsily at a vest pocket. It took a few tries, but I finally managed to grasp the small, green box and pull it out. With the last of my strength, I squeezed the trigger. The C-4 explosives I had planted in each room of the mansion before my capture detonated with a deafening boom. The entire west wing of the building was transformed into an inferno.

The force of the blast threw the girl backward, and I heard a sickening crunch as she slammed into the stone wall surrounding the compound. I wanted to smile at having wiped both Darko and the child creature from the face of the earth, but my facial muscles wouldn't respond.

Unfortunately, my satisfaction was ended prematurely. Watching the flames as choking, black smoke poured forth from every window, a lone figure emerged from the front door of the mansion. The figure moved through the devastation unscathed, as if surrounded by an impenetrable bubble. Sparks appeared in the air close to the figure, ripples spreading out from them. I realized that Jason was shooting, and the bullets were bouncing off some sort of shield.

Whoever, whatever it was, approached me purposefully.

As it came nearer, I groaned inwardly, my lips and vocal cords no longer able to make a sound. Darko. How was he doing this?

Before I could contemplate the strange sight further, he reached me and knelt down. Putting his face close to mine, he whispered, "You have done well, Miss Hayes. Now we shall see who you really are." At that, my consciousness shut down, and I plunged into a deep well of peaceful silence.

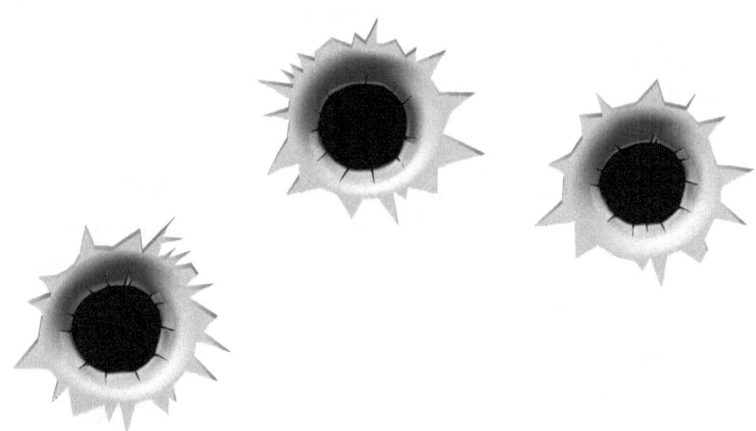

Chapter Two

A DULL ACHE crowded my consciousness, nudging me awake. The more I tried to ignore it, the more insistent it became, until the throbbing was the only thing I could think about. I tried to take my mind off it by inventorying the rest of my aches and pains.

My face was swollen and cheeks stiff with dried blood from a cut on my temple. A piercing burn on my neck screamed at me as blood pulsed through my jugular. The worst was my shoulder as it swelled within my constrictive body armor. A small movement of my arm confirmed that someone had pushed the dislocated bone back into its socket, and I was forever grateful I had been unconscious when it had been done. Finally, rough hemp rope scratched and burned the sensitive skin of my wrists and ankles.

Despite the sweat trickling down my temple, my back felt cool. My fingertips found the unforgiving surface of polished stone. I was stretched out on a slab, tied down with the bonds that scratched my skin raw. They were well-knotted, leaving no room to wiggle my hands free.

Slippered feet shuffled along a bare floor, soft as the crinkling of tissue paper. I could make out the familiar creak of leather and buckles as well as the faint smell of gun oil. All of these sounds had a hollow, echoed quality to them as objects clinked and clattered while a sharp crash sounded close to my head. I tried hard not to wince and give away my awakening.

Dammit. How the hell had I gotten myself into this mess? More importantly, how the hell was I supposed to get myself out of it? Where were Daniel and Jason? If they had followed my orders back at the compound, they would have been outside the gates when I had been taken. I knew Jason had tried to save me from Darko by shooting at him yet couldn't penetrate whatever was protecting him. It sounded pretty crazy to call it a "deflector shield"—that made me think of Star Trek.

The compound was probably a smoldering heap of ash now, so Darko must have moved me somewhere else. However, Daniel and Jason wouldn't have allowed him to take me away in a vehicle without trying to stop it.

What if Darko had killed them? That would mean no one knew where I was and there would be no cavalry coming to the rescue. That thought was momentarily terrifying, until I quashed it. I had been in worse jams, although not by much, and I wasn't about to give up without a fight.

I replayed every interaction I'd had with Darko since he had first approached me about this job back in New York, trying to find what I had missed. Daniel had dug deep into his background, using all of the electronic resources at his disposal, which were fairly considerable. It had all checked out.

Either Darko really was legit, or he had enormously vast resources to pull off a con on this scale. And to what end? What did he need from me? Sure, I was a soldier, a sniper, and quite talented at kicking ass—if I do say so myself—but there were plenty of other soldiers who were at or even above my level.

Other than my military skills, I didn't have much that set me apart. I didn't even have important connections that Darko could leverage. The best I had was a close contact in the U.S. Government's Procurement Department, which was less than impressive or useful.

I lifted my eyelids just a crack so no one in the room would notice. It was difficult to make out many details through my lashes. All I could see without moving my head was a flat, featureless wall the color of sand. Opening my eyes fully, I got a complete picture of the absolutely shitty predicament I was currently stuck in.

I was in a small, rounded cave, lying opposite the opening. There were lit torches mounted in sconces every few feet along the wall. Their flickering glow cast eerie dancing shadows on the rough hewn stone. It was slightly cooler in the cave than it had been outside, but I was still covered in a sheen of sweat. It was entirely possible that the sweating was due to fear rather than humidity though.

On either side of the cave entrance stood two guards— human this time, or so they appeared. They were wearing standard issue camouflage and bulletproof vests, holding

AK-47 assault rifles across their chests, fingers close to the triggers. I could see at least three more armed guards outside, patrolling by the entrance.

My eyes darted around the space, looking for monsters in the shadows. I would be at their mercy in my current condition, and I doubted they even knew what mercy meant. I had barely escaped the last ones with my life. If that little girl had wanted to kill me, she could have done so with no trouble at all. I desperately hoped I was surrounded only by your everyday human scum of the earth.

I shuddered involuntarily when my eyes landed on a hideous monstrosity in the room. A crone was busily moving around the stone slab I was tied to. She wore a tattered robe of deep black with the cowl turned down so I could get a good look at her unfortunate features. She looked like a creepy old woman from nightmares and horror films. Her face was deeply wrinkled and as pale as death. Her baggy eyes were bloodshot, rimmed with wet redness. One eye was enlarged and milky white, clearly blind, and her dirty, gray hair was sparse and stringy, sticking out of her pate in clumps. Her teeth were brown and crooked with gaps in places where many of them had rotted away.

Around her neck, she wore an amulet that immediately drew my attention away from her appearance. Hanging from a heavy chain rested a circle of gold. It had nicks and dents around the edges that hinted at significant use across generations. The gold was etched with swirls and shapes that weren't recognizable to me as anything more than elaborate decoration. They enrobed an aquiline gem, the deep greens and blues of a tropical sea. In its heart, I thought I saw movements as subtle as smoke and shadow.

Vertigo overwhelmed me, the sensation of drowning in those watery depths, and I yanked my gaze away quickly. I was breathing heavily, my heart racing.

The old woman placed leaves, twigs, and powders upon smoldering coal briquettes in the bowls that were evenly spaced along my stone slab. They released the pungent odors of sandalwood, masala, cinnamon, and lavender. They weren't unpleasant individually, but when the fragrances combined, it overwhelmed my senses, making me lightheaded and slightly nauseous. I took deep breaths to stave off the sensation that I was suffocating, yearning for fresh, cool air.

Just when I thought I had the nausea under control, Darko appeared at the cave's entrance. He looked almost comically out of place in this dank cave, wearing his neatly tailored suit.

"Miss Hayes, I trust that you are comfortable?" He smirked, approaching my altar.

"Well, it's no Ritz Carlton, and the bed is a bit firm, but as long as I get the free breakfast in the morning, I'm good," I retorted in that same falsely pleasant tone.

"I do apologize for the less than luxurious accommodations, but I will make every effort to ensure you do not have to suffer these conditions for much longer. The Bruja has become very efficient at these ceremonies. After all, she has been officiating sacrifices and blood rituals for hundreds of years." When he nodded his head toward the old woman in what looked like a sign of respect, she did nothing to acknowledge his complement.

"Oh, good. I feel better knowing an experienced professional is handling my blood sacrifice. Hey, since we are having such a pleasant conversation, why don't you let me in on why you are doing all of this?"

He gave a brief chuckle. "Do you think this as a James Bond movie, Miss Hayes? Should I go off on a lengthy soliloquy, revealing all of my dastardly plans, buying you precious time until you are able to free yourself or until the cavalry arrives? None of those things are going to happen, so you may want to take this time to come to terms with your fate."

Never! I hissed in my head, startling myself with the ferocity of my own thoughts. I had been on the verge of falling prey to my fears until I had heard that single word.

I turned away from Darko so he couldn't see the defiance in my eyes. I needed him and his goons to believe I was defeated. I brought forth crocodile tears and trembling lips.

He must have bought the act because he simply said to the Bruja, "It is time. Please begin."

I took a deep breath. The clock had run down, and I was no closer to an escape plan than I had been when I awoke.

The Bruja stood over me, her arms held high, the sleeves of her robes sliding to the shoulders. Stick-thin arms were threaded through with blue veins. Her eyes lifted to the ceiling and her soft voice steadily became stronger and louder. At first, I thought she was speaking Spanish, but I knew a little Spanish and couldn't make out anything of what she was saying.

She lowered her arms and reached into her robes, withdrawing a wicked-looking knife. It must have been twelve-inches long with a blade made of obsidian, so black it seemed to absorb the light around it. Its ornate handle was carved of jade, depicting a woman on her hands and knees with the obsidian blade protruding from her open mouth. The handle was tightly wrapped with a red, leather cord. I didn't know the significance of the knife, but I could take a pretty good guess that it was some type of sacrificial weapon.

I stared wide-eyed at the object as the Bruja held it point down over my chest. Her chanting steadily grew to a crescendo while my heart palpitated rapidly and my breathing became so loud it drowned out all other sound in the room. My chest wrenched at the thought of that knife plunging into it. I desperately wanted to curl into a fetal position to protect myself; however, I was completely immobilized by the ropes.

Far too soon, the knife plunged downward. I squeezed my eyes shut and tried to turn away, hoping death would come quickly.

The pain was sharp and searing … but I felt it on my wrist. I looked down at my arm, which was being held by the Bruja in a vice grip. She set the knife on the stone slab near my shoulder, apparently no longer needing it.

The cut was deep, maybe dangerously so, my blood flowing steadily as the Bruja collected it in a roughly-crafted clay bowl. The room spun and my head felt like it wanted to float off my shoulders.

A thought entered my sluggish brain that the bowl was filling up very quickly. She would need to hurry and grab another. Apparently, the Bruja decided one bowl was enough because she dropped my arm unceremoniously when it was full. I could feel the thick, warm liquid dripping off my fingertips.

She then lifted the bowl above her head with more chanting. I rubbed my eyes and forehead in an effort to clear away the cobwebs when it slowly dawned on me that my wrist was free. The Bruja had cut through my bonds when she had sliced into my wrist. I quickly dropped my arm again, hoping no one had noticed. The Bruja was still looking up to the ceiling, and the two guards were dutifully watching outside, ignoring the proceedings. Darko was intent on the bowl of blood in the Bruja's hands, his eyes focused and shining.

She placed the bowl on the table next to me and removed the mesmerizing blue amulet from her neck, submerging it in my blood. Darko leaned in a little closer, his face alit with eager anticipation.

When the Bruja removed the amulet from the bowl, the stone absorbed my blood like a thirsty sponge. In a matter of seconds, every trace of blood was sucked into the heart of the gem, turning it from an aqua blue to a deep indigo.

Darko sucked in a breath and looked down at me with a shit-eating grin on his face. He had opened his mouth to say something when his expression quickly transformed into shock then anger. He turned away from me to face the cave entrance. That was when I noticed three precisely placed holes in his back that looked curiously like they had come from a long-range assault rifle. I had no idea how he was still standing, let alone fiercely screaming to his guards.

"They have come for her. Kill them!"

All the guards ran into the surrounding jungle, searching for the attackers. When I heard the sounds of rapid gunfire, I took that as my signal to act.

While Darko's back was turned, I reached up with my free hand and grabbed the Bruja by the neck of her robe, slamming my forehead into her much more sensitive nose. As she staggered backward, stunned and bleeding, I grabbed the knife that was lying at my shoulder and quickly sliced through the rope binding my other wrist.

Darko came at me as I fully sat up, and I took the opportunity to jab my free elbow into his jaw. However, he barely seemed to take notice of the blow, shaking it off. As his eyes landed on mine, I wielded the knife menacingly at him. The gunfire sounded closer, and Darko glanced quickly toward the cave entrance, considering his next move. I could almost see his train of thought. He could stay in the cave and spend precious minutes trying to subdue me while my team got closer to our location, but there was a good chance they would come crashing through the entrance with semi-automatic weapons at any moment.

Although it appeared a few bullets shot at a distance caused him no harm—for some incomprehensible reason that I put off trying to assimilate until another time—I was willing to bet a full magazine shot at point blank range wouldn't be nearly so easy to walk away from.

I desperately tried to hide the fairly obvious fact that I was bleeding out and struggling to stay conscious. I held my wounded wrist behind me, trying to block his view to the amount of blood I had lost already. Showing weakness to a predator was a sure way to get killed, and Darko was king of the jungle right now. It was taking all my strength to keep my eyes open and my mind focused, but I couldn't hide the rapidly draining color from my skin. Darko was no dummy;

he noticed it too. He must be a gambling man because he knew when to hold them and when to fold them, and he decided on the latter.

With a sudden smile, he said pleasantly, "Miss Hayes, until next time, it has been a true honor and pleasure." He gave me a small bow, turned, and vanished from the cave. No, I didn't mean he walked out; I meant he literally vanished. Poof, one second there, the next second gone.

I was too tired to even blink in disbelief; as a result, I merely slumped back on the table, unable to hold myself upright anymore. The knife slipped from my hand and clattered to the floor.

My mistake was in forgetting that a threat still existed in the room. The Bruja had evidently recovered from my head butt, and quiet as a whisper, she crawled around the base of the stone table until she reached the knife I had dropped. She rose up over me, clutching the blade in two hands, ready to put all of her strength into plunging it through my rib cage and into my heart. A look of pure pleasure crept across her hideous features, the smile making her look even uglier.

I didn't have the strength left to even attempt to defend myself. My injuries had turned into an incessantly painful throb, pulling me steadily into unconsciousness.

Before she could take her vengeance on me, I heard a single shot, and the Bruja fell across my chest. For such a frail looking woman, she had some serious weight to her, like her paper-thin skin was hiding thick muscle.

With one last monumental effort, I ran my hands over the old woman's neck until I found the chain. My fingers landed on the mysterious amulet. I don't know why, but I had an overwhelming urge to claim it. It had my blood; it was mine. I didn't have the strength to pull it off her; instead, I just clutched it tightly, unwilling to let it go.

I turned my head to the cave entrance and saw Jason's beautiful figure standing there with that familiar cocky grin on his face and a rifle casually slung over one shoulder. I was safe now that Jason and Daniel had found me, so with a contented sigh, I gave myself permission to slip into a dreamless abyss.

Chapter Three

MY EYES OPENED to the dim grayness of morning in the minutes before sunrise. The diffused light barely illuminated the forms of an unfamiliar dark cherry wardrobe, an overstuffed armchair, and an unfamiliar man lying naked in bed next to me.

For the past seven nights since the crazy events in Mexico, I had been drinking myself into a stupor and looking for temporary comfort in the beds of strangers. It was my way of trying to avoid thinking about what had happened and what I had seen, though pushing those images from my mind was easier said than done.

I couldn't remember where I was or whom I was with. I thought his name was Tom ... or Tim ... no, Tony. I had picked him up last night at one of my favorite local watering holes. He had been there with colleagues, celebrating the landing of a big new client. I had struck up a conversation then pretty much ignored everything he had said to me in return. I hadn't been interested in talking.

I rolled out of bed, trying not to bounce the mattress or disturb the blankets, and hunted for my clothes in the pre-dawn light.

"Hey, babe. What are you doing?" a husky voice sounded from the heap on the bed.

"Oh, hey. Good morning," I said softly, startled by his awakening. "You know, it's still really early. You should go back to sleep."

"Are you bailing on me?" he asked, sitting up and taking notice of me as I slid on my underwear.

"I … um … no."

"You won't even ask for my phone number so you can lie and promise to call me?" he asked, trying to sound like he was joking, but I could hear the slight edge in his tone.

"No. I was just … I just have to go … to work."

"It's Saturday morning. Where do you work?"

"I'm, uh … a consultant … for a movie studio. They're based in California, so the work schedule is off because of the time difference."

"California is three hours behind us, not ahead. It's only two-thirty a.m. there." He was a persistent bugger.

"Fuck it. Look, Ted—"

"Todd."

"Todd, sorry. I had fun last night, but—"

"Hey, we can grab some breakfast and talk," he quickly interrupted. "You know, get to know each other better?"

"That's sweet, but really not necessary." I finished dressing and found my purse slumped in a corner of the room.

Making my way to the bedroom door, I was stopped as Todd reached out and took hold of my arm.

"Holy shit!" he yelled as I reflexively twisted his arm behind his back and applied pressure.

"Oh, God! I'm so sorry," I said, releasing him like he was on fire. "It's just habit. I, uh ... take self-defense classes. You know, a woman alone in the big city ..." I trailed off sheepishly. "I'm just going to go now."

There were days when I really wished I was more eloquent and could come up with exactly the right thing to say to get out of those kinds of awkward situations more easily. Nevertheless, I wasn't really one for conversation. When you didn't have many friends to talk to, your conversation muscle grew pretty weak.

IT WAS A cool spring morning, yet the air held humidity and the promise of a warm day to come. I walked slowly through the streets of New York City, enjoying one of those rare moments when the sidewalks weren't crowded with people. In the early hours of a Saturday morning, with the sun just starting to rise above the myriad apartment buildings and skyscrapers, it almost felt as if I were the only person left in this giant metropolis. I smiled at the peace and aloneness, though only for a moment. Aloneness quickly turned to loneliness.

I always got a little despondent after one of my trysts. I missed the warmth of a human body against mine, that fleeting feeling of connection, but I wasn't built for emotional entanglements, so I pushed the longing aside. Then I craved Manhattan's mass of bodies that would crash around me like a tidal wave. Even if I was unable to connect with people, at least I would always feel like I belonged in some way among the anonymous millions.

Walking, I shook out my stiff legs, stretched my arms over my head, and rolled my shoulders. I still had some soreness from Mexico, but I was healing rapidly. The bruises on my face were now barely visible, and I no longer needed bandages or a sling for my dislocated shoulder. I certainly wasn't one hundred percent, but one week after Jason and Daniel had rescued me from that cave, I was feeling much more like myself.

Thankfully, the boys had the forethought to radio in a chopper before attacking the cave, just in case we needed a speedy exit. It had come in handy for getting me to a hospital in Mexico City before I bled out. After I was stabilized, they had flown me back to New York to recuperate at home.

During my year in Manhattan, I lived in some filthy hovels in questionable neighborhoods that were the size of a small closet. A military pension didn't go very far in NYC, but as my freelance business had taken off—mercenary has such a negative connotation—and my income increased exponentially, I had finally saved enough money to buy the apartment of my dreams. I lived in a dramatic duplex on East 11th Street and Broadway in Greenwich Village, only a few blocks from Union Square Park to the north and Washington Square Park to the south.

"Morning, John," I said to my doorman.

Even though John had seen me do the walk of shame on many mornings, I still blushed when I greeted him. He was never judgmental though. As always, he gave me a pleasant "Good morning, Miss Hayes" and a tip of his cap.

I made my way up the stairs to the fifth floor penthouse. The building had an elevator, but I could use the exercise since my injuries had put me off my workout schedule that week.

A small smile touched my lips as I opened the door to my apartment. God, it felt good to be home. Opening the front door, I looked straight through my apartment to a wall of sixteen-foot high floor-to-ceiling windows that flooded the airy, open space with sunlight. The apartment was a perfect rectangle, long and narrow, only fourteen feet wide, but forty feet long from front to back. The main level was a single great room with a modern open kitchen on the right and a living room/dining room combination straight ahead. The only bathroom was just to the right of the front door, with an enormous travertine-tiled walk-in shower. My bedroom was up an open staircase off the living room in a loft area. The bedroom also had that rarest of NYC amenities—a walk-in closet.

My favorite feature, however, was the exposed brick wall on one side of the apartment. It was the perfect backdrop to display my framed movie poster collection from some of my all-time favorites: *Star Wars: A New Hope*, *Indiana Jones and The Raiders of the Lost Ark*, *The Lord of the Rings: The Return of the King*, *The Matrix*. The brick wall was the only remnant of the building's old bones when it had been a boarding house in the 1800s, giving it character and history.

Being in the penthouse, I also had access to a rooftop deck, but since the building was only five stories, the roof didn't afford dramatic views of the city. During certain times of the day, it got enough sun for a few hours of sunbathing before shadows from the surrounding buildings spilled over it.

I kicked off my red heels, followed by the rest of my clothing, and padded naked across the hardwood floors and up the stairs to my bedroom loft. Gathering a clean change of clothes, I made my way back down to the shower. I rarely closed the curtains on my windows. There wasn't much need since the building across the street was a warehouse that stored carpets for the rug store downstairs. Maybe the occasional warehouse worker managed to sneak a peek at me and got a good show, but I had never noticed anyone moving around behind those windows; therefore, I didn't worry much about it.

As I passed the kitchen after my shower, I noted that the digital clock on my stainless steel oven read seven fourteen a.m. When I had been in the military, I was forced to become a morning person, regularly woken up at four a.m. for a ten-mile run. Since being discharged, my body clock had been significantly reset. Almost all of my jobs took place under the cover of darkness, usually followed by a night of hard partying to celebrate the victory. I had become a very late riser, often not falling out of bed until late afternoon … when I was in my own bed.

Knowing I could use a few more hours of shut-eye, I made my way back upstairs and crashed.

I AWOKE AGAIN at four thirty p.m., dressed in a pair of dark jeans and a loose, white peasant top that hung off one shoulder, and slid on my favorite black boots. They were soft, knee-high leather with heels that were high enough draw attention to my legs yet not so high they impeded running or fighting. In fact, my boots were outfitted with steal tips in the event I needed to participate in an unexpected brawl. I wore my dark hair long and wavy. Then, after a little blush and lipstick, I was ready to go.

There was really only one place I ever went when I needed to either unwind or party, depending on my mood—The Raines Law Room. Raines was only six short blocks from my apartment, but it wasn't an easy place to find unless you were specifically looking for it. It was a bar in the speakeasy style of the 1930s. Its entrance was under an unmarked black awning and down a flight of stairs from street level. In order to be granted access, you had to ring a bell next to the unassuming door and be escorted inside. Once you were in, it was a sight to behold: all dark and plush, covered in velvet, and exuding sexy with a drizzle of cognac. It felt exclusive and sophisticated, but most importantly to me, private and discreet.

The space was segregated into four distinctly designed rooms. The Kitchen, lined with sophisticated black cabinetry, trimmed in cream and topped with white marble, where guests could wait for a table or watch mixologists prepare drinks. The outdoor Garden with its trellises, fresh herb plants and park benches that were illuminated in candlelight during the evening hours.

When I was feeling particularly social, I liked to spend time in The Lounge. There were always impeccably dressed businessmen congregating on the room's Chesterfield sofas and around its wood-burning fireplace, sipping drinks and congratulating each other on some job well done.

Most of the time, though, I headed straight for The Parlor and one of the high-backed, chocolate velvet banquettes enclosed by a set of opaque curtains. The curtains were sheer enough to allow me to observe the bar that ran the length of the opposing wall yet didn't allow an observer to see inside. I was a frequent enough regular that I rarely had to wait for a banquette even on the busiest of nights, and tonight was no exception.

"Welcome back, Miss Hayes. We haven't seen you in a few days," said the hostess, Lauren, with a pleasant smile.

"Hi, Lauren. I was traveling overseas on business." I returned her smile. Although I knew her by name and had seen her every week for more than a year, I didn't know anything about her, and I wasn't all that certain what that said about me.

"I hope you went somewhere fun," she said, leading me to my usual banquette in the Lounge—the one situated closest to the exit, just in case I needed to make a hasty retreat.

"Not really. I was tied up working most of the time and didn't even get the deal done in the end." I supposed that was technically true.

"I'm sorry to hear that. I'm sure you'll have better luck next time." She gave me a polite smile, placing a drink menu on the table as I slid into the curved banquette.

She had started to walk away when I called out to her. "Hey, Lauren, are you from New York originally?"

She paused, looking over her shoulder at me. "No, I'm from Oklahoma. I want to be an actress, so I've been working hard to get rid of the accent. Did you notice it?" she asked, frowning, her eyes worried.

"No," I said at once. "I was just curious."

"Oh, okay." She hesitated, as if she were about to say something more, perhaps to seek further assurances, but then thought better of it and walked away with less bounce in her step than she'd had before. And that was one of the many reasons why I tried not to take an interest in people. It always backfired on me in one way or another.

When my waitress came over, I ordered an Arsenic & New Lace and made no attempt at small talk. She brought me my drink within minutes and closed the curtain when she left, plunging me into my own Fortress of Solitude. I leaned in to take a sip of my gin and absinthe concoction, satisfied with the burn that sent warmth radiating through my body.

Reaching into my shirt, I pulled out the chain that held the mysterious amulet. It was a difficult piece of jewelry to hide well, given its size, which is why I had chosen to wear a loose-fitting top. I turned the amulet over in my hands, taking in every detail. Running my fingers over the smooth stone at the heart of the amulet, I swear I could feel a very subtle vibration. It felt like the thrumming of a live electrical wire, although perhaps that was just my imagination. I traced the swirls etched into the gold, thinking not for the first time that the patterns seemed distinct, some of which repeated.

Perhaps they weren't simply decorative. Maybe they were some form of writing.

Just then, the curtain enclosing my banquette was jerked aside, and I found myself looking upon the human equivalent of a Greek god, or so he seemed to think of himself. Jason Ryker stood there with his usual smirk, knowing full well the effect he had upon every woman, and even some men, who'd had the fortune to look upon his magnificence. I supposed that wasn't an entirely fair characterization of his ego. He was certainly aware of the fact that all eyes turned to him when he entered a room, and he took quite a bit of enjoyment from it, but his egomaniac persona was more for humor value than because he actually thought of himself as the embodiment of male perfection.

Jason was tall, about six-foot-three, and built like a fighter, broad and muscular. He didn't have the bulk of a football player and also didn't have the leanness of a runner or swimmer; he was somewhere in between. He had golden skin and dark wavy hair, hinting at his Latino heritage, even though his eyes were a pale green. They were all the more striking against his full, dark lashes. His features were strong and chiseled, but it was his stunning smile that drew people in. Infectious and warm, it set off the dimples in his cheeks and made his eyes crinkle at the corners.

That full wattage smile was now directed toward me, but I faced the challenge and tried not to respond in kind. He was impossible when he thought he had a willing audience. "Hey, sugar!" he drawled, over-emphasizing his Texas accent. "You look hotter than two rabbits screwin' in a wool sock."

I stared just at him, having never really gotten used to his creative southern colloquialisms.

A smaller, slighter figure slipped out from behind Jason and into the booth to sit on my left, giving me a warm hug. No one else except Daniel would have been able to get away with that kind of uninvited physical contact.

"Hey, little bro." I hugged him tightly in return.

"You scared the frack out of me," he said in a rush. "What happened? I saw … I don't know what I saw. I mean, I think I know what I saw, but …"

"Take a breath, Danny." He must have been worried. He didn't even berate me for using my old nickname for him. Years ago, he had made me start calling him Daniel instead of Danny because it sounded more mature. "I am feeling much better, by the way. Thanks for asking." I smirked in amused disapproval.

He looked abashed for not having asked after my well-being, given the injuries I had sustained. Jason snickered, enjoying Daniel's discomfort, as he slid into the banquette on my right. Jason was an ardent fan of schadenfreude, taking pleasure in the pain of other people.

"Your bodily condition is always top on my mind," Jason said with a wink, making an obvious show of looking me up and down. "And you are looking quite healthy to me."

I gave him a light jab with my elbow while Daniel ignored the exchange. He was used to Jason's ridiculous, over-the-top flirtations.

The waitress came by and took beer orders for Jason and Daniel and a refill order for me, closing the curtain again on her way out. As she did, the mood in the banquette became more subdued.

I looked down into my empty glass, wishing the waitress would hurry and bring me another. I wanted the added liquid courage before starting this conversation. I needed to know what they had seen, what they had experienced. I was hoping they had seen the same things I had so I would know I wasn't going crazy. At the same time, if they had seen those things and they were real, what did that mean for the world? I couldn't even fathom the implications of it at that moment.

I took a breath and steeled myself for their answers either way. "I need you guys to fill in the blanks for me. What happened after … after I came running out of the house?" I couldn't bring myself to say, "after I was bitten by a little snake girl." God, that sounded completely ridiculous.

"I'll show you mine if you show me yours," said Jason, waggling his eyebrows, but with curiosity and expectation in his eyes.

I supposed it was only right for me to get the ball rolling. I played back for them everything I had experienced that night in the compound. I considered holding back or glossing over the description of the creatures that had attacked me, worried they would think me completely insane, but I knew I needed honesty from them, and they deserved nothing less from me. After all, we were in this together, and we needed to share information if we were going to figure it out.

After I finished my story, I looked expectantly between the two men. Jason gave nothing away, his poker face firmly in place, whereas Daniel looked concerned yet thoughtful.

"Ghouls," he said after a few moments of silence. Jason and I shot him a questioning look. "What you described," he clarified. "Those creatures sound like a description of ghouls. Geez, didn't you guys ever play *Dungeons & Dragons*?"

That got a reaction from Jason. He snorted in derision, as if he would never in his life have been caught dead acting in such a geeky fashion as to play fantasy role-playing games.

Ignoring Daniel, I turned to Jason. "Tell me what you saw."

Jason was quiet, looking off in the distance, as though he was trying to find the right words. When he started speaking, it was slow and deliberate, but he used a calm, matter-of-fact tone, like he was giving a military field report to a commanding officer.

"After I took out the hostiles guarding the grounds so you could gain access to the compound, I moved to a higher position on the ridge overlooking the front of the building to be in a position to cover your exit if needed. A little girl emerged from the house twenty-six minutes after you went in. I saw her head for the gates and figured Daniel would pick her up since he was waiting for you just outside the perimeter. But she was just hanging out by the compound wall. I was about to radio Daniel to go in and retrieve her when you came out. You were running at break-neck speed, and two seconds later, a large, reptile-like creature emerged from the house, hot on your heels."

I had to give him credit; he didn't even hesitate when he said it. There was no sign of uncertainty, surprise or embarrassment. He was a soldier through and through.

"It sort of looked like a Nidoking," Daniel interrupted.

"A what?" Jason and I asked at the same time.

"A Nidoking. It's a reptilian Pokémon that causes damage by smashing things with its tail." We both stared at him in silence. "What?" he asked, turning up his hands in a bewildered shrug at the exasperation evident on our faces.

Jason gave him a withering look then continued. "I took it down with five rounds to the head and neck. Tough sucker. Then I saw you approach the girl and figured you would take her out of there. I didn't really see what happened next, but you went down. I didn't realize the girl was a threat until you blew the C-4. I figured you wouldn't have risked her life with an explosion that close unless you meant to."

I nodded, affirming his suspicions.

He continued, "That's when things got a little weird."

"*That's* when it got weird?" I asked. "And here I was thinking it was odd that I had been attacked by ghouls and a Pokémon."

With a quick, cheerless smile, he continued, "That guy walked right out of an inferno without even a singe and deflected an entire clip of ammo. Then he picked you up and started to carry you off. That's when Kung Foo Panda here"—he nodded at Daniel—"ran in to kick his ass."

"It didn't work so well," said Daniel, dropping his head. "Even while he was holding you, he blocked every one of my kicks and punches single-handedly then just waved his hand, and I felt this wall of energy slam into me. It threw me back about one hundred feet and knocked enough wind out of me that I couldn't recover on time to get to you. When I was finally able to get back on my feet, you were both gone."

"I was watching it all," said Jason, "but I didn't see what happened either. It was like you were there one second and gone the next. When that guy waved his hand, my night vision goggles just shorted out. They went completely white, like someone had turned on a spotlight. But, when I tore them off my head, it was still pitch black outside, and you were both gone."

"I didn't see any flare of light," Daniel said.

"So, how did you find me in that cave?"

"That was just pure luck," Jason answered. "You know we had a chopper on standby about five miles away, so we radioed the guy. He picked us up within ten minutes, and we flew in a spiral, increasing our distance, and looked for signs of life. It was hard to see through the canopy, but as the sun started to come up, we saw Jeeps parked in a clearing. I guess, even if the guy who had you could travel instantaneously, his hired muscle couldn't. So we rappelled from the chopper and tracked them on foot until we found the cave. About six, heavily-armed guards stood on patrol, but we had the element of surprise, camouflage and long-range rifles. The rest is history," he said with satisfaction, leaning back in his seat and putting his arms behind his head. I thought he even used the movement to flex his biceps for a quick, obnoxious display of his musculature.

"Okay," I nodded, satisfied I at least knew as much as they did about what had happened. "Daniel, in the future, we'll need a way to track each other in the event something like this happens again."

"Sure," he responded, perking up at the prospect of a new project. "I can have GPS chips sewn into our armor, or maybe affixed to our weapons. I'll have to think of the best place to put them, but I'm on it."

I had first come across Daniel Parkson when he was a twelve-year-old kid being fostered in the same home I had been assigned. The first day I had met him, he was wearing a *World of Warcraft* T-shirt, playing X-Box in the dingy basement, and in desperate need of a haircut. I would soon learn that every day was pretty much identical to that one.

Daniel was also a computer genius. He had hidden behind his electronics as a way of shutting himself away from our foster father. I soon became Daniel's protector and surrogate mother, and when I had turned eighteen, I promised him I would get him out. As soon as I had finished basic training and was assigned to my first military base, I had kept that promise.

Daniel pointed at my hands and the amulet that I was absently caressing with my thumbs. "What's that? You were clutching it with a death grip when we found you. We couldn't pry it out of your fingers." His line of questioning brought my attention back to the object.

"I have no idea," I whispered, turning it over in my hands for the thousandth time, getting lost in its etchings.

Daniel's voice broke into my thoughts. "Can I see it?" He asked it innocently enough, and I had absolutely no reason to question handing it over for his inspection, but a shadow welled up in my mind that was suspicious, possessive. It caused me to clutch the amulet tighter and lean slightly away from Daniel.

This is ridiculous, I thought. Next thing I knew, I'd be calling it "My Precious."

I forced my fingers to relax and handed it over.

Daniel inspected it in the same manner I had, then shrugged and handed it back. "I have no clue, either, but maybe you can take it to an expert."

I raised my eyebrows. "What, like a museum or Sotheby's?" I had no intention of putting it on display or auctioning it off to the highest bidder, no matter how ancient and priceless it was.

"Hell no. What would they know about something like this? It's clearly tied to ritualistic magic. I was thinking you should take it to that shop on 53rd, Alfreda's Antiquarian Bookshop. The owner is very knowledgeable. She has a large collection of ancient texts that might contain some relevant information."

With a sparkle in his eye, as if he was trying to hold back a laugh, Jason said, "Isn't that a witch store that sells crystals and shit like that?"

"Yes," replied Daniel, offended, "but they sell a lot more than that. They have a whole section in the back where they sell legitimate mystical objects. I'm telling you, the owner is the real deal, an expert. What can it hurt to stop in and have the necklace checked out?"

Not wanting to cause an argument, I simply told Daniel I would think about it. He seemed satisfied by that response and all but stuck his tongue out at Jason in a childish "I win!" gesture. Daniel then excused himself to get to his Friday night X-Box Live gaming session of Halo.

As soon as the curtain closed behind Daniel, I could all but feel Jason's artificially inflated ego deflate. The real man came out as his piercing gold eyes met mine with something sincere behind them, and even more than the crazy Mexico mission, it utterly terrified me.

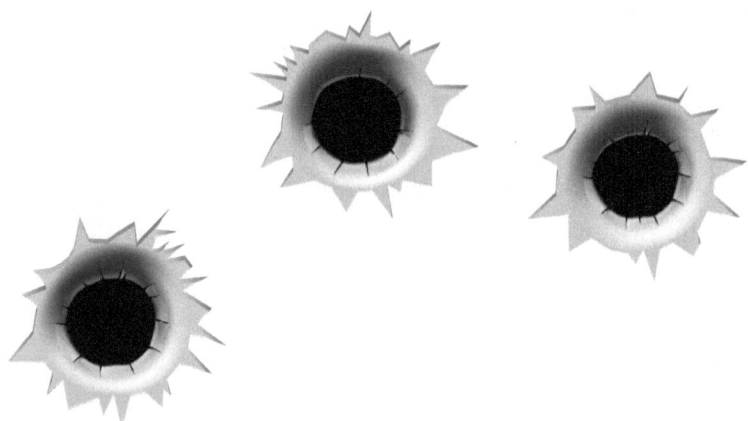

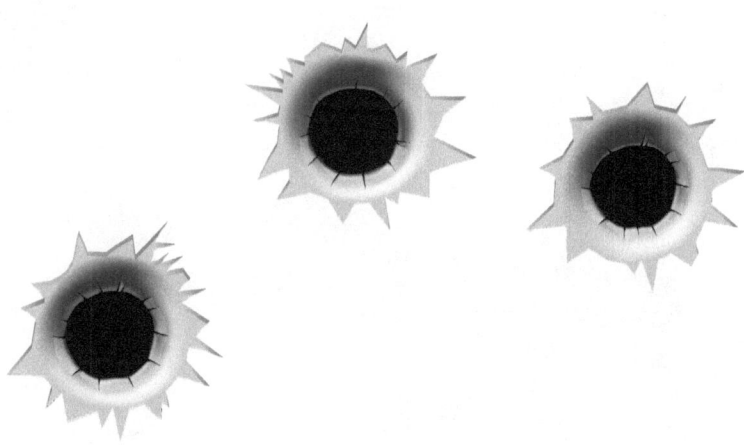

Chapter Four

"REMEMBER GOING THROUGH basic training together?" he asked with a smile

"Yeah, of course," I responded, unsure where he was going with this.

"Man, I really didn't like you back then," he recalled with a smirk.

"That's just because you couldn't handle being beaten by a girl," I quipped in return. "I bet I can still do more pull-ups than you."

"Maybe," he laughed. "You know, it wasn't until we were forced to team up for Sandhurst that I really started to respect you. I realized then that we were far better together than we were apart."

"Mmm," I responded noncommittally, staring down at my drink.

Sandhurst Military Skills Competition was a two-day competition among international military teams in activities such as obstacle course navigation, weapons handling, and rifle marksmanship. Jason and I had known that, in order to win, teamwork was going to be an essential element of the challenge. We had entered the competition as enemies and finished it as allies, the competition bringing us together like nothing else ever could. We had learned to trust and rely on each other and became inseparable after that.

"Emma, we've been together a long time, and most of that time has been really good, then it became amazing … or, at least I thought so. I know things haven't been that way between us lately, but you know how I still feel about you."

I took a long pull of my drink, eyes laser-focused on the ring of condensation my glass had left behind on the table.

When I didn't respond, he continued, "I was really worried about you this time, Em. I've never seen you hurt before. I didn't think it could ever happen. I don't want to lose you."

I knew he was no longer talking about the mission.

"You're not going to lose me, Jason. We've been friends for a long time, and that's not going to change. We're just going through a rough patch. We'll get past it."

He turned away momentarily, although not before I saw the flash of frustration and disappointment in his eyes. That was not what he had wanted to hear.

"Look, Em, we moved past friendship a while ago. I know getting close to people isn't easy for you, but this is me we're talking about. I've always had your back. You know you can trust me."

"Jason, it's not about trust."

"Then what is it about?" he said, his voice rising. In the next instant, he looked slightly apologetic at the outburst and brought the volume back down. "I just want things to be like they were before."

"So do I, Jason. I made a mistake when …"

Just then, the curtain swung open and a new waitress appeared, all tall and leggy. She took one look at Jason and her demeanor changed from professional to sultry. She put a hand on her hip and took a deep breath to accentuate her ample assets, tossing her blond hair behind her shoulder.

"Hi, Jason. I haven't seen you in a few days. I've missed you," she said with a pout on her bright pink lips.

"Hey, Lacey. How ya doing?" He couldn't stop from eyeing her up and down appreciatively; however, his voice held annoyance at the interruption.

"Oh, I am doing fantastic. Is there anything I can get for you?" She shifted her hips provocatively.

"Sure, how about another beer?" Jason shook his empty bottle.

"It would be my pleasure." She took his empty and turned to leave when I stopped her.

"I would love another drink, too. Thanks, sweetie," I said with a saccharin smile. She shot me a look that she had probably used a million times in high school to bully and intimidate the less than popular girls. I simply blew her a kiss and added, "Now I know why you're Jason's favorite waitress. You're so attentive."

She stormed off in a huff.

"Was that really necessary?" Jason asked.

"She brought it on herself. Next time, maybe she'll stop being such a dick tease and just take my damn drink order."

He knew better than to argue with me, instead conceding the point.

"So, what were you saying before we were interrupted?" he asked.

"I was going to say I made a mistake taking our relationship to the next level. I knew it wouldn't work out. I guess I just wanted to see whether it was possible to thaw my inner ice princess. Now I know."

"You didn't give us a chance. If I did something wrong, just tell me what it is and I'll fix it. We can make this work."

I sat there in silence, unable to look him in the eye. Shouldn't I feel loss, or guilt, or even jealousy? For the most part, I only felt uncomfortable with continuing this conversation. Jason meant the world to me, and I would die to protect him, but I didn't want to date him.

"Is this because of Lacey?" he asked.

I really didn't care about Lacey, or any of the other women who threw themselves at him, so I merely shook my head, fidgeting with my empty glass.

"Goddamn it, Em! Just say something, anything. I can't stand the brick wall treatment."

"I'm sorry, Jason. As much as I want to —as much as I tried to —I just can't." Not wanting to be the cause of all of that hurt, I tried to soften the blow. "I don't know… Maybe I just need some more time. It's been one hell of a week, and I have a lot to think about." That seemed to have given him the small crack in my armor that he was looking for.

"Yeah, I can do that. I can give you more time. I'm not saying you need to fall head over heels in love with me immediately, but I know that, if we spend more time together, you'll get there." Of course he would think that. No woman had ever not fallen for him.

"Maybe, but I think we should keep it to friendship for the time being." That set him off again.

"This is bullshit, Em. You would rather go around fucking strangers than spend time with me? How does that make any goddamned sense?" Trying to regain control over himself, Jason took a deep, calming breath. "Just come home with me instead. I promise I won't rush you into a serious relationship you're not ready for. I only want us to spend time together."

I wanted to say yes. I really did. Jason was amazingly good-looking, funny, charming, and I didn't have to hide from him. We did the same thing for a living, so I didn't have to lie to him about who I was ... so why did I?

"I can't do that to you, Jason. I can't lead you on like that, not knowing if I will ever be able to return your feelings. It wouldn't be right."

With a bitter laugh, Jason responded, "Since when do you ever care about what is right? You're the most amoral person I've ever met. It always amazed me that you joined the military when you have such a hard time doing the right thing and following orders."

"Well, sometimes those orders are stupid. Anyway, that's why I'm my own boss now, and I'm really good at what I do, morals be damned."

"I don't know if I find that hot or disturbing," he deadpanned.

We both smiled, enjoying the momentary truce.

"Look, Em," he said quietly. "I told myself I would be patient—I would wait for you to be ready. I wanted to let you come to me, but after this week … I don't know. Maybe I just need to grab life by the balls and make it happen. So … So I thought I would try the more direct approach tonight."

"I understand. Mexico was … different. It was strange and downright terrifying, like nothing we have ever experienced before." I stared at the dark curtain in front of the table, losing myself in the memory. "Jason, when they had me tied down to that table, I thought that old woman was going to plunge a dagger through my heart, and my greatest fear wasn't the actual dying part. It wasn't even the pain, however fleeting that would be. It was the powerlessness. I was completely vulnerable and helpless, immobilized like that. I had no options left."

While I began to drown in those feelings, Lacey chose to return with our drinks. As much as I disdained her, I could have given her a big sloppy kiss for her perfect timing. She didn't offer any pleasantries, just roughly placed the drink on the table before me and spun away with a flip of her platinum hair. I greedily drained my entire glass, feeling like I needed it to swallow those roiling emotions that had threatened to overtake me.

It seemed to work. The heat of the alcohol burned through the worst of those feelings, leaving them a hard pit in my stomach. My head started to have a pleasantly fuzzy sensation, and those fears, inhibitions, and uncertainties began to fade into the background. I had a few drinks in me, and it had been a very long and insane week, capped by an emotionally charged conversation with Jason. I was feeling particularly weak in that moment.

Regardless of everything I had just said to Jason, I had a need to connect with someone who knew what I was going through, to have someone on my side telling me they were there for me and it was going to be okay. I was getting tired of holding up the wall between myself and the rest of the world. It would feel incredibly good to give in to him, to feel his warmth against me, his strong arms wrapped around my body, his full lips on mine. Perhaps I should just go home with him tonight and not worry about hurting his feelings. He was a big boy, after all.

I must have looked at Jason with more heat in my eyes than I had meant to convey because he responded in kind instantly. "Emma," he said, his voice growing deep and husky with desire.

With no more warning than that, Jason grabbed me by the upper arms and drew me in to him. Without thinking, I tilted my head to the side, allowing him access to my mouth. He lightly brushed his lips against mine, giving me an opportunity to pull away should I want to. I didn't.

I didn't know what had come over me. Maybe it was simply the alcohol coursing through my system, dropping my inhibitions. Maybe it was because I was craving the warmth of human contact. Maybe it was because I needed to feel alive, especially in light of the events of the past week. Maybe it was all of those things. Regardless, I leaned into him and deepened the kiss.

He responded immediately.

It was a good kiss. His lips were soft. He was unhurried and controlled. His hands loosened their grip and gently made their way down to my waist. His arms wrapped around me, drawing me closer. I didn't resist. My mind had gone blank. All I could think of was how good it felt, how easy it would be to simply give in to him. When I thought of what he might do to me, my skin burned with desire, and I pressed closer to him, forgetting all of my arguments against doing this.

Then they all came flooding back against my will. How would we be able to work together and make tactical decisions if we were in a relationship? We wouldn't be able to remain objective. It would put both of our lives, including the lives of anyone else involved in a job, at risk.

However, even more than that, there was always something else holding me back. Although I cared about Jason, I could never make myself love him. A part of me refused to allow the emotion. I didn't know if it was because he wasn't the right guy for me, or if it was because I was incapable of loving someone. I feared it was the latter.

These thoughts came to me in a rush, and as they did, I pulled away from Jason. He looked dazed, his lips still swollen and red from our kiss. Then confusion and eventually frustration crossed his face. He didn't need to say anything; I knew exactly what he was thinking. It must have shown on my face too, because he didn't even attempt to talk to me about it.

Instead, he said, "Emma, you know how I feel about you. I don't want to wait quietly on the sidelines while you figure this out in your head. I'm not giving you an ultimatum, because I will be here for you no matter what, but I am going back to my place. If you are interested in seeing where this could go, you can come over and spend the night with me."

Before I could react, he placed another urgent kiss on my lips, as if he was afraid it might be our last, and then slipped out of the booth and through the curtains.

What the holy hell was I supposed to do after that? Anxiety sprung up unbidden in my mind. Being in a real relationship with someone was much too dangerous. It was safer to form no romantic attachments. Doing so would not only save my life, but could save the lives of anyone else that cared about me.

How dare he put me in such a terrible position? Was I supposed to follow him just for the sake of not losing him? How could he ask me to make such an important decision with no time to consider it? Perhaps, if I really felt something for him, I wouldn't need the time to consider it. I would just know. Or maybe that was merely something made up by Walt Disney and only happened in fairy tales. Shit! I could sit there all night, debating the pros and cons of this choice, and still not come to a decision. I simply needed to stop thinking and act.

I slid out of the banquette and moved purposefully through the curtains and into the main room of The Parlor. My feet carried me forward, but instead of taking me to the front door of Raines, they walked me straight into The Lounge. I needed another drink.

I found a waitress and ordered a dirty martini then made my way to the wood-burning fireplace and leaned against the mantle where I stared into the flames. My drink arrived in short order, and I took a sip, appreciating the perfect balance of dry and salty. I decided I would finish my drink then make my way outside to see where my feet took me.

Before I was able to take another sip, I felt the fine hairs on the back of my neck stand at attention. It felt as though an arctic breeze had blown into the room, sending shivers up my spine. I was being watched.

I took a breath, composing myself, and then very naturally turned to glance around the room, keeping a bored look on my face. My eyes skimmed past a man sitting on a Chesterfield sofa in the farthest darkened corner of the room. I stopped my gaze on two men standing nearby who were generally attractive and would have drawn my attention on any other night. I looked them up and down, assessing their assets, and then acted like I was dismissing them for one petty reason or another.

Then I allowed my eyes to rest upon the stranger in the corner. His gaze met mine, and I gave him a drunken smile.

Perhaps it was paranoia, but I wondered if he was here specifically looking for me. He seemed out of place in the room, and his expression held more curiosity than desire. Through years of experience, I had found paranoia kept me alive when I should have gone the way of the dodo. Taking a guess, I assumed he could have been one of Darko's lackeys, trying to flush me out so Darko could finish what he had started.

I decided to try to find out what this guy's ultimate plan was, hopefully without getting myself killed in the process. I made my way through the room toward him, purposefully weaving and "accidentally" bumping into one or two patrons along the way. His wary and calculating eyes followed me the entire time.

I stopped in front of him, jutting my hip out and placing one hand on my waist. I gave him a lopsided smile, perfectly playing the drunken girl looking for a one-night stand.

"Hi," I slurred. "I couldn't help noticing you sitting alone here and thought I would come join you. Do you mind if I sit?"

He didn't speak, simply nodded his acquiescence. Now that I was close enough to get a better look at him, my instincts screamed he was dangerous. He probably stood a couple of inches shy of six feet and was lean. He sat very still and controlled, ramrod straight, giving me the impression of someone with personal discipline who knew how to handle himself. His hair was cut short, almost in military style, and his eyes were a stark ice blue, not revealing anything of what might be going on inside his head. His nose was narrow, and he had high cheekbones. His sharp jaw was covered with a closely trimmed beard. Overall, he would have been an attractive man if it weren't for his seriously intense demeanor.

I took a seat next to him on the Chesterfield, close enough so my thigh touched his, and placed my hand just above his knee, trying to throw him off a little with the physical contact. It seemed to work because he blinked when I touched him and started to pull away slightly.

"I haven't seen you here before, and I'm here all the time," I giggled and then delicately hiccupped. "What's your name?"

While he cleared his throat, shifting in his seat, I got a sense of cruel satisfaction at watching him squirm. "Alex," he answered.

"Hi, Alex. I'm Jasmine," I lied. "It's *very* nice to meet you." I slid my hand a couple of inches higher on his thigh.

He shifted uncomfortably, looking as though he wanted desperately to escape. "Do you maybe want to get out here? My place is only a few blocks away," I drawled.

If Alex left with me, I would try to lure him to a less populated area of the city where I could question him and then take him out without anyone noticing. I just had to hope he wasn't some monstrous creature in disguise.

As Alex turned to face me and stared at me hard, his frozen gaze boring into mine, I tried to keep my eyes unfocused like I was inebriated and let out another little giggle. I leaned into him to place a sloppy, drunken kiss on his lips.

He immediately pulled back and stood up. "Thanks, but no. I have other plans tonight."

I stood quickly, purposefully losing my balance, and he grabbed my arm to keep me upright, allowing me to measure his strength. He would be formidable in a fight, although not as strong as those creatures I had encountered in Mexico. I was willing to bet he was no more than your above average human from a physical strength perspective. However, he carried himself as if he were skilled in combat, so I would need to catch him off guard to get the upper hand if it came to that.

I acted indignant at his rejection, spinning on my heel and stalking away unsteadily. As I approached the exit, I gently placed my drink down on a table, straightened my back, and confidently sauntered out with a small smile on my face. I knew he was going to follow me, and I was going to be ready for him.

Chapter Five

MY SOFT BOOTS were silent on the pavement as I made my way quickly and purposefully toward a quieter area of the city. This neighborhood was free of sidewalk cafes, bars, and restaurants that would draw large crowds of diners and partygoers. Instead, it was mainly a residential neighborhood, but in a poorer part of town.

The sidewalks were partially blocked by black bags of trash waiting for pick-up, and in the warmth of the night, the odor was heavy in the air. Empty beer bottles, cigarette butts, and other detritus had collected along the curbs and in the gutters.

The buildings were stark and lifeless, missing the colorful flowers, plants, and strings of lights that were commonly seen on apartment building balconies throughout the city. An old collection of battered-looking cars were lined up like soldiers beside the curb. The street was devoid of life except for one resident sitting on the front steps of his apartment, drinking a forty ounce out of a paper bag, and he didn't pay any attention to me or anything else going on in the neighborhood. No one around here would ever call the cops if they heard suspicious noises outside of their windows. They trusted the cops less than they did the criminals.

There were a few narrow alleyways between apartment buildings that were dark, damp, and smelled of rot. No one in their right mind would ever purposefully wander down one ... except for me that is. I knew this area fairly well. I had scoped it out a couple of years ago, looking for places close to my apartment where I might need some privacy for purposes such as this one. Those in my line of work tended to find themselves the target of revenge-seekers every once in a while, and there had been a few occasions when someone had unsuccessfully attempted to follow me home. I slowed my steps and kept walking in a deceptively drunken unsteadiness down the street, listening hard for the footsteps I knew would be behind me.

Ah! There they were. *Click, clack, click, clack.* Men were so predictable.

I didn't want to give away that I had heard him, so I maintained my casual pace, appearing oblivious and unworried to the danger following me. As I got closer to the corner of the block, I turned right into an alleyway then let out a noisy sound of frustration, giving the impression I had mistakenly turned down this way when I had really meant to take the right turn at the corner only a few feet beyond the alley entrance.

I stopped walking and threw my hands up in exasperation. I heard someone approach from behind and slowly, deliberately turned to face Alex.

Except it wasn't Alex standing before me.

This man exuded deadly intent, with anger and maliciousness rolling off him in waves. It wasn't the first time a man had looked at me like that, but something else about him disturbed me. I couldn't put my finger on it; it confused me.

The seconds dragged into years as we stood glaring at each other. He didn't so much as twitch or blink, eyeing me like I was a particularly complex puzzle he was trying to figure out. The entire time, he gave me no excuse to pull my gun and blow him away. Why hadn't he tried to take me by surprise and attack me while my back had been turned?

He watched me with black eyes as deep as pools of midnight oil, tinged with a little hatred and a lot of crazy. He was dressed in black from head to toe: black leather pants and a tight, black T-shirt that showed off a defined chest and arms as well as a narrow waist. His clothing was covered in some sort of odd body armor that actually looked like a thin layer of black chain mail. The entire ensemble was covered by a long, leather coat which made me think of *The Matrix*. How very cliché. It also looked out of place on such a warm night, until I noticed it was purposefully being used to hide something he had strapped to his back that I couldn't quite make out. His dark hair was long, cascading to his shoulders in light waves, a few strands falling into his eyes. He would actually be quite beautiful in his ferocity if it weren't for the scary, haunted look in his eyes.

When he finally spoke, it was in a voice that was lighter and more pleasant than I had expected to hear coming from someone who looked like him. "Do you know me?" he asked.

I took a moment and scrolled through the bad guy database in my head, coming up blank. I was certain I had never seen him before yet weighed my options carefully. I had no qualms about lying. After all, it was almost a pre-requisite for my job. However, they were usually educated lies so I wouldn't get caught. Getting caught in a lie was simply bad for business, not to mention bad for survival. If I appeased him by telling him I did remember him, I wouldn't have any information or knowledge to back up that statement. I feared that, regardless of the answer, I would set off a hair-trigger response in him, and things would descend into chaos very quickly.

I didn't really have much of a choice; therefore, I shook my head very slowly in the negative. "No," I whispered, waiting for the other shoe to drop.

His eyes closed briefly, and an odd expression of sadness and relief crossed his face so quickly I thought I might have imagined it. When he opened his eyes a moment later, though, any humanity I had seen in them was gone. They were filled with merciless malice. A sneer crossed his full lips, and I felt unexpectedly hurt to see it on his face.

Anticipating violence, I casually shifted into a fighting stance.

"Take her," he said seemingly to no one in particular, but I could feel that prick at the back of my neck.

Turning around, I saw dark forms detach themselves from the shadows, like grease oozing down a wall. I immediately placed my back to the wall where I could keep a view of

Mr. Tall-Dark-and-Handsomely-Insane as well as whatever was about to come for me. As I did so, I slipped my right hand under my peasant top and pulled a handgun fitted with a silencer from my waistband, sliding off the safety and chambering a bullet.

New York had some of the toughest gun laws in the country, and I followed them all. I had licenses for all my guns, a permit to carry a concealed weapon, and I didn't keep any assault weapons within state borders. I was happy to comply with the law because it also meant it was harder for the criminals to access illegal weapons. Sure, the more powerful scum of the city could manage to skirt the laws, but only a relatively small handful could manage it. As a result, I didn't come up against such powerful assault weapons very often, which was one of the benefits of living in New York.

I couldn't yet get a good look at what was coming for me, although I was pretty sure it didn't need an assault weapon to be lethal.

What emerged from the shadows were not human, but they also weren't like the ghouls I had fought in Mexico. They were less substantial, like living extensions of the shadows they had crept out of. Any details or features were obscured by the darkness around them. What they lacked in physical presence, they more than made up for in psychic. The unseen was almost always more terrifying than the seen.

My feet felt like lead posts drilled into cement as insidious, cold tendrils burrowed into my mind. How could I fight off something as insubstantial as shadows? I was used to fighting for my life in all sorts of extreme situations, but never against an enemy like this. I didn't know anything about these things to give me an advantage. They were going to kill me, and I would never know why. Doubt and fear began to creep in through the cracks in my armor, feelings I had thought I conquered long ago, though perhaps had only shelved for a time.

One of those shadow demons reached out a long, clawed hand toward me, snapping me out my pity party. My weapon was up in a flash, more out of instinct than purposeful defense. What good would bullets do against shadows?

Rather than fire, I dove to the side, away from the reaching claw, dropped into a roll, and sprung back to my feet directly in front of their master. In response, handsome-evil-guy reached over his shoulder for what I now recognized to be a sword hilt, but I was faster.

I dropped again and took out his legs with a sweep kick. As he fell to his knees, I came up behind him, wrapping my arm around his neck and shoving the end of my Glock into his temple. His shadow minions rushed forward, but he halted them with a raise of his hand.

"I've had about enough of this shit. I want answers, and I want them now!" I snarled, pressing the gun harder into his temple. "Who are you?"

With an almost amused tone, he responded, "There was a time you wouldn't have needed to ask that question. My name is Zane Shayde. I am the High Commander of Lord Gabriel Marduk, our Protector and Savior. I have been dispatched to bring you back to Urusilim, preferably alive, but dead will do just as well."

With false calmness, I leaned down and whispered in his ear, quoting one of my favorite lines from the movie,

Philadelphia. "'*Now explain it to me like I'm a four-year-old.*' Everything after your name sounded a lot like gibberish to me."

"I'm not here to explain anything to a traitor such as you," he spat with contempt. "I would just as soon slit your throat and have done with it, but our Lord may have some use for you yet. However, if you were to resist, you may give me no choice in the matter."

"I think you must be mistaken. I don't know who Lord Marduk is or what Urusilim is, but I am not playing your games. Take your friends here and leave before you get hurt."

The sound of a thousand nails scratching across a dusty blackboard emerged from the two shadowy forms standing ahead of us. It pierced my senses like an ice pick to the eardrum. The sound blew through the self-denial I hadn't even realized I had been clinging to. I had been in denial for days, trying to explain away what had happened in Mexico in a military fashion, never really stopping to accept or internalize what I had experienced. I had seen, but I hadn't really believed … until now. This wasn't a physical enemy I understood and could fight with traditional human weapons. I shivered with the knowledge that I was in way over my head.

Zane chuckled, "You will learn soon enough that this is no game, traitor."

I never really did well with fear. It seemed to be a useless emotion at best and a dangerous one at worst. I had a natural coping mechanism that quickly transformed fear into anger. And anger I could do something with.

I snarled between clenched teeth, "I am most certainly no traitor. I fought for my country in more wars, skirmishes, and covert missions than I can count, so don't you dare accuse me of betraying what I love."

"*What you love?*" he repeated, his voice becoming soft and distant, as if trying to grasp a wisp of a memory. His hands slowly lifted to the arm I still had wrapped around his throat, and he held my forearm with a gentleness I never would have expected from him. He slowly began to rub my sensitive skin in an almost thoughtless way, as though it was something he had done a million times before. I squeezed my eyes tight and bit back a gasp at the sensation, but the fine hairs on my arms responded, and my heart sped up a touch.

"I'm not talking about your service in this world," he continued in that soothing voice. "I am talking about what you did to our world. There are some that will never forgive you, those who would be content to allow you to stay lost to us. Others want you found to exact retribution. And still others believe you were in the right and look to you as a symbol for their cause."

I blinked in utter confusion, my mouth opening and closing, though no sounds would emerge. I had so many questions that I wanted—needed—to bombard him with, but all that came out was a weak, "What are you talking about?"

That was all it took to set him off again.

In one fluid motion, Zane shot up, breaking out of my chokehold, which had been flagging anyway given the distraction of the conversation, not to mention his touch. He spun to face me and forcibly pushed me back against the brick wall of the alley, my gun flying from my hand. I realized in that moment that I had never really had him dead to rights. Given the strength and physical prowess he had just demonstrated in that one simple move, he could have avoided my chokehold or broken free from it fairly easily. He had allowed me to put him in that position and had held back his shadow demons from clawing me to ribbons when they could have had me. The question was why.

Rational thought quickly fled as he pressed his body against mine, holding me firmly in place. He towered over me by at least a foot. Immobilizing me might not have been his only objective though. He pushed his leg between mine and pressed even closer, holding my wrists above my head. I fought against his grip, but I couldn't be sure whether I gave it my best effort.

That snarl was back in his voice, his hot breath on my neck, as he bent his head closer to my ear. "You dare question me, traitor … destroyer of worlds? I could have my shadow demons split you from neck to groin while you slowly die trying to stuff your steaming entrails back inside your worthless carcass." Zane's body was saying something entirely different from his words.

This guy was a serious lunatic and all the more dangerous for it. I needed to get him back to a more stable frame of mind.

"Zane," I said gently. He stiffened at the sound of his name on my lips, or at least the parts of him that weren't already stiff did. "I know you could easily hurt me, and I know you haven't yet. I'm sorry I don't know what you're talking about. There's a lot about my life that I don't remember, but I would like for you to help me understand. Maybe, if you explain it to me, we can work this out, and we can both walk away from this in one piece."

His body relaxed against mine, his voice shifting again to a softer tone. "Gods, how I've missed you," he breathed.

He nuzzled my neck, his breath searing my skin. Then his lips pressed against that sensitive spot behind my ear, sending a shiver along my spine that had nothing to do with fear. He felt my reaction and took it as an invitation, his mouth moving along the column of my neck. I struggled, trying to free my wrists from his iron grasp, but it only caused him to press harder against me.

His presence was overwhelming, and his effect on me was terrifying. Were my struggles meant to escape or to move against him more provocatively? How was it possible that I didn't know the answer to that question?

He kept speaking to me as if he knew me … intimately. Did he know me from before my car accident? Did we go to high school together? Maybe we dated once upon a time. What the hell was I thinking? I didn't go to high school with a guy who could command shadow demons, for cripes' sake!

Maybe he was lying about knowing me. I certainly couldn't trust him to tell the truth when he was there to kill me … or seduce me…, I couldn't really tell what his plan was at this point. My goal was to kill him or, at the very least, capture and torture him for answers, but maybe I should just rip his clothes off and take him right there in the filthy alley. If I was being completely honest with myself, the thought wasn't entirely unattractive.

He ground himself against me, and my brain almost short-circuited as I felt his desire through his leather pants. He pulled away from my neck, looking into my eyes. We were almost nose-to-nose, and I was shocked at what I saw. His expression was filled with desire, longing, sadness … and recognition. He did know me, but from where?

His hands came free from my wrists and moved down the length of my arms, causing my skin to catch fire. They slid to my shoulders and grazed gently against my chest above my breasts, which were now heaving slightly as my breathing increased. His eyes raked across my body, and he made a soft moaning sound.

I took advantage of the moment and threw a right hook, hitting him squarely in the temple. He staggered back, giving me enough freedom to lift my knee and nail him in the groin. He doubled over with a grunt, his face turning blood red, glaring up at me with eyes that held murderous intent. That had brought him back to his senses—or away from his senses, depending on how you looked at it.

I pushed off the wall, attempting to make a run for it; however, his shadow demons had his back. They closed in on me immediately, pressing me back to the wall as I tried to avoid their striking claws. Their screech came again, painfully piercing my brain as ice flooded through my body. I realized the noise was speech.

Careful, girl. Marduk would be greatly displeased with us if we let anything happen to the mage. We have worked too hard and come too far to allow you to destroy this alliance. Marduk might need you, but we do not.

When it stopped speaking, I found myself doubled over, clutching my head. The silence in my mind washed away the agony, and I was able to straighten, although it felt as if frost coated my brain. The creature had given Zane the time he needed to recover, and before I could react, Zane was on me again.

"You dare try to manipulate me, you harlot? You will never sway me from my commanded duty! I will make you regret your treachery." His long, nimble fingers closed around my neck and began to squeeze.

My eyes widened in shock and fear, but I was unable to do more than squeak with the increasing pressure on my larynx. I clawed at his hands and face, trying in vain to get him to relax his grip. Finally, my thumbs found his eye sockets, and I pushed. The soft orbs gave way beneath my fingers, but only for a brief moment. He pulled his head back and turned away from me so I lost contact, yet his grip on my neck never wavered.

My flailing arms grew heavy, falling limply at my sides. I tried to get them to obey me, but they were like immovable lead weights. My legs buckled, and Zane followed me down to the ground.

His face became fuzzy as blackness crowded in at the edges of my vision. I had always thought I would go out in a blaze of gunfire. I had never expected I would be throttled by a hot guy in a grimy back alley only a few blocks from my apartment.

Fear crept in then, like an uninvited rodent scurrying silently into a house after dark, burrowing its way behind the walls.

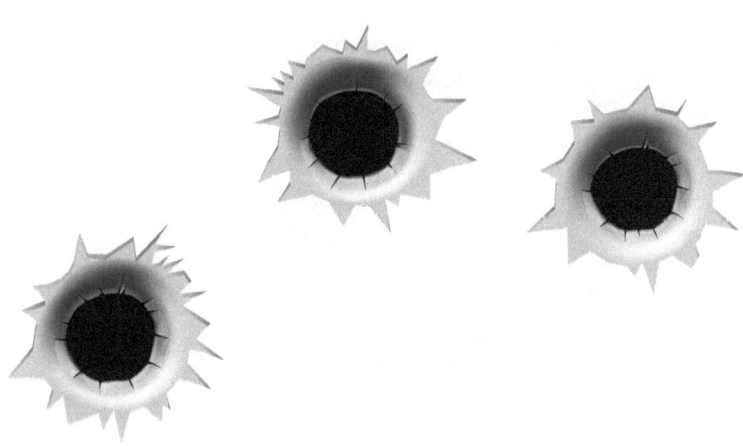

Chapter Six

I MUST HAVE passed out because, when I became aware of my surroundings again, it was the smell that hit my nose first. It told me that I was still in the alley. The sounds of angry male voices came to me next. My heavy lids fluttered opened, and the excruciating pain that pulsed through my head made me question whether remaining alive was a good thing.

Relying on discipline, training, and more than a little experience, I forced the pain down deep to be dealt with later. The solid surface of the brick wall was at my back, so I used it to stagger to my feet. When my vision cleared, the tall, lean figure of Alex emerged out of the darkness at the mouth of the alley.

He entered the narrow space cautiously, eyes alert and darting around, taking in the scene before him. He held a long, smooth shaft of wood in his hand, holding it in front of him. If he was planning to bash someone's skull in with it, that wouldn't have been the best grip to use. *Amateur*, I thought absently.

Zane was facing Alex and hadn't noticed my awakening, but I was blocked in by Zane on one side and the shadow demons on the other.

"Zane, let her go," Alex said in an authoritative tone.

"You know him?" I directed the question to Alex, my voice raspy and hoarse as I tried to speak through my damaged larynx.

Both men ignored me—typical.

"Alex, my old friend," Zane said, not sounding friendly at all. "I was wondering when you were going to show up. I knew the Council would send their favorite attack dog for her. So, what's the play: kill, capture, torture, or maybe the Council's favorite … manipulate?"

Alex's eyes darted to me then back to Zane. "You have the Council wrong, Zane. I am not here to hurt her. They want her protected."

"It doesn't matter what they want. She belongs to Marduk, and you know it. I'm just taking her back home where she belongs. He will decide her fate."

"That's not going to happen," Alex said, not sounding at all intimidated. "You know that, after what happened, this is no longer a family matter and is the responsibility of the Council."

Confusion morphed into frustration. How dare these two Neanderthals stand there and discuss my fate as if I wasn't even present?

While Zane and Alex were occupied in their my-dick-is-bigger-than-yours contest, I looked around for my weapon, finding it about twenty feet away, lying between the two men. I then remembered the sword strapped to Zane's back, which was in perfect reaching distance. I had never wielded a sword before and knew that, if it came to a fight, I would lose miserably. However, all I had to do was brandish it well enough to make them think twice about attacking me, giving me enough time and space to make my way to the Glock.

The sword slid free of its scabbard in one smooth pull, letting loose a light chime. It was a large sword, not like those Japanese blades that ninjas in the movies used. This was more like Conan the Barbarian's sword, yet it wasn't as heavy as it looked.

Using two hands, I hefted it with only a little effort, finally getting their attention. When Alex and Zane turned to face me in surprise, I swung the sword in a figure eight, hoping I didn't look like a complete novice.

"Emma," said Alex, as if he were trying to calm a spooked horse. "I'm here to help you. Give me the sword."

I snorted in response. *I know, not very lady-like of me.*

Zane wasn't quite so accommodating. "You had your chance to die peacefully," he snarled in his Mr. Hyde persona. "I'm done negotiating."

Negotiating? Was that what he thought of what had happened between us only moments earlier?

Leaving me no time to be further affronted, Zane commanded, "Take her!"

His shadow demons wasted no time closing in on either side of me. Alex made a move forward, presumably to stay true to his word and help me, but Zane blocked his path.

Unworried and uncaring about what happened to the two of them, I focused my attention on the shadows.

They might not have had brains to speak of, but they weren't stupid. They came at me together, claws bared. As they approached, I was able to get a closer look at them, although their full features never really came into focus. The most I could make out were glowing yellow eyes in long, gaunt faces, with flowing shadowy cloaks hanging from their skeletal shoulders.

I had nothing to wield against them other than Zane's sword. Therefore, as claws slashed at me, I raised the weapon in an attempt to block them. I didn't expect it to work against these insubstantial beings, but relief washed through me as steel clanged against talons. Their bodies might be shadow, but those claws were solid enough to rend, tear, and sever the life from my body.

I swung the sword wildly. It arced through the air with no technique and even less control. *Thrust, parry, slash.* I struggled to think through the right movements, the most solid stance, the best grip. My over-thinking made my movements choppy and uncertain, but I had been holding my own until one of the creatures saw an opening and slashed my left side.

I cried out as a spike of icy pain speared through me. Zane and Alex both paused in their fight as they heard me. I hadn't been paying much attention to them until this point and saw they now both held wooden staffs and were sweating and panting. How were they fighting each other with sticks, while I got stuck with the actual deadly nightmares? Not fair at all.

"Don't kill her!" Zane reminded the creatures.

Alex noticed the trouble I was having with the sword and said, "Don't think. Let your instincts take over."

Asshole, I thought. How the hell did wielding a broadsword for the first time ever—and against shadow demons, no less—come as instinct to anyone?

Ignoring both men, I focused on defending myself and retrieving my gun, which was being kicked around unceremoniously by the two men as they fought each other. Why was nothing ever easy?

The area right below my ribs where I had been injured was wet with blood and becoming numb from cold. There wasn't much pain anymore; however, I was losing the use of those muscles to hypothermia, limiting my movements as I tried to wield the large sword with two hands. The bleeding slowed as the area grew colder. Shivers set in, racking my body as my core temperature dropped a few degrees.

I blocked another slashing attack from the creature on my right and ducked as the claw of the creature on my left passed over my head. I knew they wouldn't kill me, but Zane had said nothing to stop them from maiming or crippling me. In any case, I had no intention of allowing them to capture me either.

I went on the offensive, slicing the sword through the air, cutting uselessly at shadows. Landing another blow on the claws of one demon, it let out a piercing shriek, but whether it was in anger or pain, I couldn't tell. It gave the creature extra motivation that it probably didn't need, since I was losing anyway. It came at me in a fury before I could recover, slashing my shoulder.

My left hand fell away from the sword limply as a deep freeze spread down the length of my arm and up into my collarbone. The sword tip clanged on the pavement before I could compensate for the weapon's added weight in my single hand. Although, let's face it, if I couldn't wield the damn sword well with two hands, there was no way I could do it with one.

With fluid grace, the second shadow demon swept in and sliced ribbons into the back of my right thigh. With a cry, I fell to my knee, my quickly numbing leg no longer able to support my weight.

'Using the sword as a crutch, I staggered back to my feet, placing all of my weight on my good leg. The shadow demons held back, knowing defeated prey when they saw it. However, I wasn't quite ready to concede just yet.

Taking a calculated risk, I hefted the sword and flung it with a great heave at the creature closest to me. I didn't wait for it to react, spinning, lunging toward the Glock that had come to a rest against the alley wall about twenty feet away. I landed a few feet short, crawling the remaining distance as the shadows came for me.

A cold talon wrapped around my ankle and yanked, dragging me farther from my goal. It tore through my jeans and into my calf, freezing my left leg. I flipped onto my back. If I was going down, I didn't want the final blow to come from behind.

Limp and defenseless, the enemy rose up over me. Knowing I would be taken and tortured for God only knew what purpose until death finally took me, fear once again reared its ugly head. It crashed through me like an unending tidal wave, adding to the ceaseless cold that was creeping progressively through my body, turning me into a literal ice princess. That made me think of Jason and Daniel.

A fresh assault of despair washed over me. I would never see them again. They would never know what had happened to me. I would disappear without a trace, and that would kill them. They wouldn't rest until they had found out the truth. And what if they did learn the truth? That would put them squarely in the crosshairs of a powerful supernatural enemy they couldn't hope to fight, let alone defeat. They would follow me into death, and I couldn't accept that.

The overwhelming fear transformed into overwhelming anger as I rebelled against the thought of danger coming to my friends, but I was still physically frozen, prone on the ground. The only exception was my right hand ... and the warmth that now radiated from the center of my chest.

Looking down, a deep indigo light pulsed from under the thin material of my torn top. It was radiating from the amulet. I had been wearing the thing around my neck for days, had probably examined it a hundred times, and I hadn't gotten any closer to understanding its use or significance. Now, at the time of my greatest need, it had chosen to come to life. Was that what triggered it?

I reached a shaking hand inside my top and pulled it out. The light pouring forth intensified and spilled into every corner and crevice of the alley. The shadow demons that had been looming over me screeched and wailed more sharply than any other sound they had previously made. Just when I thought my eardrums would start bleeding, the creatures disappeared. Whether they had fled to safety or had been obliterated, I couldn't say, and I didn't really care. I was simply relieved to be rid of them.

The light in the amulet gradually died out as if it, too, knew I was safe from harm. When all was dark again, an intense weariness flooded through me. All of my energy reserves had been depleted, and I was running on fumes. All I wanted to do was close my eyes and sleep for days, but I still had Zane and Alex to deal with.

Digging deep into sheer will and determination, I pulled myself along the cold concrete floor to where my gun still lay. Grasping the Glock in my hand was probably the same feeling a child had when snuggling a security blanket. I propped myself into a sitting position against the alley wall and placed the gun in my lap.

While debating whether I even had the energy to lift it, I finally got a good look at what was happening between Zane and Alex , and I was completely unprepared for it.

Although both men were bearing long, wooden staffs, they weren't using them to bludgeon each other. Instead, odd-looking symbols that covered the smooth polished wood were glowing brightly, throwing what looked like blasts of energy at each other. Streams of white hot lightning flew from Zane's staff, only to crash into an invisible barrier erected in front of Alex that shimmered almost imperceptibly when struck. A few motes of liquid fire splattered to the ground, alighting the drier pieces of trash, which burned out quickly. Alex returned in kind with a volley of ice shards that Zane countered with a wave of his staff, redirecting them to harmlessly hit the alley wall.

The energies being thrown around the tight space of the alley formed themselves into swirling ribbons of flame, jagged forks of ice, and glittering bursts of dust and ash. For a time, I could do nothing except gape at the power, intensity, and sheer magnificence of the attacks.

Blinking rapidly, I attempted to pull myself back to the reality of the situation. Looking more closely at the two men, I realized neither appeared to be in very good shape. Zane staggered on his feet after deflecting the last attack, looking for all the world like he was about to pass out. His skin was pale and glistening with sweat, looking like thin parchment stretched over hollow bones. Dark circles hung under his eyes, and he was breathing heavily.

Zane pulled it together and countered, throwing another attack at Alex, who fell to one knee, cradling his arm when the energy hit the shield he had been holding in place. Deflecting the blow had clearly caused him physical pain, even though it had never actually touched him.

This was ridiculous. These two were at a stalemate, and they couldn't keep up the volleys much longer. Someone was going to throw a blow that the other would no longer be able to avert, and then the battle would be over. However, it was impossible to guess who would luck out in the end. I didn't like those odds, and I was prepared to fix the game in my favor.

Zane had tried to kill me and come very close to succeeding. I knew he wouldn't give up until he had completed his mission; as a result, my life would be in danger as long as we both kept breathing. I wasn't certain where Alex stood, but he hadn't yet posed any threat to me. If he did, I would take care of him at that time, but until then, I had no good reason to kill him.

I wrapped my weak fingers around the handle of the Glock and raised my arm. Between the exhaustion and the uncontrollable shivering from the shadow demons' icy attack, I was struggling to take steady aim. When I got a clear shot, however, I took it.

The sound of the Glock's discharge was a loud crack, painful to my ears. Although the gun was fitted with a suppresser, in the enclosed space of the alley, the sound of the shot was magnified and reverberated off the walls.

My aim had been off. I hit Zane in the shoulder instead of the head. He went spinning with the force of the bullet and slammed into the opposite wall, dropping his staff and clutching his wound, blood leaking out from between his fingers. He looked at me wild-eyed and in pain as I kept the weapon aimed at him. However, I simply couldn't hold it any longer.

The exhaustion and cold won out, my arm falling heavily to the ground. I didn't release it from my grasp, but I wouldn't be able to will my arm back up again if I tried.

Zane wasn't in any better condition than I was. He was spent from the battle as well as blood loss and didn't even make an attempt to try to recover his staff. He probably didn't have the strength left to lift it anyway.

Alex recovered from his shock at the gunshot and ran to Zane's side to assess his wound. With a relieved sigh, he said, "The bullet is lodged in your shoulder, but it missed anything vital. You'll live as long as you get medical attention." He tore off a piece of his shirt to use as a tourniquet on the wound.

"That'll slow the bleeding enough to buy you time until an ambulance arrives." He pulled a Smartphone from his pants pocket and dialed 9-1-1. When he was done, he stood and came to me.

Looking up at him in confusion, I asked, "Why did you just do that? Why are you trying to save him when he would have killed you without hesitation?"

He knelt by my side. "Emma, that is a very long story, one we'll have to save for another time. Right now, let's get you out of here so we can fix you up."

He hefted me into a fireman's carry. Although it was the easiest way to carry a person, I was surprised he was able to manage at all, given his own current state of fatigue and burnout. He wasn't moving fast, and his breath was coming in heavy pants, yet he somehow managed to make his way the few blocks to my apartment.

You had to love New York City; no one even gave us a second glance.

Chapter Seven

I AWOKE THE next day in my own bed, surrounded by the pleasant scents of rosemary, basil, pine, and other aromas I couldn't immediately place. Opening my eyes, I found my wounds slathered in some sort of green paste, which was the source of the fragrance. I also took note that I was completely unclothed except for the Hello Kitty underwear and black bra I had been wearing yesterday, my torn and filthy clothes strewn across the floor. I was grateful Alex had saved my ass, but I figured he could have thrown away my clothes or, at the very least, tossed them into a corner rather than simply leaving them unceremoniously lying about. Men were such slobs.

I tested my limbs and was immensely grateful when they responded. The numbness was gone, replaced by the dull ache of muscle soreness. I used my hand to wipe some of the paste from the wound on my calf, revealing angry red lacerations, although they weren't deep enough to have torn muscle as

I had feared. The flesh wounds would heal and likely leave behind some thin scars yet no permanent damage. I had no doubt the shadow demons could have inflicted much more serious wounds, but they must have been holding back based on Zane's orders to capture, not kill.

I wasn't entirely certain what the paste was meant to do, but I guessed it was for healing or pain relief. I would have to remember to ask Alex.

I climbed slowly out of bed and stripped the sheets. As much as I liked the smell of the poultice, I didn't want to sleep in green puree. I threw my torn clothing into the trash and grabbed a clean outfit, making my way downstairs to the shower.

Stopping short at the kitchen, I groaned in annoyance at the mess. Alex was nowhere in sight; however, the sink was piled high with dirty, encrusted pots. Stems, leaves, and other scraps littered my white granite counters along with the dirty knives and spoons used to cut, chop, and mix the concoction. Alex clearly hadn't even tried to tidy up after himself. Maybe I was being overly sensitive, but it felt like he had left this mess on purpose. I didn't even know the guy, and he was already trying to irritate me. I seemed to be on everyone's shit list these days.

Despite that, when I saw him again, if I saw him again, I would have to thank Alex for getting me out of there last night and taking care of me. I had so many questions, and he had just disappeared without even leaving a note or a phone number. The only place I could think to look for him was back at Raines, but it wouldn't open until this evening. In the meantime, I did have another stop I needed to make today that I was hoping would yield some answers.

Sighing in resignation, I made my way to the shower.

I emerged from the bathroom thirty minutes later, clean and dressed in jeans and a vintage Star Wars T-shirt, armed with my Glock and a wicked combat knife that I had slid into my boot. I didn't want to get stuck again without a back-up weapon.

I got to work, scrubbing pots and wiping down counter tops. When my apartment was back to its usual spotless condition, I grabbed my purse and headed to midtown.

THE SUN WAS shining and the air was warming up quickly as I picked my way through the throngs of tourists in Times Square. Even though I had lived in Manhattan for years and walked through this area hundreds of times, I still couldn't help looking up in awe at the massive video screens cycling through movie trailers and advertisements; billboards of male underwear models plastered onto the sides of buildings; and flashing marquees for Broadway theater productions.

Hundreds of people were lined up at the TKTS booth, hoping to land discount tickets to their favorite musicals. Knock-off costumed characters of Elmo, Mickey Mouse, and Cookie Monster were trying to earn money by getting their photos taken with children and even some adults who saw the humor value in it. The Hard Rock Cafe and Toys R Us had lines that spilled out the front doors.

It was just another ordinarily extraordinary day in New York City.

A few blocks past Times Square and two avenues to the east, I found what I was looking for. A hanging sign swung gently in the light afternoon breeze above a shop entrance. Gold lettering on the sign's midnight blue background identified the establishment as Alfreda's Antiquarian Bookshop. Below the name was a beautifully intricate drawing of a tree with its curling gold branches extending out from a slender trunk to form a canopy of mesmerizing swirls. In the heart of the tree's trunk was a single blue gem that glittered in the sunlight.

This was the shop Daniel had recommended I visit because they might know something about my amulet. I'd had no intention of coming here when he had first mentioned it, but after last night, I needed to learn more about the object I wore around my neck. I had to tread carefully though; there were killers after me, and I didn't want to draw undue attention to myself or to anyone else, for that matter, by flaunting the medallion.

As I stepped through the front door, a small bell tinkled delicately, announcing my presence. The store wasn't large, and a clutter of numerous mystical books and other paraphernalia filled every available space. Yet, rather than making the shop feel cramped and claustrophobic, it felt welcoming and cozy.

Honey-colored shelves lined all of the walls, floor to ceiling. They were filled with books about magic, Wicca, philosophy, meditation, divination, and more. Other shelves were packed tightly with apothecary jars in an assortment of shapes, sizes, and colors, but all were labeled neatly with names like Adder's Tongue, Devil's Bone, Dragon's Blood, Horehound, and Unicorn Root. Chest-high shelving units stood in the middle of the store, overflowing with crystals, wind chimes, beads, bowls, tarot cards, and other magical and spiritual trinkets. The air was scented heavily with sandalwood, vanilla, and other perfumes from the incense, candles, and oils available for purchase.

The high-pitched musical voice of a woman who sounded more like a twelve-year-old than a twenty-something-year-old resonated from the checkout counter at the back of the shop. "Hey there!" came the bubbly welcome. "Feel free to take a look around. I don't want to hover over you or be too overbearing, so I'll stay back here. But you just let me know if there is anything I can help you with."

"Okay, thanks," I responded, grateful I would be able to approach the discussion in my own time instead of being forced into a falsely cheery chat with the checkout girl.

I walked slowly through the store, making a show of peering at all of the shelves, as if I were truly intrigued by their contents.

"Hi, again!" came that same cheerful voice from directly behind me. I was uncharacteristically startled by her sudden appearance. It wasn't often someone could sneak up behind me without my awareness. "I know I said I would stay back there, but then I thought you might need some help, and maybe you were too shy to ask, and I didn't want you to leave here and think you got bad customer service, so I thought I would pop over and see if you had any questions or were looking for something in particular."

I stared at the woman as she was speaking, wondering when she was going to take a breath. She had made it through that entire speech in one lungful—impressive. Despite her tendency toward verbosity, she was quite striking. Anywhere besides New York City, she would have easily stood out in a crowd.

Her hair was a bright, burnished red that most women achieved only from a bottle yet appeared to be natural on her. It shone like silk under the fluorescent lights, and she wore it loose and full to just below her shoulders. She was boyishly slim with an athletic grace and several inches shorter than me, but the four-inch bright green stilettos she was wearing compensated for her lack of height. Her eyes matched the color of her shoes; however, what drew my attention was the tattoo she had centered on her forehead. It was made of curving lines that appeared to represent a flame and was the same shade as her hair. It was startling yet beautiful.

I realized I was merely standing there staring at her. "Um, I like your tattoo."

"Thanks!" She smiled widely, showing perfect white teeth, framed by full lips painted an alluring red. "You have no idea how many comments I get on it. Most people who come in here tell me they love it, but every once in a while, I'll get some stodgy old fart who tells me I ruined my beautiful face with it, and when I'm old and wrinkled, I'll regret it. I don't worry too much about that though. It'll be a while before I get old enough for wrinkles."

"Oh … um … yeah, it's—"

"Oh, my, where are my manners? My name is Lilly Alfreda, and I own this shop. So, is there anything I can help you find?"

I forced what I hoped looked like a friendly smile on my face. "Yes, I could use some help. My grandmother recently passed—"

"Oh, no! I am so sorry. I would be devastated if I ever lost my grandma. She practically raised me. Were you close to her?"

"Who? Oh, my grandmother. Well, she—"

"What am I saying? Of course you were close to her. If you hadn't been, you wouldn't be so upset. I can see the grief all over your face. It causes premature aging, you know."

"What?" Had she just told me I looked old?

"My grandma is an amazing lady. She is ancient, but so wise. Just the other day, I was asking her advice about this guy I met—"

"I'm sure she gave you some very sage advice," I said, trying to steer the conversation back on topic. "As I was saying, my grandmother passed and left me all of her belongings. She was quite an odd bird, really into religion and spirituality—"

"Do you know what religion or form of spirituality she was interested in? You know, you don't have to be religious to be spiritual. I find it really interesting that she was both—"

"Lilly, please!" The extroverted and bubbly shop owner was beginning to grate on my nerves, but I still needed her help.

I plastered the false smile back on my face.

"I'm so sorry," she apologized. "I know I talk too much sometimes and go off on tangents and share too much information—"

"It's not a problem, really." Rushing to get the words out before the next interruption, I said, "Listen, I found a necklace of my grandmother's with some foreign writing on it and a gemstone in its center. I can't read it or identify the stone, but a friend told me you might know something about it."

"Oh, is that all? Sure, I can take a look at it. Did you bring it?"

I freed the amulet from under my shirt and held it out to Lilly. I had no intention of removing it. If she had tried to steal it, it would require me to hurt or kill her. Thankfully, she made no move in that direction. She reached out slowly, a look of awe crossing her features as she gently took the amulet in her hands. She inspected every surface closely, and for the first time since I walked in, the store was filled with silence.

"Well?" I asked after several peaceful minutes had gone by. As much as I enjoyed her not talking, I did need answers.

"Huh? Oh! Yes," she blurted as if she had completely forgotten I was standing there. "Um, what did you say your name was again?"

"I didn't. It's Emma."

"Nice to meet you, Emma. You mentioned that a friend referred you to me. Who is your friend? I like to thank those that give me referral business."

"I'll let my friend know you're appreciative. So, what do you know about the amulet?"

"It's a pretty special piece. How did your grandmother come to own it?"

"She won it in a poker game on the Titanic."

Lilly's eyes grew wide. "Seriously?"

"No," I said, taking some perverse pleasure at teasing her, but it served her right for prying. I wasn't about to give her the real story behind the amulet. "Lilly, if you know something, I would appreciate you sharing it with me. If you don't, I will find someone more knowledgeable."

"No! Don't do that. I mean, there's no need. I do know something I can tell you. But first, would you like a cup of tea?"

"Lilly," I said in warning.

"Okay, okay. But I have to warn you, this is going to sound strange."

"I have a high believability threshold. Hit me."

"I've only ever heard about it in stories, if it is what I think it is. But it matches those descriptions exactly. It's called the god-stone. It appears in an ancient myth my people have about the creation of the world."

"Your people?" I asked, growing wary. She could be referring to her ethnicity or religion, but I doubted it.

With hesitation, Lilly brought her hand up to hover near her temple. She appeared nervous and uncharacteristically shy. Then, with resolve flashing in her green eyes, she brushed her flaming hair behind her ears —her very *pointy* ears.

"Everyone who sees them thinks they are prosthetics or some sort of costume or role playing prop," Lilly said. "They're not. Go ahead, you can touch them."

I didn't really want to. It seemed too ... intimate. Regardless, I reached up and tugged on one of the tips. She gritted her teeth with a look of determination on her face. I hadn't pulled hard, but she appeared uncomfortable at the contact.

"I'm sorry if I hurt you," I said.

"No, it's not that. They're just … sensitive."

"What are you?"

"Well, technically, I'm an elf, but I prefer the term 'fae.' It sounds much more bad-ass, don't you think?"

"I think you should be true to who you are."

"Wow, now you sound like my dad. So, you're not surprised, or you still don't believe me?"

"I believe you. I've been confronted by more inhuman creatures this week than you can shake a stick at. You, my friend, are actually a breath of fresh air in comparison to those things."

"It's true, then? The Monere are coming into this world?"

"The who?"

"It's the name given to the class of monstrous creatures in Urusilim."

"I take it the elves are from Urusilim, as well?" She nodded. "You can tell me all about the place another time. Right now, I need to know more about the amulet."

"Oh, yeah, sure. Sorry for yet another tangent. So, as the story goes, there was once one world ruled by a number of gods. They were all different; some were benevolent and peaceful, others jealous and treacherous. Since they couldn't agree on what creature should inhabit their one world, they decided to each create one living thing in their image, which became the humans, fae, ghouls, goblins, trolls, elves, demons, angels, and the like. And, for a time, all of these creations lived side-by-side in peace.

"Then, as time went by, the inhabitants of this world began to war with each other for control. For many of them, it was not within their nature to be peaceful. There were great wars beyond what has ever been seen since. Millions were slaughtered or enslaved, and the land was all but destroyed.

"The gods, not wanting to see the annihilation of their greatest creations, realized it wasn't possible for these creatures to live together, so they created the god-stone to separate the worlds. Each of the gods poured a little bit of their blood into the stone to imbue it with the tremendous power it needed to tear the world apart. The stone was a focus point for the collective energy and power of the gods. They used it to separate the world into multiple realms with impenetrable barriers between them to prevent those walls from ever being torn down.

"Over the millennia, many of the inhabitants of those realms have forgotten they used to be one. Sure, there were still wars within each world, but without the collective might of so many different beings, those wars were destructive within acceptable limits.

"As for the god-stone, no one knows what happened to it, but the stories say it was given into the protection of one of the more peaceful and reasonable gods, where it was locked away so it could never be used again."

Lilly ended her tale, and I stood there transfixed. Was it possible? Could this really be the same stone as in the myth? I wasn't really one to believe in legends and fairy tales, especially those that involved religion and deities. However, stories came from somewhere, and usually, a nugget of truth was buried deep within them. The trick was trying to figure out where that truth lay. At this point, after everything I had seen and experienced over the past week, I found I was becoming much more open-minded.

"How did your grandmother get it?" Lilly breathed.

I shook myself from my reverie and responded with the first thing that popped into my mind. "I think she had a friend of a friend who was an archeologist and found it during a dig in the Sahara desert in the 1920s," I lied, thinking of the opening scenes of *Stargate*. I watched too many movies. "Can you read the writing?" I asked quickly, before she could further question my explanation.

"No. I can tell it's an ancient language by the type of alphabet used, but I can't read it. Hey, my grandmother is sort of a specialist in ancient writings. Would it be okay if I had her look at it?"

I tensed, preparing for the inevitable fight when she tried to get me to leave it with her or simply tried to take it from me with force.

She must have noticed my sudden shift in body language because she immediately sounded apologetic. "I mean, I can take a picture of it with my phone to show her and get your number so I can call you with any additional information."

I didn't want more people than necessary to see the amulet, especially now that Lilly had confirmed its value, even if I still didn't know the truth of it or how to use it. Although, perhaps the writing could give me a deeper insight into the object. Maybe it was some sort of ancient instruction manual, like the cover stone in *Stargate*. I smiled internally at the connection and nodded in agreement.

"Perfect!" she exclaimed in her excited girly voice. She pulled out her iPhone and took a photo, and then we exchanged numbers. "My grandma is going to be so excited. I think she can really help you out. She is sort of the matriarch of our clan. She is very knowledgeable and remembers all of the old stories. If she can't give you answers, I don't think anyone can …"

"Thanks, Lilly," I shouted over my shoulder as I practically ran to the exit. "Talk to you soon." I stepped into the humid New York City air and gladly plunged into the sea of humanity.

Chapter Eight

I DECIDED TO walk home via 5th Avenue, taking the opportunity to browse the storefronts. It was rare that I ever had a need to dress up—hell, even business casual was usually unnecessary—but I still appreciated nice things. I did get tired of wearing camouflage and black military armor all the time.

As the day wore on, the heat increased. With the deep freeze of winter only a few weeks behind us and still fresh in my mind, the warmth felt like a loving blanket wrapped around my body. I reveled in the feeling of the sun on my shoulders and took my time as I made my way downtown.

I peered in the windows of Armani, Gucci, and Cartier. I admired the glittering Harry Winston diamonds, the amazing Prada stilettos, and the supple leather Louis Vuitton bags. If I really wanted to treat myself to one special item, I could take my pick, but I never did. There didn't seem to be any point in buying myself something so stunning when I would never have the opportunity to use it. I didn't get out much.

I was gazing in the Versace window, appreciating a sheer lilac dress that was only strategically opaque, when I felt that familiar tingling sensation on the back of my neck. Someone was watching me. I used the reflection in the glass to search for my tail. With the throngs of people going about their business, it was difficult to pinpoint exactly who might be following me, but I was able to narrow down the list to a handful of potential suspects loitering across the street. I wouldn't be able to know for sure until I started moving, though.

I took my time perusing from store to store until I reached Saks Fifth Avenue. Once again, I stopped at the department store window, making a show of admiring the display of elegant, beaded silk gowns. Instead, I inspected the reflection until I identified my shadow. *I got you*, I thought with satisfaction.

Across the street stood a man wearing dark blue slacks and a matching sports jacket with a white button down shirt. He wore no tie, and his top button was undone in a casual look. He held a cell phone to his ear, as if he were engrossed in a fascinating conversation, although every few seconds, he would glance in my direction just to be sure I hadn't started walking again.

He looked nondescript with dull brown hair, neatly trimmed. He was of average height and average weight, with the facial features of an every-man. He wasn't the type of person who would draw any attention at all. In fact, he looked quite bland, which is what made him the perfect spy.

He was one of the suspects I had taken note of at the Versace window where he had been pretending to be looking at something on his phone's display. It was time to turn the tables and make the hunter the hunted. I needed to get him someplace that gave me leverage and privacy yet wasn't too far away. I wanted to get this guy before he realized I was on to him and made an escape. The spot I had in mind held its risks since a lot of people would be around, but it also had some deep, dark places that would work quite nicely.

Keeping my unhurried pace, I continued a few short blocks and cut left onto East 42nd Street. Ahead of me was my destination—the iconic Beaux Arts building that was the home of Grand Central Station.

I stepped between the enormous Corinthian columns with the statues of Mercury, Hercules, and Minerva looking down on me and into the breathtaking space of the main concourse. Thankfully, it was a Sunday, which meant the train station wasn't filled with hundreds of thousands of weekday commuters. Instead, there were probably only tens of thousands of tourists.

I made my way down the marble staircase, picking up the pace as I hurried under the vaulted ceiling with its giant painting of the zodiac. I couldn't look behind me to see if he was still following for fear of giving myself away, so I forced myself to keep my eyes forward.

Increasing my speed, I dove into a crowd that was making its way out of the nearest train tunnel. As they swallowed me, I turned sharply to the left, ducking behind a marble column, and waited.

My tail passed the column, his head swinging back and forth, eyes darting around the space, desperately trying to find me. I slipped in behind him and pulled my gun, wrapping an arm around his waist and pressing myself against his back. I slipped the gun between our bodies where it couldn't be seen, placing the muzzle to his spine. To the casual observer, it would look like a tender moment between lovers.

He wasn't much taller than I was; as a result, I was able to easily whisper into his ear, "Don't turn around, and don't try to make any sudden moves. Just keep walking in the direction I steer you. If you don't do exactly what I say, I'm going to sever your spine with a bullet. Understand?"

"Yeah, I understand," he responded in a working class British accent that reminded me of Burt from *Mary Poppins*. I would give the guy credit; he was pretty calm about the whole thing. His voice was steady, and his body remained relaxed, which put me on high alert. However, he did as I said.

I walked him through the vaulted archways of the terminal until we reached an unmarked steel door I knew was an employee access tunnel with a keypad lock. I looked around to be sure we were alone before releasing his waist. Keeping the gun to his back, I used my free hand to quickly enter the pass code and was relieved to find the old code still worked.

I had been assigned to Grand Central briefly in a military guard unit when someone had called in a credible terrorist threat a few years back. I had learned a lot about the secret rooms and tunnels beneath the terminal since I had to secure each of them. This particular doorway led down a sterile white corridor to a little used service elevator.

I pressed the button, and the elevator doors squealed open in protest.

My prisoner, who had been cooperative until this point, balked at the prospect of entering the aging lift. "Where are you taking me?" he asked. I could feel his muscles tense and twitch. "Are you going to try to kill me?"

"That depends. Do you want to die? Because, if not, I would strongly recommend that you answer the many questions I have for you."

I body checked him so he stumbled through the doors, hitting the far wall of the elevator. I followed him in, keeping my gun pointed at his chest, then pressed the only button inside the elevator that would take us to the bottom of the shaft, fifteen stories below ground. The doors slid shut, and with a jerk, the elevator began moving.

It was only when my prisoner began to change that I realized it might not have been the most brilliant idea in the world to cage myself into a small box suspended over open air with a complete stranger. I had once again forgotten I was potentially dealing with a supernatural enemy, and I shouldn't have assumed my tail was only a normal human being.

The man standing huddled in the corner straightened to his full height of only 'five-foot-ten, and his eyes began to glow a pale yellow.

"I'm more of a lover than a fighter ..." he said, his voice becoming deeper and rougher with every word. I heard the snapping of what I realized were his bones, and his skin bulged and rippled as if something living beneath it was trying to get out. His face elongated, and wickedly sharp teeth extended from what was quickly becoming a muzzle. "But I can dish out a pretty good disemboweling," he completed in a growl before the transformation of his mouth prevented any further human speech. His clothes tore away as his limbs bulged and bent. He fell to all fours as course, gray hair sprouted over his entire body.

Cold terror bled through my body, filling my veins with ice as I tried to remember all the rules I had seen in movies about taking down a werewolf. I had no way of knowing whether there was any truth to them, but it was all I had to go on. Unfortunately, the bullets in my gun were made of steel, not silver.

He completed the transformation from man to wolf in a matter of seconds, although even before then, I had put three bullets into him. I continued to hold out hope that I could interrogate him; therefore, I didn't aim for his head. Instead, I blew out his knee, trying to incapacitate him.

I was surprised when the creature actually let out a yelp of pain as a spray of blood and cartilage hit the back wall of the elevator, and the wolf's leg collapsed under it. He still had three good legs, though, and he lunged at me with snapping jaws.

I got off another two shots, but they went wide, missing him as he barreled into me. I managed to keep hold of the weapon, but the wolf's jaws clamped down on the gun. Unfortunately, the muzzle was not pointed into his mouth; thus, pulling the trigger would just put a bullet harmlessly into the wall of the elevator.

I needed the gun though. I wasn't about to let go of it. With my free hand, I punched the wolf square in the muzzle, raining repeated blows on its face, my hand going numb as my knuckles split and bled, but I kept hitting him. His eye was a bruised and swollen mess, and blood poured freely from his nose.

When I felt his jaws loosening, I pushed past the pain in my hand and hammered him with one final fist to the nose, throwing my entire body weight behind it. He released me, and I brought up my gun, but he was changing again.

Thinking he was shifting back into a man and conceding the fight, I held my fire. Instead, his muzzle sharpened and hardened into a point. His gray fur sprouted feathers, and his arms extended into broad wings that flapped wildly. His injured leg was less of an impediment now that he could fly.

He lifted from the floor and dove straight for me. I ducked, instinctively raising my arms to protect my head and face. He hit the wall behind me yet recovered quickly and flew at me again.

Staying low, I tried to get a bead on him with my gun, but he was moving too fast. The cramped elevator wasn't large; however, this form made him quicker, more capable of tight turns, and gave him more room to maneuver since he could take advantage of the air space above my head. He launched at me with talons bared and sliced through my forearm as I shielded my eyes. The pain was sharp and intense, and blood flowed freely from the lacerations.

The elevator continued to descend, and I knew it would be only seconds before we reached the bottom and the doors opened. If he flew out of the elevator in this form, I would lose him and my chance at getting some answers. He could easily elude me in the large, dark space we would be entering; consequently, I had to subdue him, and I had to do it fast.

When I ducked against his next swooping attack, he entangled his talons in my long hair, attempting to pull my head up to peck out my eyes. I kept my head low and reached up, grabbing onto his skinny bird legs with a vice grip. He subsequently flapped wildly, trying to lift off, but I held on tight, pulling him downward. Hair that was still tangled around his talons tore painfully from my head. I struggled against the powerful down strokes of his wings while he threatened to escape my grip.

Once I wrestled him down far enough, I released one leg and grabbed a hold of a wing, quickly followed by the second wing. He tried to pump them furiously, but I managed to launch myself on top of him. He fell to the floor under the weight of my body, and I pinned his wings beneath my knees.

Reaching into my boot, I freed the knife hidden there and plunged it through the bone of his wing with such force the knife drove into the elevator floor, pinning him like a butterfly in a display case.

A piercing screech rose from the bird's throat and gradually turned into the wail of a man as he shifted back into human form. He was naked beneath me, sweating and panting in pain from the knife that was impaled through his bicep.

Just then, the elevator chimed gently, announcing we had reached our destination, and the doors slid open, revealing the darkness beyond.

Chapter Nine

"WAKE UP, SLEEPY head." I lightly kicked the unconscious shape shifter in the leg I had shot. He jerked and let out a moan of pain.

He had passed out soon after the elevator doors had opened. I used his torn clothing as tourniquets for his knee and bicep and then dragged him into the abandoned train car that sat waiting on unused tracks.

This railway tunnel had once connected to the glamorous Waldorf Astoria hotel as a discreet means of transporting the hotel's more famous guests, like presidents, dignitaries, and the occasional celebrity. The train car was heavily armored yet pocked with rust and falling into decay from disuse. Access to the tunnel from the hotel had been cut off decades ago when the Waldorf walled over the entryway. I doubted any hotel employees still alive would remember it had ever been there.

I didn't bother restraining the shifter, since I had nothing to tie him down with. He wasn't in any condition to escape anyway. I found the circuit breaker and turned on the limited power supply. It was enough to get the train doors open and cast dim light throughout the cabin. I propped him onto one of the rotting cushioned seats and placed a larger remnant of his jacket over his naked lap. It wasn't out of respect for his privacy; I did it to lull him into a little bit of comfort before I really put the screws to him.

"What's your name?"

He just groaned again, his head lolling against his chest and his eyes unfocused. Another kick, harder this time, brought a higher level of awareness back to him, and he screamed hoarsely. That was better.

"What is your name?" I asked him again, louder and more slowly than the first time.

After a brief struggle to regain muscle control in his neck, he managed to lift his head and look at me. "Eddie," he panted, gritting his teeth.

If he was going to be cooperative, there was no need not to be pleasant.

"Hi, Eddie. I'm Emma. I'm actually happy to make your acquaintance." He contorted his face in pain and confusion. "I've been looking for answers, and you are going to be the one to give them to me."

He took a deep breath and sat up taller, which drew another wince from him. Once he had gotten himself settled more comfortably, he smirked, noticing the coat in his lap. "Sorry, love. Did me huge doinker make you uncomfortable?

I only get that reaction from the prudish types. Most times, the birds really love it."

So, he was the joker type.

I shifted my hips seductively and purred, "Oh, I am far from being a prude." As I leaned in, his eyes affixed themselves to the Star Wars logo pulled tight across my chest, with the S's curved around the sides of my breasts.

Slowly, I dragged the tattered jacket off his lap and slid my hands up his tensed thighs. It got the reaction I was looking for, which made it all the more fun when I placed my knife at the base of his "doinker."

He let out a high pitched wail that sounded like it had come from a six-year-old girl and scrambled backward on his seat, trying to get as far away from the blade as possible, but he had no room to maneuver. He had forgotten his injured arm, and when he placed his weight on it, trying to push himself away, he almost sobbed at the pain and injustice of it all.

"Does that mean you're ready to talk now?" I asked sweetly.

"Yeah, yeah, yeah!" He nodded furiously. "Just get that shiv away from me todger, and we can talk."

I didn't move until I felt satisfied he had received the message. Then I stood, keeping the knife held loosely in my hands.

His eyes never left the blade. "Are you planning to use that?"

"Do you plan to make me?"

He took a deep breath and blew it out slowly, his shoulders sagging as the tension left his body. That smug smile made an appearance again. I had a feeling it was his factory default setting.

"I would love to make you do all sorts of wicked things." He winked.

I rolled my eyes. "Okay, Eddie, get your mind out of the gutter. Why were you following me?"

"Maybe I just wanted to find out where you lived so I could watch you get undressed through your window." He jerked violently as my blade suddenly lodged in the seat between his legs. "Bloody hell! Have you gone barmy?"

"Why were you following me?"

"Someone hired me to keep tabs on you. That's sort of what I do. It's easy for shape shifters to move around unnoticed. We can be anybody or anything you want."

Knowing where that innuendo was going, I quickly cut in. "Who hired you?"

"Sorry, love, I can't tell you that. I like breathing."

"I thought you also liked shagging, but maybe I was wrong about that." I lowered my eyes to the knife, and he instinctively covered himself with both hands.

He leaned his head back in frustration and muttered, "This bloody job has really gone pear shaped."

"Did Vincent Darko hire you?" I asked.

"Darko?" he responded, sounding genuinely surprised. "How do you know of Vincent Darko?"

"I'm the one asking the questions. What do you know about him?"

"I know all I need to know, love. Never met him personally, but the bloke has a reputation, and not a good one. He's powerful; can't say what he is, though. Nobody seems to know that. I take that to mean anybody who's seen the real Darko under that human mask is dead. I got no interest in knowing the man beyond that."

"So if he's not the one who hired you then who did?" I asked nudging the knife blade to make my point.

He was thoughtful for a moment, weighing his options before coming to a decision. "No point in living if I can never get between the legs of a good lass again, is there? Gabriel Marduk hired me."

There was that name again—Marduk, the man Zane worked for. This guy was throwing multiple henchmen at me. Why was he so interested in me?

"Tell me about Marduk. Who is he?"

Eddie squinted at me with suspicion. "Let me ask you a question, love. What's your game?" I cocked my head in confusion. "I may not know much, but I do know you are quite familiar with Marduk. Are you trying to put one over on me?"

Why would he think I knew Marduk? Could I get Eddie to reveal more by pretending I knew what he was talking about, or should I come clean and admit I was completely clueless?

I leaned casually against a seat, trying to look like I knew a lot more than he did. "Humor me. What do you know about Marduk?"

He considered the request for a moment and seemed to think it was reasonable. "I get it. You want to know what I know. Fair enough, love. Marduk is one impressive bastard. Came up from nothing and is now vying for leadership over Urusilim. I think he'll get there too. Got a lot of support from our kind, but who else would we support, really?" His eyes held a solemn, faraway look for a moment before he shook himself out of his reverie. "Anyway, he seems quite interested in you. Why else would he go through the trouble of sending so many of his best men through the gate?"

"The gate?" I asked, forgetting I was supposed to be sly about my questioning. His sharp look made me realize I had blundered. Clearly, I was asking lots of questions that were common knowledge where he came from. I quickly corrected myself. "Why do you think he's interested in me? What did he tell you about me?"

He shrugged, allowing the redirection in questioning. "Dunno. All he said was he wanted to know where you were going and who you were working with. Oh, and if I saw you using any magic." He said that last sentence with complete nonchalance, even going so far as to slump back down in his seat and remove his hands from between relaxed legs. I merely blinked, trying to process that new piece of information.

"Why would he think I could do magic?"

Eddie let out a snort that turned into a soft chuckle. When he realized I wasn't laughing along with him and still looked utterly dumbstruck, he stopped and straightened. "Are you serious? What the bloody hell is going on? You're acting like you know nothing."

I could try to keep up this charade, but I knew so little at this point that I couldn't even fake it. Eddie was working for the enemy, and I had absolutely no reason to trust him, but a part of me was warming up to the shape shifter. He was being honest with me, and he had made no attempt to escape or attack, even though he wasn't restrained. Even his crude sense of humor was growing on me. I couldn't get too comfortable with him, but maybe I could at least make him more comfortable with me.

I took the subway seat next to him, sitting close enough so my thigh touched his. The casual contact didn't get past him, as I had known it wouldn't. He caressed my legs with his eyes until I started speaking again.

Walking that fine line between obvious flirtation and skilled seduction, I kept my eyes lowered while I rubbed my hands along my inner thighs absently. "Eddie, I have to tell you something, but I need to know I can trust you."

"Uh, yeah, love. You can absolutely trust me." To add to his sincerity, he placed his hand on my knee.

Hook, line and sinker. Men—even inhuman shape shifters—were so predictable.

"I was in a car accident ten years ago, and I can't remember anything of my life before then."

He surprised me by jerking sharply back to reality, but his hand never budged. "Ten years ago?"

I nodded. "Why?"

He quickly recovered. "Oh, no reason. It just made me think about where I was ten years ago," he said with a nervous laugh.

"Oh, yeah? And where were you?"

"Well, if you really must know, I was fifteen years old then. A boy, really, but I already had the appetites of a man, if you know what I mean." He nudged my arm playfully, and I couldn't help smiling in response. "Anyways, there was this human lass in my village who was a few years older than me and more beautiful than a field of wildflowers." He looked wistfully into the distance as if he could picture her perfectly. "This was back when humans and non-humans could live side-by-side in the same village. I wanted into her britches as much as any other hot-blooded boy in that town, but she wouldn't give me the time of day. I knew all I had to do was get her alone so I could show her my ... ahem ... assets, if you will. So I shifted into a beautiful white stallion she couldn't resist riding, and I carried her into the forest. I stopped by a stream, and before she could dismount, I shifted back into a boy, and she landed square on top of me in all my naked glory.

"Here I was, convinced she would take one look at me and jump my bones. Instead, she screamed bloody murder and some passing hunters heard it and sicced their dogs on me. I knew I couldn't outrun them, so I shifted into a dog, too, hoping the pack would take me in as one of their own. Well, it worked better than I thought it would. Some of the dogs got it in their minds that I was some kind of bitch in heat. Let me tell you, it did not end well for me."

We both burst out in laughter, enjoying a rare lighthearted moment of connection between two people.

Before we could lapse into comfortable silence, I tossed out another question. "Eddie, do you know Zane Shayde?"

"Ah, love, I wouldn't want to see a totty like you tangled up with a wanker like Zane. He's dangerous, not to mention completely insane. I heard he was a true mage once, a long time ago. Powerful, too. Folks say he would have been appointed to the Mage Council one day if he hadn't gone crazy during ... well, never mind. Those self-righteous mage arses exiled him without a second thought. Marduk took pity on him, tried to heal his mind. It didn't work entirely, but Marduk took him in anyway; that's how powerful Zane is. I feel bad for the bloke, but I still wouldn't cross him."

Eddie was absently fingering the knife still lodged in the seat between his legs. I noticed the movement, readying myself for any sudden moves, but strangely, I didn't feel threatened. Instead, I leaned in closer, eager to have my next question answered.

I rested my hand lightly on Eddie's arm, drawing his attention back to me. "Eddie, why does Marduk want me?"

His eyes softened, and a smile of genuine concern touched his lips. "Love, I'm sorry to be the one to tell you this, but he won't stop until he has you. He needs you. Unfortunately, I think he benefits whether you're alive or dead, so he's not overly concerned how you come home."

"Home?"

"Yeah, *our* home," he emphasized. "Urusilim." He took hold of my hand, squeezing it firmly with genuine conviction in his eyes. "You're one of us. You should come back with me. Marduk will protect you, fight for you, like he fights for all of us. He told us you could be our salvation against those bloody humans and mages who would see us all dead ... or you will be our destruction if you side with them against us."

His hand felt warm and soft around mine. I made no move to withdraw it. "Us?"

"Sure, those of us who aren't human, the Monere." That was the term Lilly had used to refer to evil, monstrous creatures. Was Eddie really one of those? He didn't seem all that evil to me.

I drowned in the chocolate brown pools of his eyes. God help me, he was telling the truth or, at least, the truth as he believed it to be.

He released my hand and turned away. "I'm sorry, love. You must think I've gone barmy. Maybe I've said too much, but there's something else you should know … about who you are."

Just then, a spray of blood hit my face from the gaping hole in Eddie's neck.

I leapt to my feet, pulling my gun and focusing the muzzle on Alex, who sat calmly in the shadows at the far end of the train car, a wisp of smoke trailing from the end of his staff.

I squeezed the trigger and took the shot.

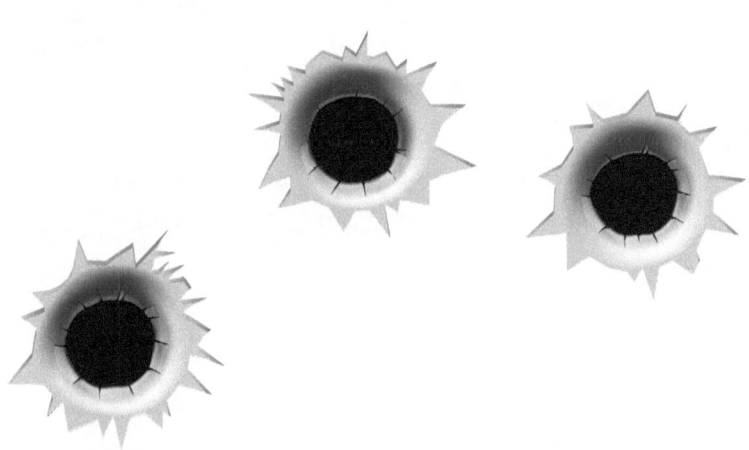

Chapter Ten

IT WAS CLEAN and straight, aimed squarely at Alex's chest, but with a flick of his wrist, the bullet was deflected, harmlessly hitting the wall.

"What the fuck, Alex?" I screamed in rage and confusion.

Alex slowly got to his feet, looking completely unconcerned, and nodded toward the body. "He was about to kill you, Ash."

His wrong use of my name momentarily startled me, but I had bigger concerns at the moment. I glanced over my shoulder at Eddie's body, being careful to keep the gun on Alex. Psychologically, it made me feel better to have a weapon in my hands, regardless of how useless it actually was. Eddie was slumped over in the seat, rivulets of blood running down his bare chest and pooling between his legs. An unfamiliar stab of remorse speared me. I hadn't wanted him to die.

It was then I noticed the knife in Eddie's hands. He had pulled it from the seat without me noticing.

"Shape shifters are notoriously manipulative and cunning. He was trying to take your guard down so he could strike before you had a chance to defend yourself. I have seen good men and women fall prey to these creatures."

"You don't know he was going to kill me," I protested, but even I could hear the doubt creeping into my voice.

"Do you really think a shape shifter could be so easily captured and detained?" Alex spat with contempt. "Those bastards are incredibly difficult to kill. He wanted you to question him so he could feed you lies and lead you further from the truth without you even realizing it was happening."

Could that be true, or was Alex the one feeding me lies? Eddie did have the knife in his hands. Had he only been fidgeting with it as he had been doing during much of our conversation, or had he intended to use it on me? I didn't have the answers, although I did know enough to understand I couldn't trust any of them. I needed to figure out what was happening in this fucked up game. Until then, I would play along and hope somebody let something slip.

I forced myself to calm down, at least on the outside. On the inside, I was roiling with anger and confusion; however, I wouldn't let Alex see that.

"How did you get in here? How did you find me?" I questioned, hoping he thought I had accepted or completely forgotten the body slumped on the seat behind me.

"I followed you and your friend here."

"How is it that I can sense everyone else who follows me except you? For that matter, how did you get down here? There is only one access point." I gestured to the elevator doors that still stood open.

"I wouldn't be much of a mage if I wasn't able to pull off a few tricks here and there, now would I?"

"I'm still the one holding the gun, Alex. You can do better than that."

He scoffed at the meaningless threat yet relented anyway. "That elevator shaft is not the only way in. A friendly old man at the train station was compelled to tell me a story about an old entrance to these unused tunnels from the Waldorf hotel. The hotel was surprisingly willing to allow me to redecorate by knocking down some of their walls." He smirked. It was clear to me that he had used some sort of influence to get information and access to this tunnel.

"As for your heightened senses, you may not even realize it, but you use small amounts of your magic to enhance your natural abilities. You can sense people watching or following you; you are slightly stronger and faster than the average human; and you have more acute vision, so you're more capable with long-range weapons. There are probably other things, but I haven't been watching you long enough to learn all of your secrets. But, as a mage, I have the ability to shield myself from your senses; for that reason, I could follow you and sit here undetected."

I slowly lowered my weapon more from the shocking impact of his words than because I trusted him not to make a move against me. Had he really just said I was using magic? I was having a hard enough time believing Zane and Alex were using real magic, and I had seen it with my own eyes. I certainly wasn't able to do what they did. I had never demonstrated even the remotest ability to wield some mysterious power, not that I had ever even tried. Anyway, everything Alex had mentioned could be explained by natural ability enhanced by intense military training. I shook my head, putting aside his words for now. This wasn't the time or place.

"Was it really necessary to kill Eddie? Even if he had meant to kill me, I am more than capable of defending myself in a knife fight against one injured man."

"He's not a man, Ash; he's a shape shifter. And I was ordered to keep an eye on you and keep you safe. That's exactly what I was doing. I gave you a chance to extract whatever information you could from him, but I had to act when he threatened you."

I still didn't feel like I had been threatened by Eddie, although I had been so distracted I hadn't noticed him pull the knife. I supposed it was entirely possible he could have slit my femoral artery or stabbed me in the chest, taking me out before I had a chance to fight back.

"Was he really lying to me about everything?" I asked, knowing Alex had heard every word.

Alex shrugged. "Perhaps not everything, at least in his mind. People usually believe the side they are fighting on is righteous. I would have given you different answers for some of those same questions, but it's hard to say which one of us would have been telling the truth, maybe both."

That was an interesting non-answer if I had ever heard one. "Okay, then, let's hear them—your answers. And start with why you keep calling me Ash."

"Fine, but I get the first question. Were you telling the truth about losing your memory ten years ago? And I will know if you're lying." He didn't say it in a threatening way, more matter-of-fact, but I knew it for what it was.

"Yes!" I yelled, stomping in a circle with my fists clenched tightly, looking a lot like a kindergartner throwing a tantrum. "In the past week, I have been set up; almost killed in some sort of voodoo ritual; attacked by ghouls, Pokémon, and shadow demons, not to mention your psycho buddy; tailed by a shape shifter you murdered right in front of me; and then you—a complete stranger, by the way—threaten me about lying when no one has yet to tell *me* the truth!"

"Pokémon?" Of course that was what he would latch on to.

"'Never mind," I grumbled. "Just tell me what the hell is going on, or get the fuck away from me."

"Now that sounds more like the Ash I know."

"And love?" I asked, completing the cliché with a withering glance.

"Absolutely not," Alex snapped. The amount of venom in his voice startled me and left me momentarily speechless. What the hell had I done to this guy to make him hate me so much? He recovered before I did and continued as if he hadn't just skewered me with his hostility. "What were you doing at that bookshop?"

I debated whether I should tell him anything, but he already knew I had the amulet. If he hadn't seen me use it in the alley, he had certainly seen it when he had unclothed me that night. "I was looking for information on the amulet. I was told the shop owner was an expert in mystical objects and might be able to help me."

"Did you learn anything?" He avoided my gaze, moving casually about the train car as though he were more interested in his surroundings than the answer to that question.

"Not much that was useful. She only told me some folklore about the origins of the amulet. She called it ... Oh, what was it? A god-stone, that's what she called it."

Alex's head whipped around as if I had just slapped him. "Are you sure that's what she said?"

"Yes, why? That obviously means something to you."

"Maybe. What was the shop keeper's name?"

"Um ... Lilly. Lilly Alfreda."

"Alfreda, huh?" He gnawed on his lip so intently I thought he might chew it off.

I managed to wait for all of five seconds. "Alex?"

"Sorry. I'll look into it. I don't want to say anything until I'm certain."

"If you're thinking she might be an elf, consider yourself certain, because she is."

"Well, that's a positive sign. It means she can be believed. If she said it's the god-stone, it likely is. Her people would know since they were the original guardians of the stone before it was lost a millennia ago."

"She said she would try to find out what the writing on the amulet means."

"Will you let me know if you learn anything?"

"Why should I? It's not like you have been entirely forthcoming with info."

He looked almost apologetic in response to my death glare. "I will answer what I can, but you have to know I am not at liberty to tell you everything."

"Fair enough." I returned the gun to my waistband. "I can respect the need for secrecy sometimes, but don't think I'll accept a non-response gracefully. I will eventually find out everything you know, one way or another."

"I have no doubt of that, but I'm sure you can also appreciate that I must follow orders."

I shrugged. "I was never one for following orders, which is why I'm no longer a soldier. Who do you take your orders from?"

"What, no small talk first to get me warmed up?"

First he hates me, and then he is being flirtatious? I don't think I would ever know what to expect from Alex.

"Patience is not one of my virtues, so you'd better get on with it before I lose charity and temperance, as well."

"Some things never change," he muttered, shaking his head. "I take my orders from the Mage Council of Urusilim. I am fighting for a worthy cause, using the unique skills at my disposal."

"What worthy cause is that?"

"That is one of those questions I cannot answer at this time."

I frowned, not satisfied with that answer, but I had too many other questions to get wrapped around the axle on that one. "Fine. Why do you keep calling me Ash?"

He barked out a short laugh. "Because that is your given name—Ashnan. I thought these questions were going to be harder. You must be losing your touch."

Ignoring his irritating jape, I pressed on, "What is Urusilim?" I braced myself for the answer, both fearing and anticipating what Alex would tell me.

"It is your homeland, your birthplace ... and your birthright."

"How is that possible? I had a family before my accident. We lived on Long Island … I think. They showed me pictures—my parents, friends, childhood vacations, high school …" My voice trailed off as I realized how false that felt.

I shook my head, trying to clear out the litter of confusing thoughts that were crashing through my mind like bumper cars. What if I was from another world? Why did I feel so sad at the prospect of losing a childhood I didn't even remember? Maybe because I had so desperately clung to the vision of that perfect family as a way to get through the hell that followed when I had entered the foster system. I wasn't ready to let go of that small measure of comfort.

However, if my childhood on earth hadn't happened, what had my real life been like? Maybe I had a loving family on Urusilim that was still alive. I went from feeling desolate to feeling hopeful. If I had parents, even siblings … I forced the thoughts from my mind. I wasn't going to let myself go down a path that might only lead to disappointment. I had been there, done that when I had been placed into an abusive foster home after no family had come to claim me, and it hadn't been pretty.

Alex merely shrugged without offering an explanation. "I cannot answer that, but I do know you did not grow up on Long Island, wherever that is, or go to high school, whatever that is. And you most certainly did not have friends." That small comment took me aback, and I felt affronted at the implication, though he didn't seem to notice. "We lost track of you when you first entered this world ten years ago. I know nothing of your life here since then."

"Ten years?" That was around the same time I had lost my memory. I wasn't a big believer in coincidences, but I also wasn't prepared to believe that I was from a magical realm yet. "So how did I get here?"

He broke eye contact, looking everywhere other than at me, his hands wringing his staff as he paced. I recognized an immovable object when I saw one.

"Let me guess, that's one of those questions you can't answer."

His non-response spoke volumes.

"Fine," I said with every intention of finding out the information at some point. "Where is Urusilim and how does one get there?"

He stopped pacing and looked back at me. "Therein lies the difficulty. It is not easily reached. Only a handful of mages and other beings have enough power to tear a small rift in the curtain separating our worlds to allow just one person or creature through. Then it sometimes takes weeks for them to recover from the immense effort. Those who are not strong enough or knowledgeable enough in the art sometimes never recover."

"And you're strong enough to open the way through?" I asked. He appeared to be talented and capable; however, I didn't think he was at the Gandalf or Dumbledore level, given his youth and periodic erratic outbursts, especially with me.

"Someone else facilitated the opening so I could make it through. If I had attempted to do so myself, I would have been dangerously weakened and vulnerable for quite some time once I arrived here."

"So, assuming all of the creatures I have run into so far are also from Urusilim, there is a built-in control mechanism preventing armies of monsters from coming through. That's good."

"Precisely. It is impossible to open a rift large enough or long enough to move large numbers of beings. That is why you have only been attacked by a few creatures here and there. Marduk has powerful magic users in his employ, capable of sending creatures through, but they are still unable to transport an army to more easily overpower you."

"Okay, assuming I am from Urusilim, somehow I don't think that Marduk, Zane, and that creepy creature menagerie have been hunting me down just to throw me a home coming party," I challenged.

"You pose a great threat to them, and they will either need to eliminate you or turn you to their side to control you."

I felt like I was playing a game of twenty questions. Why couldn't he simply give me the entire story instead of forcing me to pull it out of him one piece at a time? It was clearly his tactic not to reveal too much too soon, and it was getting really annoying.

"Holy crap, Alex! Just spill it for Christ's sake. I told you I didn't have patience. How am I a threat to them?"

"Because you have more power than you know. Unfortunately, I am unable to bring your memories back so you can unlock those powers, since I don't know how you lost those memories in the first place." He lowered his voice to an almost inaudible level. "And I don't know if I should."

It sounded like he felt as threatened by me as Marduk did. "I lost my memory from a head injury I suffered in a car accident ten years ago," I repeated the same explanation I had been giving people for years.

"Perhaps," he responded, sounding as unconvinced as I was beginning to feel.

"What do you think happened?"

"I don't know, but ..." He shrugged and shook his head. "I don't know."

"Seriously? Is that the best you can do?"

He turned and walked a few steps away, looking uncomfortable. "I think I may have said too much already."

I quickly stepped up behind him, grabbing his arm and spinning him to face me. "How do you think I lost my memory?" I demanded. My voice steadily rose in volume as I barraged him with questions. "What kind of power am I supposed to have? What is it that you think I can do? Who am I?" I ended on a scream.

He tore his arm from my grip, his own voice rising. "By the gods, Ash—Emma—whatever you want me to call you—I don't know what to tell you. We are on the brink of war, and memory or not, soon you are going to be forced to choose a side. Unfortunately, I am forbidden from saying anything that might sway you. It has to be your choice and yours alone."

"You can call me Emma; I don't know who Ash is. And how the hell am I supposed to choose sides in a war that I know nothing about? Why should I stick my neck out for a place and people that mean nothing to me? If you're expecting me to do it out of the goodness of my heart, you're talking to the wrong person."

He nodded, looking smug and disgusted at the same time. "I expected nothing more from you."

How could he make me feel completely small and ashamed by my own words? I had never pretended to be anything more than a mercenary, and I wore that honesty like a badge. Nonetheless, it felt like Alex had just shone the piercing light of day on all of my deepest flaws, illuminating them for harsh judgment.

"You don't like me very much, do you?"

He met my eyes and didn't waver. "No, I don't, and I trust you even less."

"You don't even know me."

"I clearly know you better than you know yourself."

I supposed that was true enough. "What did I do to you? Who was I?"

He was silent for several moments, and I was beginning to think he wasn't going to answer my question. I started to turn away, believing the conversation was over, when he said, "You hurt a lot of people, Ash—Emma. But, in particular, you hurt someone who was very important to me, and for that, I can never forgive you."

Did he expect me to apologize for doing something I couldn't remember? Was I supposed to feel remorse or regret for causing him pain? Well, I didn't. I didn't even know anything about Alex or this person I had supposedly hurt. How was I supposed to care about people who were complete strangers to me? The only thing I felt for Alex right then was anger at withholding crucial information.

"Then tell me what I did, who I hurt."

This time, he stayed silent.

I screamed in exasperation, my frustrations echoing off the walls of the train tunnel. How did he expect me to walk into a war armed with no knowledge? It was my neck on the line, and I wasn't about to stick it out without a damn good reason. If he couldn't—wouldn't—help me, I could think of only one other person who might know something of my past.

Chapter Eleven

I HAD MET Benjamin Hayes years ago when I had first joined the military. He was what everyone liked to call a "paper pusher" when, in fact, he held an incredibly powerful, albeit not sexy, position within the government. He was the head of procurement for the entire United States military, ultimately controlling all purchasing decisions from six hundred dollar toilet seats to two billion dollar B-2 stealth bombers.

Our paths had crossed when I had been a member of a strategic anti-terrorist team looking at unique ways to protect the country against attacks. We had needed to work with procurement to gain access to top-secret technology to aid in our research. Given the priority of the project at the time, Benjamin had personally gotten involved.

He had been described to me as a meek-looking bulldog that would bite if provoked, and if you crossed him, your funding would get slashed. He wielded his pen and budget authority like a sword. For some odd reason, we had really hit it off. Maybe it was because I understood that, when you didn't have physical power, you used whatever means available to you not to be a victim. Ever since that first meeting, Benjamin had become almost a surrogate father to me.

I had once asked him for a favor—to use the formidable resources at his disposal to see if he could track down some living family members of mine. I simply hadn't been able to let go of the wretched hope that maybe I wasn't completely alone in the world. He had agreed, although a few weeks later, he said had been unable to find anything. Yet something about that conversation had left me unsettled.

He had been nervous, even scared, pacing and unable to look me in the eye. He had continuously glanced around the room, as if looking for cameras or bugs. I had let it go, fully intending to bring it up again at some point in the future. And it was time.

I went home from Grand Central Station to change my torn and bloody clothes, and Alex insisted on tagging along. He had proven himself useful in the past; as a result, I figured having him around couldn't hurt.

While I was in the bathroom changing, in a moment of divinely horrific timing, Jason knocked on my door and Alex answered it. I came running out of the bathroom when I heard the sound of my living room lamp shattering, and found the two of them scuffling on the floor. After I broke up the party, Jason looked abashed.

"I'm sorry. I had no right to do that," he said.

"No, you didn't!" Although, I had to admit, I got some satisfaction from the black eye Alex was sporting. He deserved it and much more for killing Eddie.

I couldn't easily explain to Jason who Alex was and why I was with him; therefore, I simply introduced him as a friend. Jason looked none too pleased, and that didn't go unnoticed by Alex. Alex graciously backed out of the trip to Benjamin's house with the excuse that he had plans to visit a bookstore.

Benjamin's main office was in the Pentagon, but he said he needed to escape Washington D.C. politics once in a while, so he kept a house on Long Island. During the train ride there, I brought Jason up to speed on the events of the past twenty-four hours. He looked skeptical yet was supportive of my need to dig for more information.

We stepped off the Long Island Railroad at the Stony Brook station. Benjamin lived in the very small, affluent hamlet of Old Field on the North Shore of the island, about an hour east of Manhattan. The sun had just dipped behind the horizon when the taxi pulled up to the home that stood gracefully at the top of the bluffs, overlooking the Long Island Sound.

It had once been a modest farmhouse on acres of pastureland. Over the decades, it had fallen into disrepair. When Benjamin had purchased it twenty years ago, he had immediately begun a multi-year project of renovations, additions, and modernization of the home. After he was done, it was a stunning estate that retained those rustic farmhouse features by using the original stone walls, doors, and furniture made of reclaimed wood from an old barn on the property as well as a grand wrap-around porch overlooking the Sound.

It was the perfect escape from the high-pressure world of Washington politics.

I paid the taxi driver, then Jason and I made our way up the bluestone walkway to knock on a set of heavy oak doors. The seconds ticked by until the door finally swung open. The man standing in the threshold was shorter than me, with a thinning head of gray hair and wrinkles that made him look older than his sixty years. His eyes were small and dark, reflecting a man who was shrewd, intelligent, and no-nonsense. He was slight, but his waistline was starting to develop a slight paunch. On first glance, he appeared to be made of stone, hard and unyielding, yet when that broad smile crossed his face upon seeing me, it erased at least ten years from his features, added a sparkle to his eyes, and warmed his entire demeanor.

"Emma, my dear! What an unexpectedly wonderful surprise. Come in, come in." He ushered us across the threshold.

"I'm sorry to barge in on you like this, Ben. I hope you don't mind. You remember Jason?"

"Mr. Ryker, welcome," he said, shaking Jason's hand. "Emma, you know you're my favorite person on this earth. You are always welcome."

"I may not be after I tell you why I'm here."

The smile fell from Benjamin's face, and the stony expression returned. He stared at me in silence for a moment, finally nodding in resignation. "Mr. Ryker, if you would be so kind as to wait in the library?" he said, walking us into a room off the foyer.

The library was two stories high with mahogany bookshelves covering every wall and a ladder that slid along a track, allowing the uppermost shelves to be reached. At the far end of the room was a hand-carved Civil War era desk, and plush sofas and armchairs were arranged before a stone fireplace that was so large a man could comfortably stand in it.

Jason grudgingly entered the library, and we left him alone to peruse the shelves with feigned interest. We made our way through the pretentious front part of the house that was only used to make an impression on equally pretentious guests. The sound of our heels echoing off the marble floors turned silent as we stepped onto the soft carpeting of the back half of the house, where the real living happened.

As we approached the kitchen, the phone rang. "Just give me a minute to answer that. Make yourself comfortable in the kitchen," Benjamin said before entering his formal office off the kitchen.

The kitchen was warm and sunny, filled with cream-colored cabinetry and stainless steel appliances. The room was dominated by a large center island with graceful curves and swirling granite in colors of cream, gold, and burgundy. Although he had a formal office, Benjamin's laptop and work papers were scattered across the island.

I casually explored the bottles in his wine rack, which happened to be located near the kitchen entrance, putting me within earshot of Benjamin's conversation. "Did you procure it? Excellent. How much does she want for it? What! That much? Okay, we'll have to take this one out of the reserve budget. It's probably better that way, less paperwork. Once you move it, make sure it's secure but accessible. Yes, put it into play. Goodbye."

I heard the soft beep of the phone being hung up, and then Benjamin joined me in the kitchen.

"See anything you like?" he asked, nodding toward the wine rack.

"Yeah. How about the Tignanello? I can't resist a good Super Tuscan."

"Good choice." He removed the bottle from the rack and searched for a corkscrew.

"Closing a big deal?"

Benjamin's head shot up. "You know me; I'm always negotiating something," he said with an uncomfortable laugh. "Enough about me. How are you? How is work?"

I had told Benjamin that I was a security consultant. I didn't want him to think less of me because of my line of work. "Work is fine, but that's not what I wanted to talk to you about."

Benjamin handed me a glass of wine, and we settled into the stools at the island. He took a long pull from his own glass then said, "Okay, I'm ready. You can talk to me about anything."

My glass clinked against the granite as I fidgeted with it, swirling the wine for longer than necessary. "I know you must have found something out about me when I asked you to look into my family years ago. I need to know what you know."

"Where is this coming from, Em? What triggered this?"

"Some ... stuff ... happened this past week. I met some people who told me I'm ... not from here. They were pretty convincing."

He didn't respond right away. He was thoughtful, merely watching me as if he were trying to read the truth of what had happened on my face. Right when his stare was lingering a bit too long for my comfort, his eyes shifted away, staring into the middle distance. "Tell me what happened."

I had spent the entire train ride debating how much to tell Benjamin. I trusted him implicitly, yet there was no way I was prepared to answer that question truthfully. "Um, I can't really go into details. It was work related, so I have to respect the confidentiality of my clients." I knew I couldn't expect complete honesty from him if I wasn't willing to give a little in return; therefore, I debated what was innocuous enough to reveal. "All I can tell you is that the name of the person who hired me is Vincent Darko."

Benjamin's shoulders slumped almost imperceptibly, and he seemed to age right in front of my eyes. "I will tell you what I know, which isn't much. It was almost ten years ago when I got a call from a friend ... someone very high up in the military. He told me about a girl who had been found unconscious in the New Mexico desert eleven months prior. He never explained what exactly had happened to you, just that you had been in a coma all that time. They had been keeping you under observation at a military hospital, and you had just woken up, seemingly with severe amnesia. They had no idea what to do with you, so they called me."

"Why you? Why not just call Social Services and turn me over to state authorities like they would have done with any other lost child?"

"They thought you might be important, I suppose. You were apparently found under mysterious circumstances, although I have no idea what that means. Anyway, I was the guy they went to when they needed things. In this case, they needed to find you a home. I actually thought about adopting you myself, but I was younger and more ambitious at the time. Work was my life, and I was unmarried. I was nowhere near equipped to raise a teenage girl."

"Why didn't you tell me any of this before?" I asked, trying not to think about how different my life could have been had Benjamin decided to take me in.

He sighed deeply, shaking his head. "What was I supposed to say—that I turned you away and you ended up in an abusive foster home for years as a result? I can't tell you how much I regret that decision."

I could see the truth of that statement in the pleading look he gave me. It wasn't worth crying over. Benjamin had been good to me, even if he hadn't raised me. I was grateful to him for that much.

"Who is this 'they' you keep referring to?"

"I'm sorry, Emma, but I can't give you names. I'm under strict orders. I shouldn't even have told you as much as I have. What I can do is warn you, though. 'They' are very dangerous and powerful men who won't hesitate to do whatever is necessary to achieve their objectives, up to and including murder. I don't know what their goals are, but based on who is involved, I can tell you this thing goes all the way to the top."

"So, what would you have me do?" I hadn't realized until right then how tired I was of being on the defensive all the time. I was usually the hunter, not the prey. It wasn't much fun being on this side of the equation. Then Benjamin dropped a bomb on me that my newest enemies had serious backing and virtually unlimited resources. Evil sorcerers from another world were one thing; the might of the U.S. government was something entirely different. I didn't stand a chance in hell of getting out of this one alive.

"Lay low, go into hiding where they can't find you. Don't poke your head up until you have figured out who you are. And, when that day arrives, come and see me. I'll help you get through this. I have a few connections of my own, and I can protect you as long as you don't do anything … reckless."

I chuckled at that. "Reckless" was practically my profession, and I was good at it. "Okay, Ben. Thanks for the advice. I promise that, if I have a sudden return of my memory, you'll be the first person I call."

He seemed pleased with that answer and gave me a warm bear hug. Releasing me, he said, "I'm sorry I can't tell you anything more. But you said this past week had been strange. What did you mean by that?"

"I was just being dramatic. It was a crazy week at work. I had a client put me in a bad spot, but I worked it all out. Everything is fine now. Look, I want you to know you have been good to me. I'm not angry or even a little upset at the decision you made a decade ago. You made the choice that was right for you at the time. You didn't know what was going to happen." I gave him a weak smile, and he returned it.

Jason and I stayed for dinner, the mood lifting as we ate, talked, and joked. Then it was time to catch the train back to the city. Benjamin called us a cab, and we left him with warm goodbyes before walking to the end of the long drive to wait for the taxi.

Instead of a cab coming for us, a black stretch limo pulled up. At first, I thought Benjamin had gifted us with a limo back to the city, but when the muscle-bound driver stepped out and opened the rear door for us, a man in a business suit peered out with cold, gray eyes.

"Miss Hayes, Mr. Ryker, my employer would very much like to speak with you. Please ..." He swept his hand toward the interior of the car, signaling us to get in.

I looked back at the driver who had stepped up behind us, blocking our path away from the car. Jason and I wouldn't have had a problem taking both of them, but the driver already had a semi-automatic pointed at my back, and as fast as I was, I couldn't dodge bullets.

I nodded at Jason, and then we stepped into the limousine.

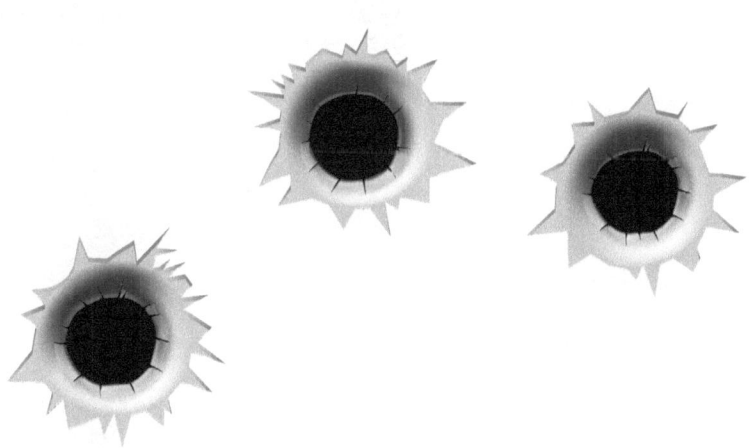

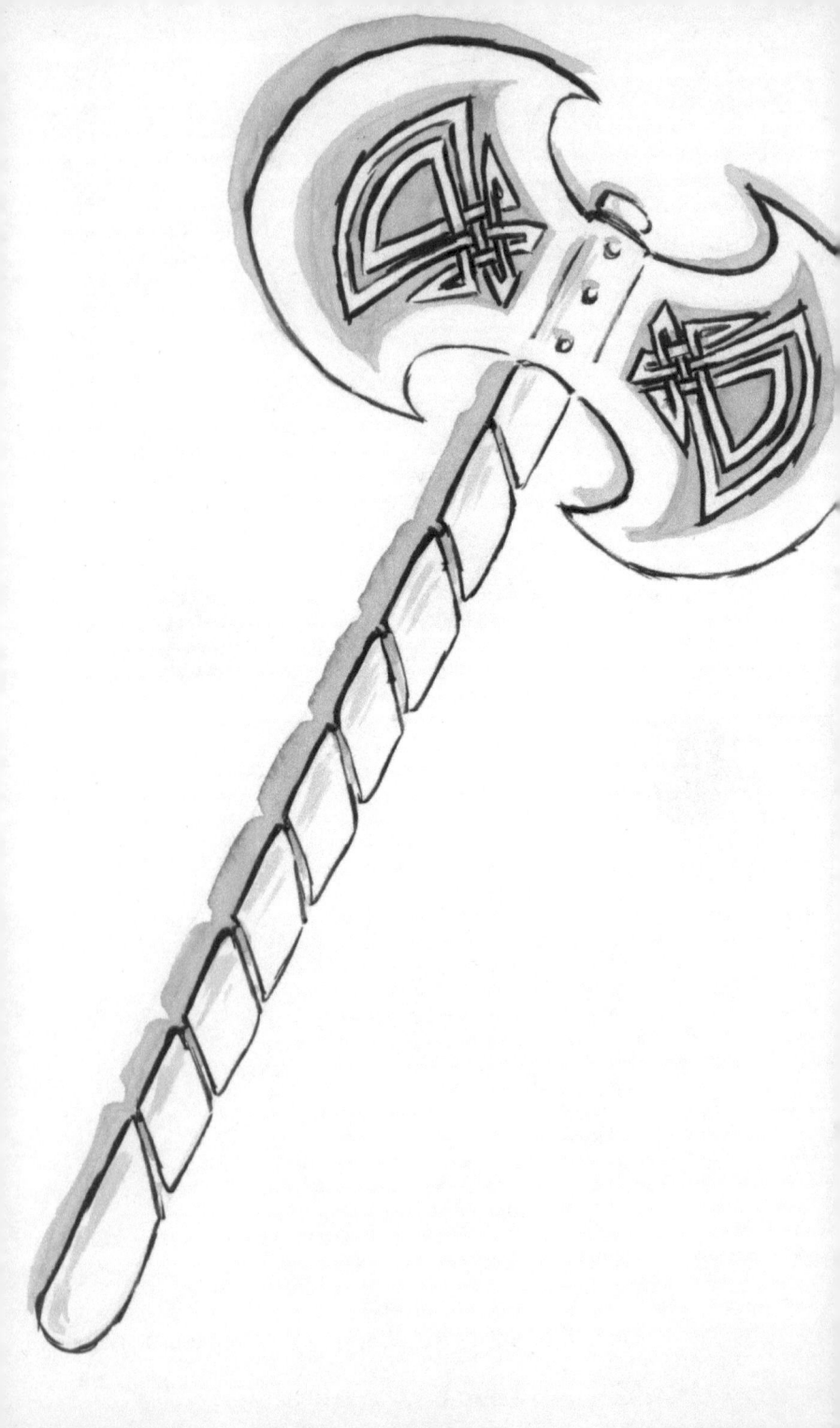

Chapter Twelve

"WHO IS YOUR employer, and what does he want with us?" I asked.

"Well, he doesn't actually want anything with Mr. Ryker, but I figured it would be easier to get you in the car if he was invited along."

"And what makes me so special?"

"I must say, Miss Hayes, I am disappointed you haven't been able to figure that out yet. But no matter. My employer will put you on the path to enlightenment."

"Oh? Are you taking us to see the Dalai Lama?"

He chuckled dryly. "No, not quite. I am taking you to see Nathan Anshar."

Jason and I exchanged a surprised glance. Nathan Anshar was one of the wealthiest men in the country. He was often considered a genius for his uncanny ability to create and build companies that caught fire then selling them for an astronomical profit. For the past several years, he had been focused on building a research incubator for the development of new medical therapies. His company was focused on developing a novel compound for the treatment of cancer. There had even been speculation it could become the next blockbuster drug if it ever made it to the market.

"So, what does he want with me?"

"I'm sure I don't know, Miss Hayes, but I think I can safely guess he wants to talk business."

"And who are you?"

"Who I am isn't important, but if it makes you feel more comfortable, you can call me Mr. Smith. I am Mr. Anshar's assistant."

"Like his secretary?" I smirked.

He didn't seem to appreciate the snarky humor. "No. I assist him. My role is primarily to handle the most challenging assignments. Often, I am tasked to deal with those who have disappointed Mr. Anshar in some way. A word of advice, do not disappoint him." Smith winked at me, but I got the feeling he was much more dangerous than I had initially believed. Anyone who worked for a man like Anshar must be quite good at his job.

We rode the rest of the way back to Manhattan in silence. I stared out the tinted windows, hypnotized by the blur of streetlights and the soft *thump, thump, thump* of the car driving over evenly spaced gaps in the roadway. Soon, I started to drift off, lulled by the motion of the car, the vibration of the engine, and the silence.

I dreamt of a place consumed in fire and ash, and in the midst of the destruction stood an impenetrable gray fortress. Its towers and turrets loomed over the desolate landscape and flew banners with a red dragon on a field of black. I heard a voice, faint at first yet growing insistently louder. *I will teach you. They cannot stand against us.* I didn't recognize the voice. It was deep and steely with an unfamiliar accent that sounded almost Russian or Slavic, though not quite. Then I was flying over the land. Far below me were glittering rivers, verdant green fields, dense forests, snow-capped mountains, and arid deserts. From this height, all looked peaceful, and I smiled at the beauty of it.

Then the ground was rushing up to meet me. I was plummeting out of control, the wind grabbing at my hair and whipping it painfully across my face. My eyes stung, and I couldn't catch my breath. As the ground came closer, I started to make out shapes and movement. The tiny specs grew, taking the shape of men, horses, and creatures I couldn't put a name to. There was fire and arrows and the sounds of clashing steel. As I fell, I could see the bright red of blood and hear the screams of pain and fear.

Looming beneath me was the greatest shape of all—an enormous red dragon like the one on the banners. It looked skyward, as if expecting me. I was powerless to stop my decent and unable to change direction. The dragon opened its mouth to reveal hundreds of serrated teeth. Terror raced through me at the thought of being chewed by that beast, but then a glow began at the back of its throat that grew brighter and hotter. Flame poured forth, spouting into the sky directly at me as I fell to meet it.

I awoke with a start. The car was slowing as it pulled into the garage under a luxury apartment building on Central Park West. The driver took a reserved spot right next to an elevator labeled "private." We exited the limo, and Mr. Smith used a key to unlock access to the elevator. The doors slid open silently to reveal an immaculate marble and mirror interior.

"No thumb print or retinal scan?" I teased at the low-tech manner of entry.

"A very good shape shifter would be able to mimic fingerprints and eyes. And, even your average human with a good knife could take those from someone who had security access."

His mention of shape shifters made me immediately think of Eddie. He had made an impression on me with his raunchy humor and sweet demeanor. Had I been wrong about him?

It wasn't until Jason elbowed me with a wide-eyed look that it dawned on me that Mr. Smith knew about the existence of shape shifters. Could this visit have something to do with the events of the past week? How was a wealthy businessman entangled in otherworldly matters?

Before I could ask Mr. Smith what else he knew, the elevator chimed to signal we had reached our destination on the fifty-sixth floor. The doors opened, and we stepped into a space that looked more like a museum than a home. The walls were covered in original Van Goghs, Picassos, and other masters, all contained in heavy, gilded frames and enclosed in glass, dramatically lit by soft spotlights above each piece. Tucked within corners and alcoves were Greek and Roman statuary, some fully intact and others missing heads, arms, and pieces from their torsos.

Placed thoughtfully throughout the large, open space were settees as well as ornately carved chairs; chests; and other pieces of heavy, wood furniture. On top of tables and chests sat decorative objects—vases, glassware, statuettes, jeweled eggs, dolls—some encased in glass and others accessible to touch. Mr. Anshar was clearly a collector of the rare and beautiful, or maybe he simply didn't know what else to do with his gobs of money.

"Mr. Anshar will be out in a moment. Please have a seat … and don't touch anything." Mr. Smith exited via the elevator, leaving Jason and I amidst the relics. I couldn't imagine how anyone, except perhaps a thief, would ever risk touching items so delicate and valuable.

"Um, where are we supposed to sit? I'm afraid to put my ass on anything," Jason said, looking around.

"Yeah, maybe we should just stand here and wait." We tried that for about a minute yet were soon drawn deeper into the room by the myriad objects, looking at everything while touching nothing.

"Do you see anything you like?" I turned at that silken voice to find the man I recognized from the cover of Fortune magazine.

He was a handsome, older man with salt and pepper hair at his temples and ice blue eyes. He still had the smooth skin of youth and could have passed for any age between forty and fifty-five years old. He carried himself with the supreme confidence of a man who worked hard and had earned his way to the top. He smiled, and his eyes crinkled charmingly at the corners.

I consciously forced myself not to get star stuck. "It's hard to choose a favorite. Everything in this room is stunning."

"Well, if there is something in particular that catches your fancy, consider it yours."

Startled and suspicious, yet intrigued all the same, I asked, "Why would you do that?"

He waved around the room, as if that offered sufficient explanation. When I didn't react, he smiled patiently and said, "I have plenty of priceless objects, and I like showing off my wealth by giving away extravagant gifts." I couldn't tell whether he was joking.

I shook my head. "Thank you, but I can't accept anything. May I ask why you have brought us here?"

"Right to business? I can respect that. Why don't we talk in my office? Mr. Ryker, you may come along if you'd like."

We followed him down a long hallway, passing bedrooms, bathrooms, a music room with a grand piano, and even a game room with a billiard table. The museum-like quality extended throughout the house with Persian rugs, crystal chandeliers, ornate furniture, and more artwork, until we entered his office. Typical of the rest of the apartment, Nathan had a massive carved desk with legs in the shape of lion claws. However, behind that antique monstrosity was a full wall mounted with rare weapons.

The objects on display were placed in historical order, with the oldest weapons starting on the left most wall and the more modern weapons ending farthest to the right. Nathan seemed to have at least one of almost every type of weapon created: daggers, swords, maces, axes, pole arms, war hammers, muskets, flintlock pistols, revolvers, carbines, repeaters, semi-automatics, and full-automatics.

The collection was behind a wall of security glass, but it was brightly illuminated, providing most of the light in the room. This was something Jason and I could appreciate much more than art. We both ogled the display like children on Christmas morning.

"As you can see, I appreciate not only beauty but power, which brings us to why I asked you here. I would like to attain your services to retrieve something that was stolen from me. But only someone with special qualifications will be capable of pulling off a feat such as this one. As such, I need to know whether you are the right person for the job." He paused dramatically, as if expecting me to know what he was talking about. I didn't. "Let me see it."

"See what?" I asked, confused.

"The amulet," he explained, gesturing toward my chest.

How the hell did he know about the amulet? A wave of panic washed through me as I scrambled my brain, trying to figure out who knew about the amulet and could have shared that information with Nathan Anshar. It left me cold, reinforcing what Fox Mulder always said, *Trust no one.* However, I was in a difficult spot. I couldn't pretend I didn't know what he was talking about when the shape of the amulet was obvious through my tight T-shirt. We could make a run for it, although I didn't know a faster way out than the elevator, and Mr. Smith and his bulky driver were likely waiting for us at the bottom.

"So the rumors are true; you do have it. I can tell by the look on your face that you are trying to figure out how to keep it from me."

"How did you know? Who told you?"

"I am a very well-connected man, at more levels than you can imagine, and believe me when I say I am not the only one who knows you have it. You're right to be cautious, Miss Hayes. There are worse things than death, and many who would use those kinds of means to possess that amulet."

"Do you know what it is? Why it is so valuable? What does it do?"

Jason placed his hand on my arm to stop me. The questions had just tumbled unbidden out of my mouth. I hadn't meant to ask them, to show my lack of understanding, but I was so desperate for answers I couldn't stop myself.

Nathan didn't look at me like I was prey, as I would have expected from someone who had just learned they held the advantage. Instead, he said, "As valuable as the amulet is alone, it is exponentially more powerful when coupled with another very special object. The amulet is almost like a brain without a body. It has no way to put voice to thoughts or actions to intentions. You will never know what it is truly capable of until you learn to communicate with it. To do that, you must find its body."

"Is that what you want to hire me to find?"

"Yes. The object I am searching for is an ancient weapon. It was once one of the most prized items in my collection." He stood, turning to face the wall of relics behind him. I noticed then an empty spot on the wall directly behind his chair. He placed a gentle hand to the glass, as if remembering the feel of the weapon in his hands. "It was stolen from me about ten years ago, and I wish to have it back."

"How will retrieving this item help me if I only have to give it back to you? Do you seriously think I'll turn over the amulet to you, as well?" My hackles went up, anticipating a confrontation. There was no way in hell I was going to turn over everything to him, especially not knowing what these objects were capable of.

He turned back to me and smiled. "Of course not, Miss Hayes. Once you retrieve it, please consider it a gift from me to you, even more so than any of the pieces you were admiring earlier. This item was almost made for you."

Was he serious? He was simply going to let me have it? There had to be another angle I was missing.

I narrowed my eyes on him. "Why would you just let me have something so valuable and supposedly powerful?"

"Because I need a skilled fighter to wield it on my behalf. What I ask for in return is your service … to me."

There was always a catch. "Sorry, but I already have a job. I work for myself because I don't make for a particularly obedient employee."

"I can vouch for that," Jason interjected dryly.

"I've been told I make an excellent boss. The benefits are second to none. I will double your pay; you'll have an opportunity to visit exotic new places and meet interesting characters; and best of all, I will teach you, train you. You will need someone to guide you in the use of your powers, to introduce you to the world you have forgotten. If you do this, I will tell you everything you wish to know, including who you are."

Shit, that was a tempting offer … but at what cost? Was this knowledge worth the price of my freedom? Given more time, would I be able to learn this information anyway? I had been piecing things together bit by bit. Sure, it was slow and tedious, but I might be able to figure it out eventually without Nathan. However, would I be able to survive that long? I was being hunted by deadly creatures, and it was more than likely they would find me and end me before I could learn enough to defend myself.

I looked to Jason for help.

"Don't do it," he said firmly. "You can't trust him. You don't know what he'll make you do, and I can guarantee the price will be too high. We'll find another way."

I turned back to Nathan, still uncertain. "How are you involved in all of this?"

Nathan sat back down slowly, interlocking his fingers and placing his hands on the desk in front of him, looking deadly serious. "Emma, I know your mother."

I took a sharp intake of breath and sprang to my feet, Jason quickly following, taking my hand supportively. Of all the things I might have expected him to say, mentioning my mother hadn't even been a thought.

"You knew my mother?" I practically shouted.

"No, Miss Hayes. I *know* your mother."

The synapses in my brain stopped firing for a few seconds, and all I could feel was a blooming sensation in my chest that I didn't recognize. When the thoughts came flooding back, I realized the unknown feeling was joy, hope. Nonetheless, as quickly as it had come, I obliterated the emotion with harsh reality.

I had assumed my biological parents were dead; otherwise, why would I have ended up here? If my mother was alive, wouldn't she have been there to protect me, to keep me with her? How had I ended up here, and did she care? The endless questions were enough to drive me mad.

When I was finally able to produce a sound, it sounded something like "uhgrgh," and then Nathan's cell phone rang. He pulled it from his pocket and put it to his ear, listening to the caller on the other end. His eyes flew up to meet mine, suddenly looking very concerned. All he said into the phone was, "Stall them," and then hung up.

"What is it?" Jason asked.

"There are federal agents downstairs, backed with a contingent of Black Ops soldiers, looking for Emma. You two have to get out of here, and you must retrieve the weapon, or all is lost. What do you say, Emma? Do we have a deal?"

There's nothing like mortal danger and an imminent deadline to refocus my priorities. I came back to my senses, my mind frantically running through my options.

Jason squeezed my hand urgently. "Emma, don't let him pressure you into a decision. For all we know, there's no one downstairs, and this is just a tactic he's using to force your hand."

Nathan's phone beeped, and he looked at the incoming text message. "Unfortunately, Mr. Ryker, this is not a ploy. They are in the elevator and will be here in less than two minutes. What's it going to be, Miss Hayes? Do you want answers?"

I no longer had a choice. As soon as he had revealed that he knew my mother, I had made my decision. "Yes, I'll work for you, but only after you tell me everything I want to know."

"Agreed, but first you must recover the weapon and bring it back to me. I will teach you how to use it." He quickly grabbed a Post-It note from his desk and wrote something on it, handing it to me. "This is where you will find it. Now, come with me." He darted to a door at the far end of the room I hadn't noticed before. It was camouflaged with the same wood paneling that ran along the length of the wall. Pulling it open revealed a metal and cement stairwell. "This will take you down to the parking garage. I have someone who can help waiting for you with a car."

Ding. The elevator signaled its arrival on Nathan's floor. Jason and I flew down the staircase as Nathan sealed the door behind us.

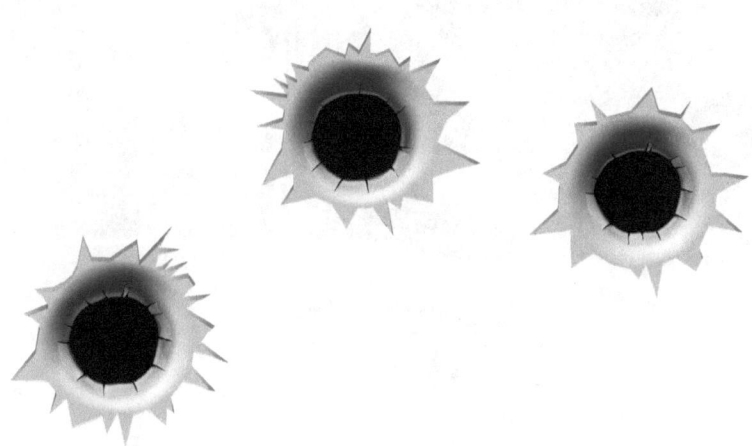

Chapter Thirteen

"WHY THE HELL is the government after you?" Jason panted as we raced down the steps. We were both in great shape, but even going down the stairs, fifty-six flights at breakneck speed was still plenty to get us winded.

"I have ... no ... idea," I said between breaths. "But, if it's really Black Ops ... we're ... screwed." Black Operations could be carried out by any qualified branch of the military; as a result, I didn't know who exactly we would be dealing with. However, these were highly covert operations involving activities that required plausible deniability because of their questionable ethics and legality. If someone classified this mission as a Black Ops, it meant someone was trying to cream our corn, as Jason would say.

When we reached the thirtieth floor, I heard dim pounding and clanging sounds echoing from the stairwell above us. "They're on us," Jason said, stating the obvious. We increased the pace, leaping four and five steps at a time, and cut corners by vaulting over the railings onto the next set of steps below us. We reached the garage level in minutes, throwing ourselves into the steel door, slamming it open. We slowed, looking around frantically for the car Nathan had said would be waiting for us.

"There's a subway two blocks from here," I urged when the car didn't immediately show.

"No way. They'll have all of the exits watched. They'll be on us as soon as we step foot outside."

Jason was right, but those soldiers would be bursting through that door in moments. The stomping sounds of feet on steps grew louder with every heartbeat. "Jason, we can't stay here. We have to hide if we can't run."

"Motherfucker framed us!" Jason shouted, punching the nearest car.

If that was true, Nathan Anshar was going on my personal hit list, if I didn't get hit first. "Jason, we need to move now!" I glanced over my shoulder at the door. It was beginning to rattle from the vibrations of men barreling down the last of the steps.

Grabbing Jason's arm, we began to run when a gray BMW M6 came to a screeching halt in front of us. The black tinted driver's side window slid down, revealing the bright red hair and flame tattoo of Lilly Alfreda.

"Get in," she shouted.

It didn't take any more encouragement than that before we were in the backseat, slamming the car door just as the Black Ops soldiers burst into the garage and opened fire on us with MP5 sub-machine guns. I instinctively ducked, moving away from the windows, but the 9-millimeter rounds ricocheted off the bulletproof glass. Lilly stepped on the gas, throwing me against the seat as she pealed out of the garage.

"You okay back there?" It wasn't Lilly's voice that came from the front seat; it was Alex's. I sat up and met his eyes as he peered over the passenger seat at me. He read my thoughts while I looked between him and Lilly. "I'll explain later."

"Yes, you will. In the meantime, I'd feel better with a weapon in my hands."

"Lift the seat cushion," Lilly directed.

Jason and I knelt on the floor and pried up the seat, finding a store of handguns, rifles, and grenades.

"I think I'm in love with you," Jason said to Lilly as he reached into the cache to caress a Kalashnikov rifle.

She giggled girlishly, which seemed incongruous coming from a woman driving a speeding vehicle through the streets of New York City at two a.m. while being pursued by government operatives.

Jason claimed the Kalashnikov, while I opted for an M16 rifle with grenade launcher, slinging a grenade belt across my chest. I also shoved two Colt 1911 handguns into my waistband and filled my pockets with extra ammunition. Our attempted escape was not going to be subtle.

Lilly was doing an impressive job of swerving around yellow cabs and cutting through intersections without killing any pedestrians. Peering out the rear window, I counted three black Ford SUVs tight on our tail. Even with the faster car, we would never escape them in these tight streets. At this hour, plenty of cars and people were still out and about. It would be a miracle if there wasn't any collateral damage.

"We can't open fire on them here. We either have to lose them or get out of the city."

"How about both?" Lilly suggested.

When she turned sharply onto 1st Avenue, heading downtown, one of the SUVs took advantage of the wider, less trafficked avenue to pull alongside us. The driver jerked the wheel sharply and rammed into the BMW. I fell into Jason as we both tumbled across the seat upon impact. Lilly kept us from careening off the road, and Jason and I took advantage of the opportunity to fasten our seatbelts.

Another of the SUVs plowed into our rear, snapping us all forward. Pain shot through my neck, and a dull ache began at the base of my skull. Lilly pulled the wheel to left, throwing us into a controlled three hundred sixty-degree spin. Before coming to a complete stop, she straightened the car and stepped on the gas. The SUV was now in front of us as we approached a section of roadway under construction, lined with concrete barriers and orange cones. Lilly sped up and clipped the SUV in the rear left bumper, causing him to swerve wildly into the concrete barriers. The entire front end of the car crumpled, and then it flipped onto its roof.

Lilly hung a sharp left onto the Williamsburg Bridge, swerving the car back and forth, trying to prevent either of the remaining SUVs from coming up alongside us. With us out in the open on the mostly deserted bridge, I unbuckled my seatbelt and rolled down the window. Then I leaned out precariously, trying to brace myself by wedging my foot under the driver seat, and opened fire with the rifle. When the bullets bounced off it harmlessly, I adjusted my aim and went for the tires.

Before any of my shots could hit home, a soldier dressed in black camouflage with black face paint stood up through the SUV's sunroof and shouldered his machine gun. I felt a hand tightening on my jeans, and Jason tugged me back into the safety of the car right as bullets came raining down on us. The rear window shattered under the barrage. It didn't break, but it was impossible to see through given all the spider vein cracks running through it.

Jason leveraged himself with his back against the front seat and used his long, powerful legs to kick out the rear window, regaining our visibility to the two cars still following us. This time, we did have to duck when gunfire erupted in our direction.

I screamed to Alex and Lilly, afraid a bullet would strike one of them through the seats. Alex was on it, erecting a shimmering shield where the rear window had been. Bullets hit it harmlessly, creating ripples in the shield like a rock tossed into a pond. That bought me the few precious moments I needed to load the grenade launcher.

"Alex, on my signal," I shouted to him over my shoulder. Taking careful aim out the back window, with bullets still flying at us, I yelled, "Now!" Alex dropped the shield. I depressed the trigger at the same moment, and the grenade streaked through the night air.

I had aimed for the closest SUV, but the driver attempted to avoid the grenade by swerving to the right. It hit the undercarriage of the car and exploded, sending the vehicle into the air and tumbling over the edge of the bridge. We were almost to the end of it, keeping the SUV from plummeting thousands of feet into the East River. Instead, it fell only a few stories and hit the sloping ground a couple feet from the water, becoming engulfed in flames.

We made it off the bridge, and Lilly took several sharp turns, bringing us to an area that was darkened perceptibly compared to the bright lights of the bridge and busy Manhattan streets behind us. The hunkering shapes of cargo ships and cranes loomed ahead, which helped me identify this place as the Brooklyn Navy Yard. She sped through the yard, weaving around shipping containers, forklifts, and other machinery.

As she came around the corner of a low warehouse building, we found ourselves barreling down the street directly toward a figure standing resolute in the middle of the roadway. The figure didn't even twitch, making no move at all to dive out of the way of our speeding vehicle.

Lilly screamed and slammed on the brakes. We were all thrown forward, the pain in my neck now shooting down my back. I was going to need some massive muscle relaxants after all that had happened.

The tires squealed and I could smell burning rubber, but we came to a stop about twenty feet from the figure. Pissed off, I threw open the back door, pulling a Colt handgun from my waistband.

"What the fuck, asshole!" I yelled, stomping toward the man with my gun aimed squarely at his forehead. My steps faltered as I got closer and the figure became recognizable. "Fuck me," I breathed. "Zane."

He was once again dressed all in black, and I couldn't help noticing how his clothing hugged his body, accentuating every curve of hard muscle. His long hair was loose around his head, and a few strands were blowing gently across his eyes.

Those eyes! They were watching me with a feverish intensity, drinking me in from head to toe. I flushed at the heat his gaze sent through my body. Even under these circumstances, his mere presence caused my body to short circuit my brain.

I could hear car doors opening, and Alex and Jason appeared on either side of me.

"Zane," Alex said, in much the same tone I had used. "Move away. We have to get out of here, or we're all dead."

Zane was unmoved by the urgent plea, making no attempt to let us pass.

"I say we just run the fucker down," Jason said.

I wasn't inclined to damage such a fine specimen, but we needed to move, and fast. The narrow road was lined on both sides with warehouses. There wasn't enough room to pass without harming him.

Just then, Lilly leaned on the horn, letting loose a long honking wail. All heads spun in her direction. She was hanging out the driver's side window yelling, "They're here!" Pinpricks of light were visible against the blanket of blackness and grew into the blinding glare of headlights as the car closed the distance. "Get in," Lilly screamed over the growing rumble of an accelerating engine.

Alex grabbed my elbow to steer me back to the waiting vehicle. Seeing Alex touch me, snapped Zane to attention. "Alex," Zane boomed. "Don't touch her. She's mine!"

Zane leapt forward, and before anyone could react, he slammed Alex in the jaw with a left hook. When Alex stumbled and lost his grip on my arm, Zane grabbed me and threw me over his shoulder. The caveman treatment stunned me into inaction, not to mention I had to place my hands on his lower back, near his perfect rear. I almost forgot I was still holding a gun and could have shot Zane at any time, but I didn't want to do that.

I clutched his waistband and slid myself forward, throwing off Zane's balance as I redistributed most of weight behind him. While he stumbled and took two steps backward, I stiffened my legs, breaking his hold on them, and flipped myself over his shoulder to land on my feet behind him.

Headlights and machine gun fire exploded in the night as the black SUV finally caught up to us. Lilly dove back into the car, and I ran in a crouch to take cover on the far side of the vehicle with Alex and Jason.

Zane didn't move a muscle, although hiding probably wasn't in his repertoire. His eyes and hands began to glow red, and he slammed a fireball into the oncoming SUV's gas tank. The vehicle went up in flames in an ear-splitting explosion that lit up the night sky like it was dawn. Then Jason was at my side, hauling me up and trying to get the passenger side door open. Billows of heat and smoke blew through the enclosed space, choking and suffocating us.

I looked up, and with tears blurring my vision, I saw the silhouette of Zane stalking toward us. I wrenched my arm out of Jason's grasp and stomped off into the billowing cloud. Jason and Alex were yelling for me, unable to see more than a few feet in front of them.

With every footfall, my anger raised another level. I was absolutely done with being treated like a pawn in everyone else's game. As a short gust cleared the air briefly, making

Zane visible, I reached him then shoved him hard in the chest, pushing him back a step.

"Who the hell do you think you are?" I demanded. "I'm not yours or anyone else's. I've faced bigger and badder assholes than you who think they can bully women with their brawn and big talk." I gave him another shove, but he continued to stand there, looking stunned at my verbal onslaught. "You barge into my life all dangerous and mysterious, claiming you know me and refusing to give me any answers, all the while threatening or seducing me—I can't tell which! Well, I've had about enough of you ... and of Alex. You two deserve each other. I'm out."

I spun on my heel to walk off dramatically when Zane caught my wrist and pulled me into him before he pressed his lips to mine. His strong hands buried themselves in my hair as he held me tight against his mouth. His lips were incredibly soft. He smelled spicy, like cinnamon, and I melted into his arms, moving my mouth against his. The kiss felt familiar, like a half-remembered dream.

He broke away first. "I'm sorry," he whispered. "You're right, about everything. I just ... can't think straight sometimes." He shook his head as if trying to clear it of confusion, looking pained. "I'm trying ... I don't want to ..."

A gunshot rang out, and Zane stumbled, falling to his knees. I reached out to help him as he struggled awkwardly to his feet. He tried putting weight on his right leg and almost went down again with a pained grunt. I saw blood dripping down his boots, leaving red footprints on the cement.

Another gust of wind blew away the billowing smoke, and Jason stood behind Zane, readjusting the aim of his gun to point at Zane's head now that he could get a clear shot.

"Jason, no!" I yelled. "He's not going to hurt me."

Turning to Zane, I said, "Get out of here before he kills you."

Alex and Lilly ran up alongside Jason, relief crossing their features seeing Zane wounded and barely able to stay on his feet. They thought we had won, that we had Zane dead to rights. Only I knew the truth because Zane was facing me, and I could see the pain and confusion disappear from his eyes, replaced by animalistic rage. We were in trouble.

Despite the searing pain he must have felt, Zane gritted his teeth and stood on his wounded leg, shoving me away from him. He raised his hands above his head and screamed unrecognizable words into the night sky. "Felhívom a vadállat!"

When Alex heard it, fear entered his eyes. "We have to get out of here. Now!" He grabbed Lilly and Jason and started dragging them back to the car, frantically shouting at me to follow.

I turned my face upward and saw a shadow fall across the half moon, blocking it entirely from view. I squinted and strained my eyes, trying to see what was there. The stars were disappearing and reappearing, and it took me a moment to realize it was because something massive and black was moving in front of them. A shriek pierced the air that left me cold. Then the shape landed heavily in the narrow roadway between the warehouses.

I couldn't make out any features until a massive fireball, much larger than the one that destroyed the SUV, came from the direction of the shadow and torched one of the warehouses. The flames cast an eerie, dancing light on a great winged beast with the body and head of a lion, sporting the spiraling horns of a ram. It had a serpentine tail that ended in a second head, though this one was a rattlesnake. All four scaled legs ended in wicked talons, and saliva dripped from a muzzle filled with sharp, crooked teeth.

I couldn't wrench my eyes from the horrific sight until it opened that deadly maw and spewed another ball of fire toward the car that was now racing toward me. The flames missed the car by mere inches, splattering the bumper with drops of some sort of flaming ooze.

Lilly brought the car to a stop, and Jason threw open the rear door, roughly pulling me inside. Lilly threw the car into a squealing three hundred sixty degree turn and slammed on the gas before the door was even closed.

I looked through the missing rear window and saw the creature beat its great wings, rising into the air in pursuit.

Chapter Fourteen

"WHAT IS THAT thing?" Jason yelled in a panic.

"A chimera," Lilly answered. "Absolutely deadly and a bitch to kill, not to mention virtually invisible in the dark, fire-breathing, and venomous."

"How do you know that? And who are you, by the way?" Jason asked.

"Lilly Alfreda. Nice to meet you," Lilly said with a smile. "I'd shake your hand, but I kind of need to keep both of them on the wheel right now." She emphasized her point by making a sharp turn onto the Brooklyn Queens Expressway.

"Lilly works at the bookshop where I took the amulet. Although, I have no idea what she is doing here tonight," I said, stabbing her with an accusing glare. When a fireball slammed into the roadway just ahead of our car, Lilly drove through the flames and smoke, leaving the car unscathed. "But we can have that conversation later, if we get out of this mess alive."

The highway was empty, but Lilly continued to swerve randomly because an unpredictable moving target was harder to hit. The chimera threw another firebomb, and Lilly avoided it by mere inches. Realizing it wasn't having much luck with this tactic, the creature tried a different approach. The chimera flew lower until it could peer through the missing rear window of the car.

"Oh, shit! It's going to blast us," I realized.

"Not if I blast it first," Jason responded. He aimed the grenade launcher I had been using earlier, but the chimera was faster. It let loose a burst of flame from its throat. Lilly tried to stay ahead of it by speeding up yet was only partially successful. The tail end of the flames still reached the back of the car. I had ducked behind the seat, but Jason was still intent on aiming his weapon, and the molten phlegm touched his arm.

Jason's scream of pain pierced the night, but the sensation also caused his hand to spasm and depress the trigger before he dropped the weapon. He landed a perfect shot right to the chimera's head, although when the smoke cleared, the creature was still coming. The grenade didn't seem to have seriously injured it, but it must have been enough of a nuisance to cause the creature to fly farther back from the car.

"Jason! Are you okay?" It sounded like a stupid question even as I said it, but I didn't know what else to say. He clearly wasn't okay. He had managed to put out the flames; however, the skin underneath was charred black and melted. He clutched his wrist, his face twisted in an agonized grimace.

The chimera came at us again, but this time, it rammed its full body weight into the side of the car, tipping it onto two wheels for a moment before the car righted itself again.

"We can't stay out in the open like this," Alex said.

"I know, I know. I'm working on it!" Lilly turned off the highway and onto the Brooklyn Bridge.

The network of steel cables that crisscrossed the historic bridge framed the roadway like a prison, making it impossible for the large chimera to fly alongside or directly above the car without slamming into the cables. The chimera was forced to pace us along the outside of the bridge over open water.

Alex shifted in his seat, pulling out his rune-carved staff. He rolled down the window, pointing his staff down toward the churning, black waters below. He muttered indecipherable words under his breath, his green eyes developing a deep luminescence I was learning signaled the use of magic.

Nothing happened at first, then a roaring began, like the sound of a freight train. It rapidly grew closer, louder. Jason and I leaned toward the window, trying to figure out what Alex was doing, when a geyser of water shot up from the East River, rising hundreds of feet into the air. It slammed into the chimera with such force the beast howled and went spinning through the air toward us.

The chimera was pitched violently into the steel cables of the bridge. Several cables snapped, and the bridge swayed slightly under the impact.

"You're going to destroy the Brooklyn Bridge!" I screamed in horror, slapping Alex in the back of the head. "Figure out another way to kill that thing without destroying an iconic landmark."

Alex gave me a withering look, clearly not appreciating the cultural heritage of New York, while the chimera was violently shaking water off itself, like a manic dog after a bath. I figured fire-breathing creatures probably didn't favor water very much.

Alex lifted his staff once again and yelled, "*Glacies*!" The water that was still clinging to the chimera's body froze into a solid sheet of ice. The beast plummeted out of the sky, unable to use its wings to stay aloft. A sickening smack sounded from below as the chimera hit the surface of the water.

"Can those things swim?" I asked.

No one replied, which I took to mean they didn't know. Even if the creature didn't drown, at least Alex had bought us some time.

I sidled up close to Jason, wanting to offer him any comfort I could, but I knew that touching him would only make it worse. I eyed the gruesome wound. "He's hurt. He needs a hospital."

"Lilly, can you help him?" Alex asked. I didn't know why he was asking her. What could she possibly do for Jason?

"I don't have what I need in the car. It'll have to wait until we can get someplace safe. The best I can do is reduce the pain for now."

"Do it. I'll take the wheel." Lilly and Alex nimbly switched places, with Lilly sliding herself lithely across Alex's lap. She then switched places with me to get closer to Jason, although there was quite a bit less rubbing when we moved past each other. We settled into our new seats as Alex came to the end of the bridge and drove us back into Manhattan.

Lilly gently took Jason's arm and pulled it from his body where he was cradling it protectively against his chest. When he sucked in a pained breath at the movement, Lilly looked at him with sympathy and hovered a hand inches above the open wound. Closing her eyes and steadying her breathing, she hummed lightly in a clear, high-pitched tone. A soft, moss green illumination emanated from her palm into the wound. Jason's pained grimace immediately eased, the creases in his forehead smoothing out and his eyes rolling back into his head at the sweet relief.

"It won't last long, maybe an hour, but hopefully, that'll be enough time to get you someplace we can help you."

"Are you kidding?" Jason said. "I could marry you right now. Thank you."

Lilly smiled shyly in response.

"When you two love bugs are done making googly eyes at each other, we have a problem," I said, bringing everyone's attention back to the chimera that was now climbing out of the river behind us, shaking off the last shards of ice.

We were moving rapidly, but it caught sight of us, breaking into a run. Lower Manhattan tended to be quiet at night since it was mostly office buildings; as a result, only a few lucky passersby got to see the giant chimera galloping down Centre Street, ripping up the asphalt with its wicked claws. The wind rushing past its body must have helped to dry off its wings because it took a great leap and launched itself back into the air. It was gaining on us rapidly.

"We're too easy of a target," I said. "We need to get underground."

"We can't let this thing follow us into a subway or a parking garage under a building," said Alex. "It would put too many people at risk."

"The tunnel!" Lilly suggested. "It's too narrow for the chimera to follow us in there."

"How do I get there?" Alex asked.

Lilly directed him to make a left onto Canal Street and go straight into the Holland Tunnel. The chimera wasn't about to let us off the hook for the stunt we pulled on the bridge, though. As we raced toward the tunnel, the creature opened its maw, and a glow began to burn deep in its throat.

"Incoming!" I yelled.

Alex swerved onto an empty sidewalk to avoid the blast, plowing over a fire hydrant, a spray of water climbing into the air. The chimera howled and changed course to avoid another soaking.

The next fireball forced Alex to sideswipe a number of cars that were parked along the curb, the flames engulfing an electronics store. We wouldn't be able to dodge these attacks for much longer. There just wasn't enough space for maneuverability on these streets.

As though the chimera could read my thoughts, it waited for us to hit the next block where construction vehicles and barriers lined the street, allowing enough space for only one vehicle to pass through. It flew in close and spit the next fireball directly toward the car.

Jason and Lilly threw themselves onto the floor, but that wouldn't protect them if the entire vehicle went up in flames. I felt completely helpless watching our destruction hurtle toward us in slow motion. Not for the first time this week, I thought this was the end.

Then Alex interrupted my desolate thoughts. "Emma, grab the wheel!"

I did as he asked without hesitation, leaning across Alex as he lifted his staff again, calling forth that shimmering shield. It wrapped around the back end of the car, and as the chimera's blast slammed into it, the force lifted our rear wheels off the ground, thrusting the car forward the last few feet into the safety of the Holland Tunnel.

The chimera touched down at the entrance to the tunnel and blew an angry blast of fire into the enclosed space. With nowhere to disperse, the heat and flame consumed the tunnel, melting asphalt and heating up the inside of the car, but Alex's shield held.

Once we were out of its reach, Alex dropped the shield and slumped against the driver's seat in exhaustion, reducing speed to give us precious extra minutes for recovery before we had to engage again.

"So, what now?" I asked. "We can't hide in this tunnel forever, and we have to get rid of that thing before the sun rises and the streets fill with people."

Lilly pulled out her cell phone and started texting. "I'll text my father and brother to come help, but it may take them a little bit of time to get here."

"We need to make a stand," said Jason, his voice weak yet determined. "On the other side of the tunnel is Liberty State Park. It'll give us some open space, with less chance that anyone will wander by. We'll never make it farther than that with this thing flying on top of us."

"Our best chance of defeating it is on the ground where it's slower and has less maneuverability," Alex agreed. "Its wings are the most vulnerable part of its body. If we can inflict enough damage on them, we can bring the chimera down."

"And how do you propose we kill it? Do you have a magic spell that can strike it dead instantly?" Jason asked hopefully.

"If I did, don't you think I would have used it by now?"

"Okay, we do this the old-fashioned way," I said. "Jason and I will shoot it out of the sky. Alex, can you figure out a way to put out its flame again?" Alex nodded. "Once it's down, we surround it and hit it with everything we've got, aiming for the soft spots—eyes, belly, mouth, wings." Everyone nodded in agreement, though without much confidence.

We all armed ourselves as the car inexorably approached the tunnel exit.

"Is everybody ready?" I asked.

With silent nods all around, Alex stepped hard on the gas, shooting out of the tunnel with tires smoking. The chimera was on us in seconds, breathing fire and slamming its body against the already very damaged car.

We made it to the park and came to a grinding halt in a lot close to the promenade along the river. We threw ourselves from the car, taking cover under some nearby trees, seconds before the vehicle was fully engulfed in flames.

Jason and I pulled out our rifles and opened fire, aiming for the chimera's wings. It was difficult to hit a moving target in the black of night, but at least some of the bullets found home. They tore through the soft membrane and boney spines, riddling the wings with enough small holes they could no longer catch air.

The creature wailed in pain and anger. It tried desperately to stay aloft; however, even the frantic beating of its wings could not sustain its flight for long, and its feet alit on the ground.

Alex stepped forward just as another fireball left the beast's mouth. Raising his staff, he called forth a gale and swept his arms forward, sending the winds straight at the creature, reversing the fireball's direction back into its throat. The creature choked and burped, coughing plumes of black smoke, then it swept out a massive claw and caught Alex in the gut, sending him flying into a nearby tree. Alex landed limply on the ground beneath the budding branches, unconscious.

Jason crept around the creature's rear, trying to attack it from the opposite side, but the snake tail swiveled, catching the movement. I screamed a warning, but it was too late. The snake hissed, baring fangs dripping with venom, and struck as quick as lightning. When it pulled away, Jason stood stunned for a few moments. Then I saw a trickle of blood slide down his throat, and he toppled to the grass.

I lifted my Kalashnikov, shifting it to semi-automatic, and fired at the snake. As bullet after bullet slammed into it, chunks of flesh were torn from the tail until it was severed from the chimera's body and my ammo ran out.

I dropped the rifle, feeling as spent and empty as the weapon, but forced my feet to move around the creature until I reached Jason. I dropped to my knees at his side, pressing my fingers into his neck, desperate for a pulse. After a few seconds, I found one, although it was slow and stuttering. I didn't know whether we would be able to defeat this creature before Jason's heart gave out.

I was thirsty for the chimera's blood, wanting to kill it for hurting Jason and Alex, but I had nothing to fight with. I clutched the amulet under my shirt, squeezing it hard, trying to hold down that old feeling of helplessness. The amulet grew warm under my hands, and I could feel that strange thrumming, like a live electrical wire. The vibration moved out of the stone, into my hands and up my arms. A sense of calm assurance flooded through me. I felt invincible.

Slowly, I got to my feet and walked purposefully straight toward the raging chimera. All sound had ceased. I heard nothing other than the rush of my own blood in my ears. I continued to move slowly, as if in a dream. The creature's head swung toward me, jaws wide, teeth bared, wisps of smoke trailing from its nostrils. It drew in a deep breath, stoking the fire in its belly with oxygen. The red glow began at the back of its throat, and I braced myself for the onslaught.

Flames shot from its mouth, and I met them with fire of my own. I held the amulet in front of me like a wand, and green tongues of flames licked out, meeting and consuming the chimera's weaker orange fire. It pressed into and around the chimera, burning its hide and searing its insides. The creature flailed and twisted, unable to escape. I felt elated, high almost, at the sheer power I was wielding. I was drunk on it, laughter bubbling up from my chest. However, as quickly as it had come, it vanished, and I crashed—hard.

I hit empty, and the green flames sputtered out as my legs gave way beneath me. The chimera was significantly injured yet not dead. It was a blackened husk, covered in melted scales and oozing blisters. It cried and screeched, lashing out blindly at anything in its path. I had nothing left, though. The chimera would kill me easily and then go on a rampage, possibly killing hundreds of people.

But death didn't come that night, the elves did. A dozen of them swarmed in with bows, arrows, and swords. I expected them to look like Legolas from *The Lord of the Rings*; instead, they were dressed in jeans, sweatpants, graphic tees, sneakers, and a couple were even in slacks and suit jackets, like they had just come from an evening out at a fine restaurant. Nevertheless, they all had long hair to hide their pointy ears.

The elves surrounded the beast, nimbly leaping in and back, randomly stabbing and hacking from so many different positions the creature couldn't get a bead on any of them. I lay on the ground unmoving, watching the butchering of the chimera by the elves. It was clear this small band probably couldn't have taken it down at its full strength, but the beast was severely compromised.

Arrows bounced harmlessly off its hide, though the swords were another matter. When the chimera was distracted, defending its rear from attack, two elves gracefully moved underneath the creature, and in perfect coordination, they stabbed upward, plunging two swords through the creature's heart.

The chimera stiffened, shuddered, and fell. I should have felt vindicated and satisfied, but I didn't. I didn't feel much of anything. I looked up at the lightening sky as dawn approached, when a face entered my vision. I met Alex's compassionate gaze.

"You're okay," I managed to croak, barely able to stay awake any longer.

"Just a bruise. Otherwise, I'm good." He smiled then cradled me in his arms, and I could feel myself being lifted off the ground.

I closed my eyes and rested my head against his shoulder, taking comfort in the warmth of his body and the feeling of his strong arms holding me. The last thing I remembered was the sensation of him resting his cheek on the top of my head before I drifted into a dreamless sleep.

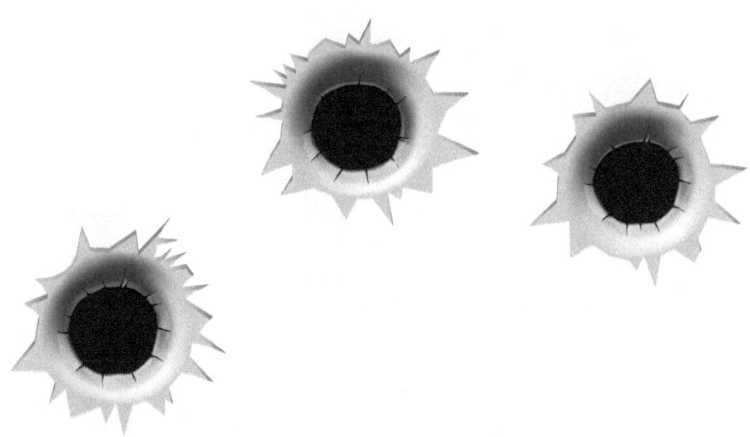

Chapter Fifteen

WHEN I AWOKE the following day, the sun was already setting. The room I found myself in was unfamiliar, and it took me a few moments to remember where I was. The night before, I had regained consciousness long enough to learn that Alex and Lilly felt the safest place for me to be right now was at the farm owned by Lilly's family, although the word "compound" was a better way to describe it.

They lived in the largest log cabin I had ever seen. Lilly had said her father and twelve brothers had built the ten-bedroom home themselves about a decade ago. Despite its size, it was warm and rustic, almost all of the materials coming from the fifty-six acres of land the home sat on. Even the furniture had been fashioned from trees surrounding the property. The rugs, bedding, and the family's clothing were all made from soft wool shorn from the flock of sheep that roamed the open grasses alongside cows, goats, horses, and chickens.

It was secure to the extent that it was in the middle of nowhere and difficult to find, and no one outside of our small group knew I was there. I didn't like the idea of hiding, but acknowledged that we needed time to regroup and figure out our next steps, not to mention eat. I was starving. Hunger and a desire to see how Jason was doing drove me from the comfort of the feather bed.

Before I had fallen into bed last night—or this morning, actually—Jason had been carried off to another bedroom to be tended by Lilly's grandmother, who was apparently a woman with great healing skills. I had wanted to stay with him; however, the wizened old woman had unceremoniously ushered me out of his room, telling me the spirits preferred to work alone, whatever that meant.

I moved down the hall to the room where they had brought Jason last night. I knocked lightly, not wanting to wake him if he was resting, but I heard a weak, "Come in."

Opening the door slowly, I peered in and saw Jason lying in a bed covered with sheepskin blankets. The curtains were drawn, leaving the room dim.

"Hey, you," I said softly. "How are you feeling?" I closed the door behind me and walked across the room to sit on the bed next to him. He looked pale and tired and had some kind of herbal-smelling wraps tied around his burned arm and bitten neck. Regardless, he greeted me with a smile.

"A little old lady with pointy ears told me I'll live, so I've either gone crazy, or I might be dead already and just don't know it."

"Neither. Believe it or not, she's an elf. So is Lilly. We're at her family's house in Cortlandt, upstate New York. They allowed us to use this place as a safe house for now, but I don't plan to overstay our welcome. When you're feeling up to it, we'll need to figure out our next move."

"I don't think I could get out of bed right now, let alone pick a fight. That snake venom really did a number on me."

"No worries. You rest as long as you need to. The bad guys aren't going anywhere. I'll work it out with Alex and Lilly, and I'll let you know the plan."

"Yeah, okay, Em. I'm going to go to sleep now," Jason responded, his voice drifting off as his eyes closed, and his breathing turned slow and deep.

I leaned forward and gave him a soft kiss on the forehead. What would I do without him? I didn't even want to think about the possibility. He was my best friend and my only link to the world I remembered. He made sense to me, kept me grounded when the rest of my world was being twisted inside out. I couldn't lose him.

I made my way downstairs to a rustic yet modern kitchen. Its centerpiece was an enormous island covered on all sides with multi-colored fieldstones and topped with a beautifully carved butcher-block slab. Lilly's grandmother was bustling around, chopping herbs and vegetables and tossing them into a tall pot on the stove while humming softly under her breath. She had to stand on her tiptoes to reach the top of the pot with her slight four-and-half-foot frame. A long, white braid that reached past her waist swung gently as she moved.

Alex and Lilly were sitting at the handmade oak trestle table with two men I assumed were her father and one of her brothers. I took the open seat next to Alex with Lilly and her brother across from us and her father at the head of the rectangular table. They had been deep in conversation over several sets of maps laid out before them, but all eyes shifted to me when I entered the room.

Alex placed a warm hand on my arm. "Hey, sleepy head. Feeling better?"

I was taken aback by the endearment. It seemed so unlike Alex, especially given his frequent animosity toward me. Did that mean maybe he didn't see me as the enemy after all?

"I'm much better, thanks. I checked on Jason, and he's doing well, too. He just needs a little more rest. What are you guys working on?" I recognized the map of Manhattan immediately, though the one underneath looked completely unfamiliar.

"Oh, my God," Lilly started in that perky way of hers. "That was crazy last night! I've never seen a chimera before, only heard about them from Gram's stories. It was fierce. I can't believe we made it out of there alive. Em, why were those government guys after you? Did you forget to pay your taxes or something?" She stopped to laugh at her own joke, and I took the opening to interrupt her.

"I don't know what they wanted. What I do want to know is what you are doing working for Nathan Anshar and how you and Alex just happened to show up together in the same car." I tried to sound casual, but I was sure the accusation was clear.

"Mr. Anshar is a friend of the family," Lilly's father interrupted. "I'm sorry we haven't yet been introduced." He threw a steely look at Lilly, and she dropped her head apologetically. "I am Therran, son of Tahltril, Lilly's father and the leader of the Thalbrar clan. This is my eldest son and heir, Lockien." Lilly's dad spoke with the authority of a monarch; however, he looked more like the head of a motorcycle club than an elven clan. He had long hair, generously strung through with gray; rough stubble covered his jaw; and he wore faded jeans and a Grateful Dead T-shirt. His son, on the other hand, looked like he had crawled out of an Abercrombie ad, wearing dark wash jeans and a gray cable knit sweater, with perfectly tousled hair and the same bright green eyes as Lilly.

With a greeting like that, I didn't know if I was expected to kneel, bow, kiss a ring, or some other such sign of deference. Instead, I simply said, "It's very nice to meet you. I can't thank you enough for coming to our rescue last night. If you hadn't shown up, I don't think we would have made it out of there alive."

"No, likely you would not have. Chimeras are not easy creatures to kill. Luckily, I have had some experience with them in the past. As for Mr. Anshar, he has been a benefactor to this family since our arrival here. We owe him much, and occasionally that means he will call on us for assistance."

Lilly jumped in with her usual enthusiasm. "Yeah, Alex had come into my store last night after you told him I knew something about the amulet. I think his original plan was going to be to threaten me with physical harm if I didn't reveal all." She winked at Alex, letting him know she didn't take his threats of torture personally. "But, if you guys hadn't noticed, I'm kind of a talker, so I had no problem telling him what I told you. Anyway, we were chatting when Nathan's assistant called, asking me to play your driver for the night, and Alex insisted on coming along. I have to say, I was pretty surprised when I heard it was you I would be driving around. How do you know Nathan?"

"Lilly," her father interrupted sternly, "you should refer to him as Mr. Anshar. It is a sign of respect."

Lilly rolled her eyes, looking like a teenager whose parents simply didn't get it. "Dad, I have told you a million times, that's not how it's done here. It's okay to call people by their first names." She turned to me and Alex, explaining conspiratorially, "I'm the only one in this family who was born and schooled on earth, so they just don't get it. My family is still stuck in the old ways. It drives me crazy. That's why I had to move to New York City, to be with normal people. I bet, if given a choice, they would go back to Urusilim in a heartbeat. Not me, though."

"Speaking of which…" I began. "How did such a large group of elves make it to Earth? I thought it was difficult for even one person to get through the rift, let alone almost fifteen."

Therran looked uncomfortable and exchanged a glance with his son, who had been sitting there silently until now. "We had some…special assistance. I will tell you the story one day, but right now, we should get back to the reason why we are sitting around this table. We have all been sharing information and trying to piece together recent events in order to determine what comes next."

That got my attention, but I filed away the question of the elves' arrival for future discussion. "What have you learned?"

Alex took the lead, which I initially thought he did to ensure I wasn't told anything he didn't want me to know, though maybe I was being unfair. Alex probably knew the most about what was happening.

"I think we can safely say Marduk is sending creatures through the rift in an effort to assist with your capture and return. I told you how difficult that is to do, which is why he hasn't been able to send armies after you. However, we aren't certain he is behind what happened to you in Mexico. The best I can tell, the purpose behind the blood ritual was to activate the amulet. I am guessing there must be something special about you that required the use of your blood and no one else's."

"What is it? What is so special about me?"

Alex merely shrugged, not answering. His non-response made me believe he knew more than he was letting on, as usual.

"I also think the ritual removed the shielding spell that we believe had been cast on you. The Mage Council and others have been searching for you for years. Then, suddenly, I was contacted a week ago by the Council with your location and a mandate to protect you. That message came only a day after the incident in Mexico."

"I suppose that would explain why all of this is happening now."

"Yes. I think it is safe to speculate that Marduk wants you alive for a reason connected to the amulet. I don't know why your own government would want you though."

"I'm just irresistible, I guess." Speaking of irresistible, I thought about Zane and that kiss in the Navy Yard, feeling my cheeks flush at the memory.

"Tell me more about Zane." Zane confused me more than anything else, if that was even possible. Although he was deadly dangerous and had tried to kill or capture me on a few occasions, I didn't fear him. In fact, if I was going to be honest with myself, I almost wanted to see him again.

Alex hesitated, his eyes fluttering around the room, looking everywhere except at me. He blew out an uncertain breath. "Zane and I were best friends once. It was a long time ago. He wasn't always like he is now. He was a good person, the best really. You knew that better than anyone. The two of you had … something. But Zane was always a private person, so I can't really give you any details."

I had no memory at all of Zane and our time together, but I knew immediately what Alex had said was true. I felt it in my soul. Zane had been mine once. "What happened to him?"

"Marduk," he said simply. "Zane was taken. Broken. I can't imagine what Marduk did to him, but whatever it was, it destroyed Zane's mind. A few years ago, the Mage Council managed to capture Zane. The most talented and powerful mages in all of Urusilim tried to restore him, but to no avail. If they couldn't do it, no one can. Zane is Marduk's lap dog, completely and irreversibly brainwashed. Zane escaped the Council and went running right back to his master."

"But it sometimes seems like there is still a sane person in there somewhere," I insisted.

Alex shook his head, giving me a look of pity. "I think you are only deluding yourself. None of us have seen even a glimmer of hope. If you think you saw glimpses of the old

Zane, it's either because he's manipulating you or because you don't remember what the old Zane was like."

"Yeah, maybe," I said, unconvinced. I knew what manipulation looked like, and I didn't think that was what was happening. The kiss had felt genuine. Besides, just because Alex had told me I had a history with Zane didn't mean I remembered it, and I certainly didn't feel it—at least, not entirely. It was more like a ghost of a feeling, similar to déjà vu. It was enough to create some passing intrigue, though certainly not enough to drive me to take an action on it … yet.

"And what about the amulet? What does it do?" I asked.

Alex shrugged and looked like he was about to tell me he had no idea when Lilly's grandmother interrupted. "That depends on you, child," she said in a surprisingly strong voice for someone who looked so frail. She continued to bustle about the kitchen, not even looking in our direction. "It has your blood; it is your essence. If you know who you are, you know what the amulet is capable of."

That sent chills down my spine. I didn't know who I was, but I knew at least some of what I was capable of, and not much of it was good. Could the amulet channel the darkness within me? If so, I didn't want to be responsible for the potential consequences. I wasn't the right person to carry an object of such power. I should give it to someone who could be trusted to do good with it, but who was that? Even if I knew any good people, would I want to burden them with the amulet?

"So, you're saying I can do anything at all with it, without limitations?"

"Its limitations are yours. What are your limits?" She must have seen the fear in my face because she continued, "No faith in yourself, eh? You will be tested, child. That is when you will find out who you really are."

Dread passed through me. I made a vow to myself then to give the amulet to someone who proved themselves worthy of it. And, if I couldn't find that person in time, I would hide it away somewhere deep and dark where no one would be able to find it.

"So, what is our next move?" Lockien asked.

When I gave him an eternally grateful glance for having shifted the attention away from me, he returned it with the hint of a smile. That was when I remembered the sheet of paper in my back pocket.

"Nathan gave this to me just before we had to flee the building. I agreed to take a job finding a stolen object for him." I looked at the blue Post-It note for the first time. On it, scrawled in neat block lettering, was the location of my next mission:

North Brother Island
Lab B13

None of us had ever heard of North Brother Island, so Lilly googled it on her iPhone.

"Wow. It's right here in New York City. It's an abandoned island in the Hudson River that used to house Riverside Hospital, a quarantine facility for smallpox victims. It looks like someplace out of a horror movie." She turned her screen around so we could all see the imposing yet dilapidated brick structure of the hospital that was slowly but surely being reclaimed by the surrounding forest. She turned back to her phone. "This says the hospital closed in the 1930s after a boat filled with patients caught fire on the river and everyone onboard died, their bodies washing up on the shore of the island. It looks like the entire island was turned into a wildlife sanctuary after that."

"Why would he want to send you there? What is supposed to be there?" Alex asked.

"He said it was a weapon of some sort, something about it being a body for the amulet. It didn't make much sense to me."

Lilly's grandmother stopped mid-chop on her onions and dropped the knife onto the floor with a clatter. Everyone's attention turned to her; however, she was staring holes through me with piercing, incredulous eyes. Then she exchanged a long look with her son.

Therran said to her, "Do you think Nathan knew where it was all along and didn't say anything? He wouldn't do that. He knows how long we have been searching for it."

"If you had found it first, would you have told him?" she asked.

Lilly's father didn't respond. His silence was answer enough though.

"What the heck are you two talking about?" Lilly demanded.

Her father gave her another disapproving look. I had a feeling Lilly got that look a lot from her family, but he proceeded to explain anyway. "If it is the weapon we suspect it to be, it is called Sharur. It is beyond ancient. Sharur is, in its most basic form, a battle axe said to have been forged by the gods in the lava pits that flow through the core of Urusilim. It was created for a fae prince who was said to have helped the gods defeat the Old One, the first god who created our world in darkness. However, some creatures still loyal to the Old One—the Monere—escaped retribution and searched Urusilim for the prince to take their revenge. To protect their loyal servant, the gods forged for him a weapon that could kill magic and open rifts in reality to allow him to escape to safety on other worlds. Yet the enemy eventually found him and mortally wounded him. Although they couldn't fix his body, the gods preserved him by placing his soul in the axe, granting him immortality,"

"And you want it why exactly?" Lilly asked her father.

The answer came to me before Therran could respond. "You think that, if you had this weapon, you could open a rift back to Urusilim." Therran looked pleased that I had been able to figure it out on my own and nodded. "But why don't you just ask the mages to help you open a rift? There are some that are strong enough to do it."

"That's true," Therran said. "However, they are only capable of sending one individual through a rift at a time, and the recovery from even that effort is significant. We believe that Sharur is the only object in existence that can open a rift large enough for long enough to send many through."

"An army," I breathed. "Marduk wants to invade earth."

"Yes, that is possible," he said. "But that is not the elves' purpose. Those of us here on Earth are refugees from the partial destruction of Urusilim a decade ago. We simply want to reunite with our families and clans and see if enough time has passed so we can successfully heal the land."

"Are you kidding me?" Lilly snapped. "There is no way in hell I am going anywhere. I can't leave my job and my friends. I have a life here—"

"We will speak of this another time." Therran nailed Lilly with a sharp look. I didn't think it was possible, but she actually shut up.

"If the government is somehow aware of what is going on, that would explain their involvement," I said as the realization dawned on me. "If they think I am going after the only object that can open a rift, allowing an invading army access to American soil, of course they are going to try to stop me. But how would they know about Marduk and Urusilim and rifts and magic?" My head was spinning with so many unanswered questions.

"They have their hands in more things than the public will ever know about. Why not this too?" Lilly said. "I watched this documentary on the Discovery Channel the other day about secret government projects. It explained that the fluoride the government adds to our drinking water is really a mind control drug, and that the government created the AIDS virus to purposefully kill gay people, and don't even get me started on Area 51—"

"I get your point," I said, unconvinced that she used the best examples, but believing that her general argument had merit.

"So now we think we may know what the government wants, but what about Nathan? What does he want with the axe?" Alex asked.

"He said he wants me to reclaim what was stolen from him, and will teach me to use it, but I don't know why," I responded.

"Whatever his reasons are, the fact that he didn't reveal them to us causes me concern," Therran said.

"What does this Sharur have to do with me?"

"It is our belief that, although the axe can be wielded by anyone as a traditional weapon, it will only share its full capabilities with the person who holds the key to unlocking them. I don't know how that power is unlocked, but Nathan seems to think you are the person who can do it."

Silence descended as we all fell into our own thoughts.

It took only a few minutes for me to make up my mind. I stood up and pounded my fist on the table, effectively getting everyone's attention. "We go after Sharur tomorrow night. We'll spend the rest of today planning our strategy, arming ourselves, and getting some much needed rest. We make our move tomorrow at midnight."

I was expecting an outburst of debate and questions, but I was only met with eyes that glittered in anticipation.

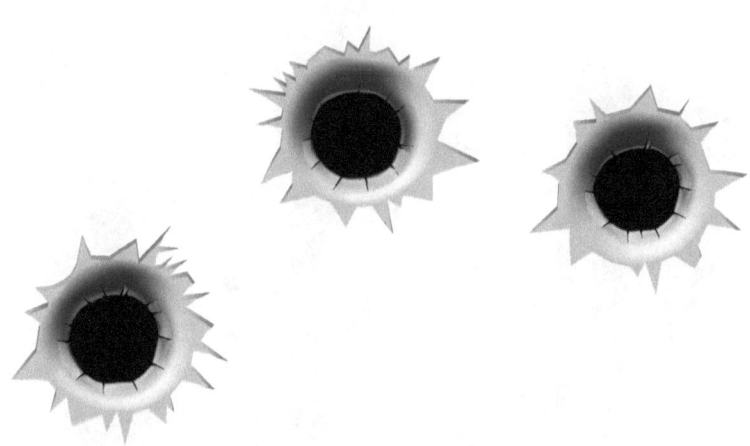

Chapter Sixteen

A TRICKLE OF sweat took a slow path down my temple and over the band of my telescopic night vision goggles. My dark hair was pulled into a heavy braid that trailed down my back, but it did nothing to help keep me cooler.

I reached under my jaw and unhooked my helmet, ripping it off my head to allow some cooler air to reach my scalp. It was an unusually hot night; the first heat wave of the year had decided to come early in the season.

I was lying uncomfortably on the deck of a black speedboat that was almost motionless on the glass-like waters of the Hudson River. There was no breeze tonight, nothing to disrupt the stifling humidity. The air was so thick with moisture it felt as if I was trying to breathe through a wet washcloth.

It had been a while since I had pulled a job in this kind of weather. Most of my work the past few years had tended to be in the deserts of Afghanistan or some other God-forsakenistan country. Don't get me wrong, that environment was no walk in the park either. I had sand in places no one should ever find sand. However, the cooler nights in the dessert brought some measure of relief to the scorching, arid days. Tonight, there was no such relief. Making it worse was the heavy wetsuit that stuck to my back and trapped the sweat close to my body.

"Lockien, what do you see?" I asked to the elf lying beside me. Whereas I needed night vision to survey the old Riverside Hospital on North Brother Island, Lockien was able to see just fine in the dark, even from this distance.

"I see four well-armed men patrolling the grounds on the south side of the hospital. It takes them six minutes to complete a full patrol," Lockien reported.

"I see them too," I said, wanting to ensure we weren't missing anything.

"Daniel, what have you got? Over," I said softly into my earpiece.

Through my goggles, I could see the bright white impression of the hospital standing stoically a few hundred yards from the shore of the river along with the blurry figures of the patrols. It would have been a bitch to go in blind trying to find Lab B13. Thankfully, Daniel had been able to locate old blueprints of the structure from when it had been first constructed. There was no room labeled "B13," but areas in the hospital's basement were specifically built as laboratories. I was guessing the "B" stood for Basement and figured that was the best place to start our search.

Daniel also assumed they must have upgraded their security system sometime recently if they were housing a valuable weapon. He had scoured his contacts until he had found the company that had done the work and learned they were a government contractor. That had told us two things— the building was a government facility, as we had already guessed, and they had probably installed one of the most state-of-the-art security systems available. Daniel had almost been giddy at the prospect of that kind of challenge; however, I had remained uncomfortable with the niggling question of why and how the government had come to possess Sharur.

In full scuba gear, Daniel had dropped into the black waters of the Hudson from the boat about two hours ago. He had come ashore on the island with his gear protected in a waterproof pack and proceeded to locate the underground wires and control panel for the system. I had probably checked in with him a half dozen times since then, but his progress was slow.

I was beginning to wonder whether we would need to abort the mission altogether when Daniel radioed back, "I'm almost in. I can disengage the alarms on the front doors, but if any other systems are inside, I would need to work on those separately. I can't just cut the blue wire and shut the whole thing down."

My shoulders slumped at the prospect of taking Daniel inside the building. He was one of the most capable people I knew, but I always had a protective streak when it came to him. He didn't have a selfish bone in his body, no ulterior motives or hidden objectives. Everything he did, he did out of genuine loyalty to me. For that reason, I wanted to keep him out of harm's way as much as possible, although it seemed like it just wasn't going to be possible this time.

I closed my eyes briefly and then said, "Understood. We're coming in."

I stood, turning to Therran and the seven other elves of his clan who made up our party. We had wanted to be sure we had enough support yet hadn't wanted so many that an ambush would be unfeasible; as a result, we had settled on twelve in total: Therran and Lockien, with their seven clan members, plus Alex, Daniel, and myself. Jason had argued, cajoled and even begged to come along, but he was still recovering, and I wouldn't allow him back in the field.

I was the only one who needed scuba gear since, apparently, elves had a talent for holding their breath. They had tried to explain to me that it had something to do with the spirits of nature sustaining them, but I had simply been happy we didn't have to find and lug the extra gear. Meanwhile, Alex had never dived before and couldn't hold his breath; however, he had assured us he could freeze the water just long enough to allow himself to walk to land. We didn't want him to waste his energy trying to sustain an ice bridge long enough for the rest of us though.

"Let's go," I said.

Without another word, eleven of us dropped into the water. If I could have sighed in pleasure underwater, I would have as the coolness enveloped me even through the wetsuit. Careful to avoid creating a wake on the surface of the water, we dived to a depth of about fifteen feet, the elves keeping up with me easily. We selected an area of shoreline where the trees came close to the water, avoiding the crumbling boat dock.

Alex and Daniel caught up with us onshore, and I un-shouldered my gear bag, gratefully stripping out of the wetsuit. We were all similarly clothed in black bodysuits with black body paint covering any exposed skin.

Reaching into my bag, I removed and assembled the parts to my M40 sniper rifle in less than five seconds, slinging it across my back. The elves carried knives and the handguns I had given them from my personal stash.

We silently picked our way through the foliage to a clearing that opened onto the hospital's entrance. The building was three stories high, made entirely of red brick. Most of the windows were broken, and where glass still remained, it was coated in decades of dirt and grime. Moss and vines climbed the walls and crept in through cracks in the crumbling stone. The place had a creepy, haunted feel about it, like the ghosts of the hundreds of small pox victims who had died there still roamed the grounds.

I un-slung the rifle and placed my eye to the scope. Taking into account the humidity and lack of wind, I aimed the weapon on the first patrolling guard who came into my sight. I took a deep breath and held it as my finger exerted pressure on the trigger. Quietly exhaling, I depressed it all the way. Although the M40 was outfitted with a silencer, one common myth is that a silencer makes a gun silent. It doesn't. Instead, it makes the gunman invisible. I used a silencer to hide the muzzle flash and disperse the sound of the shot, making it much more difficult to pinpoint my location.

The bullet found its way home, straight through the unprotected throat of the man patrolling the grounds. I watched as his head snapped back and he dropped silently.

Meanwhile, his friends on the opposite end of the building continued their patrol, none the wiser.

I chambered the next bullet and waited for the second soldier to return, but he didn't appear. That's when the rhythmic blaring of the alarm shattered the peacefulness of the night.

The. *Shit!* I looked to the top of the building and noticed the end of a high-powered rifle sticking out through the cracks of some misplaced boards covering a window. That soldier was too well-hidden for us to have noticed him when we had been scoping the place from the boat. He must have seen the soldier below him drop from my bullet and called in the cavalry.

The front doors of the hospital slammed opened, and Black Ops soldiers came pouring out. Thirty of them fanned out along the sides of the building, using the shadows, rubble, and overgrown shrubs as cover. They were all wearing night vision goggles and were armed with semi-automatics.

"Once they're in position, they are going to spot us and open fire," I said to my team. "Alex, can you blind them?" He nodded. "Our best chance is to take them by surprise. Now!" I urged him just as the soldiers completed their formation.

One minute he was there, and the next, Alex had simply disappeared. He had cloaked his presence and made a run toward the soldiers. Speed was more important than stealth; therefore, I could hear him crashing through the undergrowth. He came to a stop near the soldiers and dropped the cloak. Before they could react to his sudden appearance, Alex raised his staff high then brought it down, stabbing the end into the ground. When the wood touched earth, a blinding white light poured forth.

Anticipating it, my team and I had shut our eyes tight and looked away. The soldiers, however, had all been focused on Alex and were now grunting in pain as they frantically tore off their shorted out goggles.

With a few precious seconds bought, we rushed the hospital, opening fire on the soldiers before they were able to recover their vision.

If I had commanded a trained team, it would have been as easy as shooting fish in a barrel, but elves weren't exactly experts with human firearms. In fact, the first time any of them had ever handled a gun was the previous afternoon when I had given them their first shooting lesson. Most of their shots had gone far afield, hitting trees and dirt instead of the targets I had set up. What was going on at that point was more of the same. They were able to hit only four of the thirty soldiers before our highly-trained adversaries regrouped and returned fire.

Five of the elves went down immediately in a spray of blood.

"Alex!" I screamed.

"On it," he responded without need for further explanation. The runes in his staff illuminated, and he brought up a shield as he ran back to our position to protect the remaining members of our party. Bullets slammed into the shield. The force of that much high-powered ammunition knocked Alex back a few feet and dropped him to his knees.

"Therran, Alex won't be able to hold that shield for more than a few minutes. If it falls, we're all dead. I need to get in that building now," I said.

Therran turned to his son. "Lockien, I'll create a distraction, and you get Emma into the building and keep her safe. Do everything in your power to make sure Sharur is recovered."

Without waiting for acknowledgements, Therran knelt and placed his hands flat on the ground, chanting under his breath. I could feel a presence, immense and old, stirring awake. Goose bumps ran down my arms, despite the clinging heat.

Seeing movement in my peripheral vision, I turned toward it. The tangles of roots, vines, and overgrown plant life rustled and swayed, yet not even a gentle breeze disturbed them. Roots of oak trees dislodged themselves from the ground, and untamed wisteria vines slithered through undergrowth toward the unsuspecting soldiers. Plant life wrapped around ankles, torsos, and arms, squeezing and pulling. Screams filled the air as limbs were torn from their sockets with the popping of bones and gushing of blood.

I frantically looked at the ground around me, eyes wide, poised to run for my life. I could hear dry hissing sounds moving around me as the animated plants slid past my feet. I spun in a circle, frantic to see if any were about to attack, but they ignored me, uninterested in targeting anyone other than the soldiers.

The soldiers who hadn't been grabbed initially were smart enough to move to clearer areas where they couldn't be easily reached by the plants, and they targeted their weapons on the new threat.

"Alex, Daniel, Lockien, with me. Move!"

We kept to the forest and skirted the building until we reached a clearing that would take us the final fifty feet to the front entrance. With the guards otherwise occupied or in pieces, my small group then sprinted to the entrance of the hospital without anyone attempting to stop us.

I pulled the handle on the front doors and found them locked. "Daniel, get these open."

Daniel tore the door's security keypad off the wall, exposing the wires behind it. I was not very technically savvy, beyond being very talented with online shopping; as a result, I mostly ignored him while he disconnected and reconnected wires, fiddled with the digital keypad, and overall looked quite pleased with himself when the lock clicked open. The kid could break into a high security military installation as easily as he could hack my email, which I had also seen him do.

We slipped into the building and were confronted by a crumbling lobby. Sections of ceiling had given way, dumping plaster and debris over the concrete floors. Paint was peeling off walls, and broken remnants of chairs and tables were scattered about. At the rear of the lobby, behind a decrepit welcome desk, there was a door. It appeared cracked and weakened with time, but upon closer inspection, it was a facade covering an impenetrable steel door.

"Daniel, I don't see any control panels or locking mechanisms. How do we get this thing opened?" I asked.

Daniel gave me a confident smile and sauntered up to the lobby desk. He dropped to his knees, peering under the counter until he found what he was looking for. With the push of a hidden button, the steel door silently swung open.

Drawing my gun, I made sure the way was clear and ushered the group through. We were deposited into a sterile white corridor with smooth walls and fluorescent overhead lights. I signaled for quiet as we moved cautiously forward. If anyone or anything came at us now, we had nowhere to hide.

A few hundred feet farther down, doors began to appear, lining either side of the hallway. Each door was fitted with a small glass window, giving us a view into professional looking offices. They were neat and orderly as well as clearly in current use, with solid wood desks, computer monitors, file cabinets, and even potted trees. I tried a few handles, and all were locked. At the end of the hall, we came upon a set of elevators.

As the elevator descended, I had a hard time ignoring the nagging feeling that finding this building empty of security or even a janitor was a little too convenient.

When the elevator reached the basement, the doors slid open. A barrage of gunfire filled every square inch of the small space, but thankfully, it was empty of passengers.

From my perch on top of the elevator car, I peered through the trap door in the ceiling, waiting until the gunmen realized the elevator was empty and stopped firing. When all was quiet, I lobbed a grenade through the trap door. It bounced down the hall, rolling to a stop at the feet of the soldiers.

The explosion was deafening in the small space. Heat and smoke flooded the hallway and elevator, setting off the fire suppression system. The combination of smoke and spraying water reduced the odds of me being spotted when I dropped through the trap door to the elevator's floor; however, I still opened fire on any soldiers that might have survived the grenade blast. I wasn't taking any chances.

With the way now clear, I pulled open the stairwell door next to the elevator and ushered out Alex, Daniel, and Lockien. We picked our way over prone bodies, careful not to slip on the blood-soaked floors. This hallway looked identical to the one above.

As we came upon the first door, I peered through the small window into a room lined with shelves. Each shelf contained various-sized glass jars filled with liquid, and floating inside were objects that looked to be body parts. I recognized hearts, lungs, eyes, livers, and other less recognizable organs.

I moved on to the next room, which was similar to the first, though this one held large glass tanks. Inside each tank was a body suspended in a viscous liquid. Some looked human, but most did not. The largest tank was almost twelve feet tall and held a giant muscle-bound creature with skin the color and texture of stone. The smallest tank was no more than two feet tall, and inside was a lithe creature that looked like a cross between a human and a dragonfly with luminescent wings and a delicate, child-like face. In other tanks, I recognized ghouls and shadow demons like the ones that had attacked me. I certainly had no love for any of those creatures, but I couldn't help wondering how they had died and what they had been through before the end had come.

I tore myself from the window, feeling a bit queasy as I approached the next door. I didn't want to look, but at the same time, I couldn't stop myself. I wished I had.

The next room looked like a standard hospital operating room with computerized monitoring equipment, overhead lights and carts containing trays of surgical instruments. The room had been recently used, not yet cleaned. The instruments were covered in blood and pieces of tissue taken from the poor creature still lying on the stainless steel table.

It took me a moment to realize why it reminded me of Eddie. When I figured it out, I had to look away and swallow down the bile that threatened to come up. I could hear Daniel behind me heaving up his dinner while Lockien sputtered furiously in a language I could only assume was elven. Only Alex was silent, but when I looked at him, his expression held all the rage and disgust that the rest of us were feeling.

On the steel table was the body of a shape shifter who had been killed mid-transformation. It looked as though he had possibly been trying to transfigure into a dragon. He still looked humanoid with arms and legs, but his body was covered in a tough, scaly hide. His face was that of a lizard with a snout full of sharp teeth and a forked tongue lolling out through slack jaws. A long, thick tail protruded from the bottom of his spine.

He was in the process of being autopsied, his rib cage spread and his abdomen pulled open. Much of his skin had been flayed off, revealing the raw pink muscles and tendons beneath. The top of his skull had been removed, the brain sitting in a liquid-filled jar nearby, likely destined for the room we had passed earlier. A neat pile of intestines sat on the table next to him, and one clawed hand had been cut off, as had his manhood. The worst part was the creature's arms, legs, and torso were bound by leather straps. Restraints weren't necessary for the deceased or even the unconscious. I couldn't even allow myself to consider it.

I forcibly compartmentalized what I had seen and locked it away. Thinking about what was happening in that place was not going to help me complete the mission.

"Let's move," I commanded the others. "Don't look in the windows."

I led us more quickly down the hallway, almost feeling the palpable effort everyone made to stay focused on the task at hand. Eyeing the room numbers etched onto placards above each door, we stopped when we came to B13.

This door had no window in it, and only a retinal scan could open the locked door. I doubted any of the soldiers behind us had been given access to the room, or I would have started digging out eyeballs. I looked to Daniel for help.

"Our only option here is to go in the old-fashioned way," he said, pulling a brick of C-4 from his pack and sticking it to the retinal scan reader.

Once he had everything set up, we all moved farther down the hallway and covered our ears. The blast shorted out the security panel, and we made our way into the room.

It was small, only about fourteen square feet, and completely empty except for a pedestal in the dead center of the room. The white granite structure was polished to a high shine. A niche had been carved into it, and within that space hung the object coveted by so many. To me, it looked like any other medieval battle axe that could be found in a museum. It was a work of art, to be sure; however, it had seen better days.

It had a double axe head with curving blades on both sides of a staff made of some material I couldn't immediately recognize. It looked like wood, but it must have been incredibly durable not to have rotted away over time. The bottom of the staff was tipped with a wicked-looking spike, allowing its wielder to slice, hack and stab with the weapon. The metal was dull and lifeless, the blade chipped and scarred. Intricate scrollwork was etched into the blade face that must have been stunning at one time yet was now fading and difficult to see. This weapon must have seen countless battles, but it didn't look like it was in a condition to see any more. I was less than impressed.

How could this possibly be the weapon that had been created by gods, wielded by a fae prince, and held the power to rip apart worlds? Yet, even as I eyed it skeptically, I noticed something about it that grabbed my attention. Before I could act, Lockien pushed past me and grabbed the axe with greedy hands. I gasped, expecting laser beams, explosions, toxic gas, or some other kind of security response, but nothing happened. He lifted it out of the display, hands shaking and knuckles turning white as he clutched the axe with veneration and vindication.

"Lockien, what are you doing?" Alex asked, like he was trying to reason with a two-year-old.

Lockien looked up as if he had forgotten we were all standing there. "Sharur doesn't belong to any of you. Even with the best of intentions, you will eventually become corrupted by its power. You aren't pure enough to resist the temptation, and it will eventually lead to the downfall of both of our worlds."

I opened my mouth to argue with him then shut it again when I had a hard time coming up with a counter argument. After all, maybe he was right. I had done terrible things in my adult life. Could someone who made a living killing people for personal gain, with no consideration for who I was hurting, be considered pure of heart? How could I be sure I wouldn't be corrupted if Sharur was placed in my hands? Even if I had good intentions, did I have the right to use the weapon to influence the fate of worlds? Who was I to claim it?

All of my questions and self-doubt meant little though. I had come here to retrieve the axe, and I fully intended to complete my mission. However, what I did with the weapon after I had it was still up for debate.

Lockien clutched the axe close to his chest. "My father never intended to allow you to have it, or he wouldn't have sent me with you. Sharur belongs to my people, and we are the only ones with the strength and the right to use it."

"And how do you plan to use it?" I asked, trying to buy some time until I could figure out how to get the weapon back without hurting Lockien. Even though he didn't want me to have Sharur, he still wasn't the enemy.

"Now that the axe is in my hands, I will open the rift to bring all my people to Earth along with any others we deem worthy to share this world with us. Urusilim is damaged beyond repair, a frayed husk of what it used to be, yet Earth contains lands where we can settle and thrive. I don't want to wield Sharur against you, but I will if I have to. Even your mage stands no chance against it. So I ask of you, please hear the wisdom in my words and stand with me, not against me."

No sooner had he made the request than a crack reverberated through the confines of the small room, and a small red hole appeared in the center of Lockien's forehead.

His face went slack and the axe slid from his hands with the clatter of steel hitting tile. Lilly's brother followed Sharur to the ground.

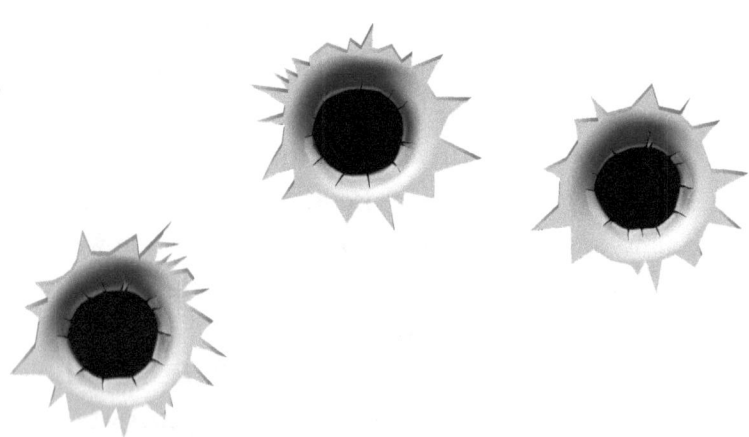

Chapter Seventeen

WE SPUN TO face the doorway where Black Ops soldiers stormed into the room, surrounding us. The sound of their boots pounding the floor drowned out my desperate whisper to Alex. "You have to get out of here. You saw what they'll do to you."

I knew Alex was drained from the shield he had generated outside. Besides, if they captured him, he would be filling the next set of jars in the other room. They were experimenting on beings from Urusilim, likely trying to discover the secrets of their biology and magical properties. As much as I feared for Daniel, he was probably the safest of all of us, being a plain vanilla human and just following my orders. Sure, they might interrogate him and toss him in prison, but I didn't think they would risk harming a genuine U.S. Citizen.

As for me, I was too valuable to kill, although I had no doubt they would use whatever other means were at their disposal to get what they wanted from me. I could handle whatever they threw at me, and maybe, if Alex got out, he could bring help.

He was standing at my back, so close I could feel the heat of him through my bodysuit. It was a comforting feeling, and even though I needed him to be safe, part of me didn't want him to leave. I knew Alex wouldn't voluntarily leave us behind; however, he must have reached the same conclusion I had. I suddenly felt the energy pass through me as he gathered it around him. It felt like an electric caress sliding over my skin.

"Miss Hayes. Exactly the person I expected to find here." The soldiers made way for the man stepping through the doorway.

He had the look of a former athlete whose best days had passed him by. A big man, most of the muscle from his youth was now turning to jelly. He was thick around the middle with the beginnings of a gut hanging over his belt. His cheeks were drooping into jowls, and his thick lips smirked in satisfaction at having cornered me.

"Who are you?" I demanded. I had to buy Alex the time he needed to gather enough energy to get out of here.

"My name is Ed Connor. I'm an envoy to the Committee on Superhuman Research, a joint effort between Homeland Security and the National Institute of Health. I have wanted to speak with you, but you have the unfortunate habit of running away."

"If you had peaceful intentions, you shouldn't have sent your soldiers after me at Nathan Anshar's office. Oh, and you just killed my friend," I spat, gesturing to Lockien's body without having the desire to look at it.

His cold eyes rested on the body of Lilly's brother. He leaned down and brushed the hair from Lockien's ears, revealing the obviously pointed tips. He waved at his team, and two men efficiently ran over, lifting Lockien from the floor and carrying him out of the room.

"What are you going to do with him?" I asked, feeling nauseous.

He merely gave me a small half-smile in response. We both knew the answer already.

Then his eyes landed on Alex. "You must be Alex Griffin. Don't look so surprised. We have files on all of you, albeit some are less complete than others. I would love the opportunity to get to know you better, Mr. Griffin, to find out what makes you tick."

My heart was pounding in my throat. *Get out, get out*, I kept screaming at Alex in my head. I didn't think he could read minds, though I was desperate enough to try. I was not sure when I had started to care about Alex or even if I really did. Maybe what I was feeling was fear at potentially losing someone who had helped keep me alive thus far. Maybe I simply didn't want to lose an ally, even if he wasn't exactly a friend.

"How do you know so much about us?" I asked, trying to keep Connor talking.

I was relieved when he refocused his attention on me. "Why, Miss Hayes, I am disappointed you don't remember me. After all, I was the first person to welcome you to Earth when you arrived. Although, you were quite incoherent and then unconscious during much of the time we spent together, so I don't suppose I can blame you. Suffice it to say, my team took good care of you and even found you a loving foster home."

"I don't think we entirely agree on the definition of 'loving,'" I said with contempt. The memories of those years still haunted my nightmares, but now I knew who to thank properly for my time in hell.

"Well, tough love is still a form of love, is it not?" He seemed to enjoy mocking me. "You really should be grateful. In fact, I would say that you owe us, and now it's time to collect. The government simply wants its property back."

"I am no one's property, least of all the government's. Didn't you know, I'm an independent contractor now."

"Emma dear, there is no need to get defensive. No one wants to hurt you. Just the opposite, in fact. We want to help you realize your full potential. We've given you ten years on the outside to figure it out on your own, and you have failed miserably. Your time is up, and now you need to come back."

Benjamin's words came back to me: "They are very dangerous and powerful men who won't hesitate to do whatever is necessary to achieve their objectives, up to and including murder." I had no doubt this man was one of those Ben had been speaking of, and I had no intention of going anywhere with him.

"Why now?"

"You heard your dead friend there a few minutes ago. They are planning an invasion of Earth. We might be able to peaceably take in a group of docile elven refugees, but what about all of the others who will come pouring forth once there is a way available to them. You have seen those creatures, and they aren't even the tip of the iceberg. What do you think will happen to Earth and humans when it is overrun by even more powerful monsters? We need all of the weapons we can get, and you are one of them, Emma. You can help us save the world."

I snorted. "I've been fed that crock of shit before, Mr. Connor. I believe it was right before every single one of my military deployments. None of them ever seemed to turn out exactly as promised."

"Our problems in the Middle East are child's play compared to what we are facing now. We acquired the battle axe years ago, knowing that, at some point, you would be ready to learn how to wield it. Now is that time. We have some allies from Urusilim who don't want that rift opened any more than we do. They have agreed to teach you in exchange for your loyalty."

I had been wondering what was taking Alex so long to make his escape, and I had suspected it was because he wanted to hear as much of this conversation as he could before leaving. He must have heard enough because the pull of energy blooming at my back increased to uncomfortable levels. I was vibrating violently and sweat beaded my forehead.

Connor must have thought I was scared because he actually tried to reassure me. "No harm will come to you or your friends if you agree to join us. I promise you that."

"I'm not going anywhere with you," I said between clenched teeth.

As if on cue, a blinding light erupted from behind me. I squeezed my eyes shut and grabbed onto Daniel, who had been standing by my side, pulling him to the floor. Gun fire immediately erupted from one or two less disciplined soldiers, and I could hear Connor screaming at them to stop shooting. I covered Daniel with my body as bullets whizzed overhead. One hit me in the shoulder, and I screamed as pain spiked down my arm. Then quiet settled around us except for panicked breathing and my whimpers. When I opened my eyes and looked around, Alex was gone.

I sagged in relief and whispered close to Daniel's ear, "Are you okay?" He nodded. "They're not going to hurt you. Cooperate. Keep yourself alive until Alex brings help. And don't worry about me. I can handle them." My voice held more confidence than I felt, but I hoped it was enough to make Daniel obey.

Strong hands reached down and dug into my wounded arm. I almost passed out as I was roughly lifted to my feet. A couple of soldiers did the same with Daniel.

"Put her in room three-three-six and secure her. The boy stays with me. We have a lot to talk about."

I WAS PLACED in a small, sparsely furnished room on the third floor of the old hospital. There was nothing in the room other than a cot with a moth-eaten mattress and the folding chair that I was sitting on. My wrists and ankles were in shackles, connected to lengths of chain that were welded into the concrete floor. I had already tested my bonds, and there was no way I was getting free on my own. Above my head was a dim fluorescent light fixture, and a single window was covered with a thick, black curtain so I couldn't tell whether it was still night.

Blood ran down my arm from the gunshot wound, but they had made no move to clean and bandage it. I guessed we weren't operating under the Geneva Convention here. My blood was seeping out at a slow rate; therefore, I wasn't in danger of immediately bleeding out, although it had made me weak and tired. Between that and simple boredom, I found myself dozing off periodically as I waited for something to happen.

It felt like several hours had gone by before Connor finally came in to see me. One of his soldiers followed him in, carrying an identical folding chair. Setting it down, he faced it toward me. The soldier then retreated to the corner of the room, placing his hand on his holstered revolver. The message was clear.

Despite the long night, Connor looked well-rested and refreshed. He took a seat in front of me, crossing his legs at the knees and placing his folded hands on his lap.

I didn't let him speak first. "Where is Daniel? What did you do with him?"

"No need to worry about your friend. He is being well taken care of. He's actually quite a technological genius. That kind of talent isn't easy to come by."

I breathed an inward sigh of relief. They wouldn't want to get rid of a valuable asset like Daniel. The best thing I could do was keep the attention off him by not bringing him up again.

"So, what is it you want from me?"

"Quite simply, Miss Hayes, we want your loyalty, and in order to achieve that, we need to know everything about you."

"I thought you already knew everything about me. Isn't it all right there in your top secret files?"

"Alas, we don't know everything."

"Well, if you want my loyalty, it would go a long way to show your good faith if you untied me and told me everything you do know."

He looked at me for a long moment then shrugged. "I'm not going to release you just yet, but I suppose we can trade information. Quite honestly, Emma, you turned our world upside down when we found you a decade ago. NASA picked up an unusual energy reading in the New Mexico desert from one of their satellites and reported it to the FBI, thinking it was a domestic concern. We sent in a standard response team, and what we found was you. You were lying semi-conscious in the middle of the desert, babbling like a mad woman. The earth around you had been displaced in a perfect circle with you at its center. We found you hundreds of miles from the nearest town, with no tire tracks or prints of any sort to show how you got there. You want to tell me how you got there?"

"I have no idea," I said, trying to hide my excitement. This was the first time I had been told anything about my past. "What did you learn about the energy reading?"

"Smart girl. You ask the right questions. It took NASA a while to analyze the data, and during that time, we kept you in a government hospital under observation. They eventually came back and told us it looked like an Einstein Rosen Bridge. Do you know what that is?"

It sounded familiar, maybe from a movie I had seen, but I couldn't place it, so I shook my head.

"It's a stable wormhole that is believed to be a shortcut through space and time. It is theoretically possible," he said, "but no one has ever been able to actually create one … except for you."

"I didn't create it!"

"Then who did?" he asked, leaning forward, placing his elbows on his knees.

For a fleeting moment, I had been absolutely certain I knew the answer, but then it just slipped out of my brain as if it had never been there.

I shook my head. "I honestly don't know."

He nodded and sat up straight. "That's what you said to us when you arrived, but I'm not surprised that you don't remember those first few weeks here. You were pretty out of it, coming in and out of consciousness, not making a lot of sense. You muttered a few words here and there. Mostly, 'father,' 'Zane,' 'I love you' … oh, and 'kill them all.'" I tried to remain impassive when he said that; however, I was sure the rapid blinking and increased heart rate were noticeable. "Beyond that, we couldn't get much out of you.

"We knew you needed care, both medical and psychological. There was a lot of debate over what to do with you. We even held a secret Congressional hearing. Folks were on all different sides of the issue, from killing you as a security risk to letting you live among us in freedom. Bleeding heart liberals," he said with scorn. He stood, stretching his legs, and began to pace the room casually. How I wished I could do the same. My muscles were cramping in painful spasms.

"Do you think you could take these shackles off while we talk? As good as I am, I can't get out of a heavily guarded building single-handedly, unarmed and injured. And any chance I can get some medical attention?"

He stopped pacing and faced me, a smile crossing his face briefly. "That all depends on how cooperative you are." He continued moving about the room. "In any case, Benjamin Hayes learned of your situation. After all, as the head of procurement, he pretty much knows everything that is going on in the government. Everyone thinks it's the politicians that make things happen, but it's really those who control the money." He winked at me. "For some reason, he took an interest in you, pulled some strings, and got the votes to release you into a foster home in return for keeping an eye on you and reporting back. But the other side had some influence over the selection of your foster family. After all, if something unfortunate and tragic were to befall you there, we would have no further need for concern."

I didn't know how to feel about Benjamin's involvement. I was grateful he had stepped in on my behalf to try to free me, but he had always told me he didn't know anything about my history. He had been lying to me for years, even failing to mention the other day that he had known about me from the start. Had he befriended me only to monitor me for the government? Was he reporting my every move back to them? Would he really betray me like that? I had trusted him, though I guessed that had been the whole point, hadn't it? The betrayal felt like a knife in my gut. I blinked back tears.

"Oh, don't take it too hard," Connor said with mock sympathy. "I have long suspected Ben was protecting you and not being forthright with the information he had promised to provide, which is why you are here today. Ben has clearly failed to draw anything useful out of you. Ten years has been more than enough time. Now I am taking over this project, and I have no intention of coddling you into submission."

Many people would have preferred the approach Benjamin Hayes had taken—building trust through friendship. However, for some reason, I understood Connor's approach better and felt like I knew what I was getting with him. I could trust Connor to always betray me because his loyalties lay with something greater than me. When putting me against his country, I would lose every time, and I was okay with that.

Even as my friendship with Ben had grown, I had never understood him. I couldn't comprehend that his interests might be for my well-being. Maybe that was why I had never opened up to him. Maybe that was why I had joined the military, to be with people whose motivations and methods I could understand.

"As it happens, I don't respond to being coddled," I said. "I am also former military and have as much loyalty to this country as you do. I have no intention of seeing it threatened by those creatures, but I can't tell you what I don't know. How do you propose recovering my memories?"

"Emma, Emma, Emma," Connor said, shaking his head. "You have already proven to me time and again that you are quite formidable. You have resisted Ben's efforts at gaining your trust for ten years; you escaped my Black Ops soldiers … twice; you allied yourself with non-humans; and you made your way into this facility. A few pretty words from you will not be enough to make me believe them. However, you raise an excellent question. How am I to recover your memories and your abilities with them?" He paced toward me like a tiger stalking its prey. "We have already established that kindness doesn't work."

When he got within arm's reach of me, I knew I was in trouble. I recognized that look in his eyes. I had seen it many times in the eyes of psychopaths around the world who claimed to be fighting for a greater cause yet were really only looking for a legal way of indulging in their fetish for causing others pain.

Connor reached out with a single finger and jabbed it directly into the bullet hole in my shoulder, digging and twisting until I let out a scream that must have been heard across the island. Tears streamed from my eyes and blood flowed freely in rivulets down my arm.

"Perhaps pain will unlock those gates in your brain," Connor said with a little too much pleasure.

I didn't have a snappy comeback. It was all I could do to keep breathing and try to remember my training. I had been trained not to reveal secrets under torture. In this case, keeping my mouth shut was easy because I didn't have the answers he wanted. However, I needed to rely on that training to get me through this alive or at least until Alex came with the cavalry. I had to believe he would come for me, but that small voice in the deep recesses of my brain kept asking why Alex would save me when he knew where Sharur was and didn't need me anymore.

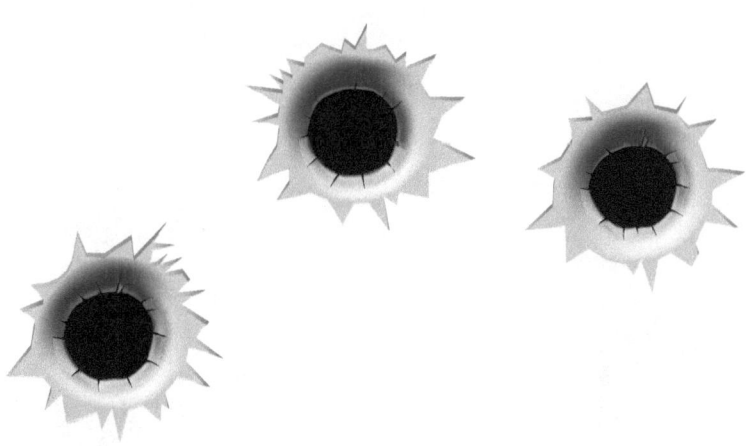

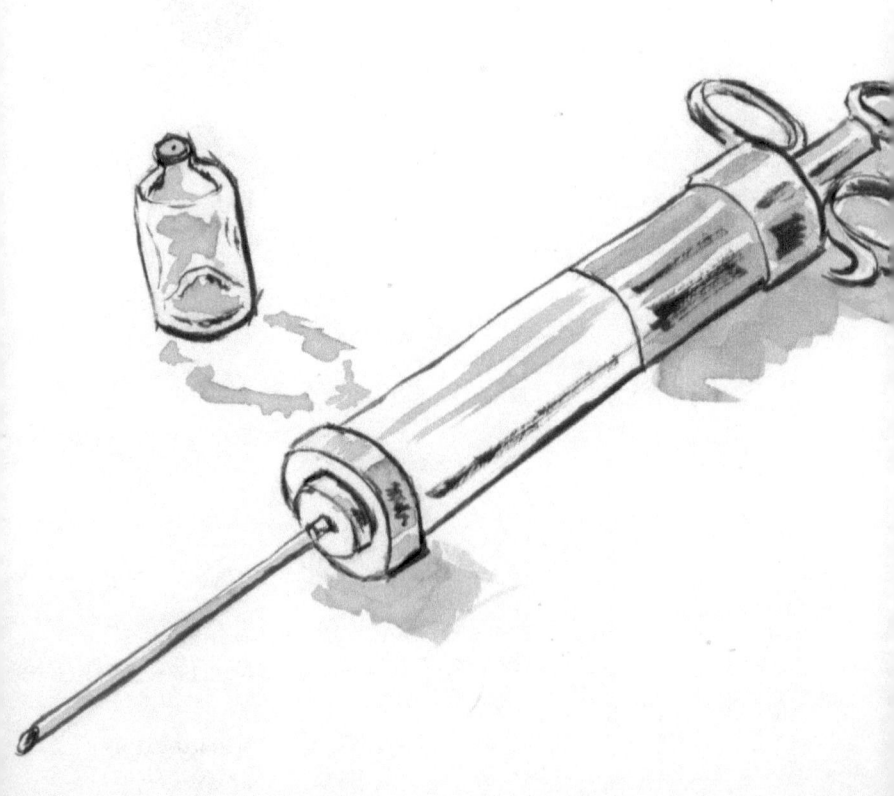

Chapter Eighteen

CONNOR DID EVENTUALLY send someone up to my room to provide medical care, which consisted of IV antibiotics so I wouldn't die of infection yet did not go so far as to remove the bullet or stitch up the wound.

Every once in a while, Connor had me unchained from the floor, only to connect my chains to hooks in the ceiling. After all, dangling me by my wrists was much more painful than allowing me to stay seated with my arms resting at my sides.

When he got particularly frustrated at my lack of cooperation, he enjoyed using me as a punching bag, but most often, he resorted to psychological techniques, helped along by water boarding, electrical shock treatments, and drugs.

In the darkened room, I had no idea how much time had gone by, though it felt like forever. I hadn't stopped holding out hope that Alex would come for me—not because I believed in him, but because of the power hope played in keeping people alive. Hope was the strongest weapon I had right now, even if it was misplaced. While Connor was playing mind games with me, I was playing them with myself.

"Emma, you know I don't want to do this to you," Connor said one day while paying me an unwelcome visit. He was dressed in his usual cheap business suit, this one navy blue with pinstripes, a white shirt opened at the neck, and no tie.

It must be casual Friday, I mused absently. I was sure his own comfort was of the utmost importance to him while engaging in a fun torture session.

"Actually, I'm guessing you've been looking forward to this all day," I managed to croak through my parched throat.

The corner of his mouth twitched almost imperceptibly, which told me I had been right. He struck me as a sadistic psychopath, hired by the government to do things normal people were uncomfortable with, like work with politicians and torture young women.

At that point, the door opened and a soldier wheeled in a medical cart draped with a white cloth. He placed it in front of me and left, locking the door behind him.

Connor removed the cloth with a flourish, as if he was doing a magic trick. I wasn't surprised to see a number of stainless steel surgical instruments lying on the cart: a scalpel, bone saw, scissors, staples, syringes. Normally, I would dismiss the theatrics as mind games 101, but given what I had seen in the basement, I had no doubt these instruments had been used many times before for procedures that might or might not have involved anesthesia.

I expected Connor to go for the scalpel first. He could use it to inflict as much or as little damage as he wanted, and if handled correctly, it could cause fairly significant pain while not being life-threatening. Instead, he went for a syringe that was as large as a fat cigar with a needle about three inches long. The clear vial was filled with a yellow liquid. He placed his fingers on the plunger and held it up to me so I could get a good look.

"Normally, I would prefer starting with the instruments first. I find they are a good way to soften up my guests, making them more … cooperative. The drugs just give them that last nudge before they pour their guts out for me, both literally and figuratively." He actually giggled, amused by his own joke. "Unfortunately, I don't have the luxury of time, so we'll skip the pleasantries and go right for the injection."

"What is it? It doesn't look like sodium pentothal."

"Hah. Truth serum is child's play compared to this. No, this beauty was synthesized from the toxin of the Lindworm, one of those marvelous creatures from your home world. It causes strong hallucinations, and you'll do anything to stop them, including telling me what I want to know."

"But I don't know anything. I would tell you if I did."

"Perhaps, but I am also hoping this serum will open up your mind and let something useful out. Now, let's get started, shall we?" He took a step closer and squeezed out a golden drop, tapping the side of the vial to ensure there were no air bubbles.

"Why? What's the hurry?"

"Didn't you know?" he mocked. "We scheduled a war, and I don't want to be late to the party."

"What? What are you talking about?"

He placed the syringe to my neck, and I struggled in vain to pull away from it. Then, with a gleeful giggle, he stabbed it into the side of my neck. Searing flames burned their way through my jugular as he depressed the plunger. I instantly clenched my teeth, trying to hold back a scream, not wanting to give him the satisfaction. It felt like the syringe would never empty and the fire pumping through my blood would never abate. After an interminable amount of time, Connor finally pulled the needle from my neck, and I slumped forward in my chair.

He leaned down to whisper in my ear, "Too bad you weren't invited to the party." He stood, and all I could do was watch his shoes as he paced in front of me, unable to lift my head. "It should be quite a sight, all of those creatures pouring through the rift and right into our trap. They'll leave the way open for us to go through to their side. I wish you could tell me what it's like there," he said wistfully. "But I'll find out on my own soon enough."

"When is that?" I asked, struggling to stay focused on his words, fighting the growing disorientation.

"Only one short week from now, under the full moon. And you are going to help make it all possible."

"How …?" I tried speaking, but my tongue was too thick, and I couldn't get the words past it. I felt drunk. My brain was coated in fog and the room spun, but I didn't care, and it felt good not to care anymore.

"How are you going to help me start a war?" he completed the question for me. "To be honest, I'm not even convinced that useless battle axe is anything more than a souvenir from the Renaissance Fair, but my bosses are convinced it's the key to opening the door between our worlds. So, my dear, I need you to tell me how it works."

I just shook my head. There was no way he would get the answers, because I didn't have a clue myself. Would he kill me if I couldn't give him the information, or would he need to keep me alive just in case they wanted to keep trying? I knew I should be worried or scared; however, I didn't feel much of anything right then.

Connor placed the now empty syringe back on the tray and picked up something else I couldn't see. He gently pushed my hair behind my ears and placed sticky pads at my temples. I was able to lift my head an inch, only enough to see that wires led from my temples to a black electrical box sitting on the cart.

"This is good for you, Emma. I know you want to uncover those memories buried in your mind as much as we do. I am just helping you to do that, but I need you to meet me halfway. Now, what can you tell me about the axe?"

"N...nothing. I swear..." It was difficult to speak, as if my brain didn't agree with my words.

"Are you sure about that, Emma? I think you know more than you are letting on. Fighting the drug will only end up hurting you. Just tell me the truth."

I shook my head, silently denying any knowledge. Then my own voice reached my ears. I hadn't even realized I had spoken. "Amulet," I croaked.

Connor's eyes trailed down my neck to my breasts, and a wolfish smile spread across face. He reached into my shirt, his hand purposefully lingering on my bare skin, before removing the amulet from around my neck. "And what does this beauty do exactly," he asked, inspecting the gem as I had done so many times before. It didn't reveal its secrets to him any more than it had to me.

"I don't know, and that's the truth," I responded. I may not have known the purpose of the amulet, but I was still terrified that it had fallen into the hands of the government.

He scrutinized my face carefully before nodding. "I believe you, but maybe there is something hidden in your past that will shed some light on this mystery. Let's start easy. What is your earliest memory?"

I did try; I really did. Connor was right; I wanted to uncover those memories, even if I had no intention of revealing them to him. I was almost a willing participant in the torture, thinking it held the possibility of unlocking my brain. Even so, nothing would come. Every once in a while, I felt like I was on the verge of a breakthrough. Flashes of memories would pass across my vision, but then they would disappear as quickly as they had come.

"I remember my foster father ... I stopped him from hurting Daniel once ..."

"Before that, Emma. I need you to go back farther," Connor said in frustration. I knew that tone of voice. It meant bad things were in store for me.

I squeezed my eyes shut and tried even harder to remember. "I see a man ... with black hair. He looks angry. He's yelling at me. He's going to burn me." I flinched away from the memory and it changed. "Zane. He's smiling. He looks happy. He's teaching me ... something. I'm having trouble understanding it. I argue with him and storm away." The image faded, replaced by a new one. This one I wasn't about to describe aloud.

It was Zane again, but this time, he was naked and underneath me. We were in an empty field under a red tree with nothing under us except soft grass. I was straddling him, moving slowly, reveling in every sensation: the feel of him inside of me, the look of ecstasy on his handsome face, the smell of sweat and sex mingling with the sweet scent of grass. Passion, desire, and possession flooded my body, overwhelming me. I heard myself let out a moan as my head fell back.

"What do you see?" Connor demanded, unable to tell if what I was experiencing was pleasure or pain. In actuality, it was a little of both.

I forced the hallucination away, unwilling to experience it in Connor's presence and certainly not wanting to tell him about it. A new vision replaced it.

"I see Zane again, but he looks different, terrified. He's yelling something to me, but I don't hear him. There is smoke and fire everywhere. He holds his hands up to me, and ... there's light and pain ... then nothing."

I opened my eyes, panting and exhausted. I was feeling confused and unfocused from the drugs, having a hard time comprehending what I had just experienced. When I looked up at Connor, he seemed genuinely pleased for the first time.

"Emma, I knew you had it in you and my approach would bring it out." He stepped up to me and placed a cool hand to my forehead, almost gently caressing the clammy skin and brushing back strings of damp hair. "I know you must be drained from your experience, but we can't stop now. We have had a breakthrough. If we push just a bit harder, imagine what we might be able to uncover." He stood and turned to the medical attendant who had been monitoring my vitals. "Give her another dose then shock her."

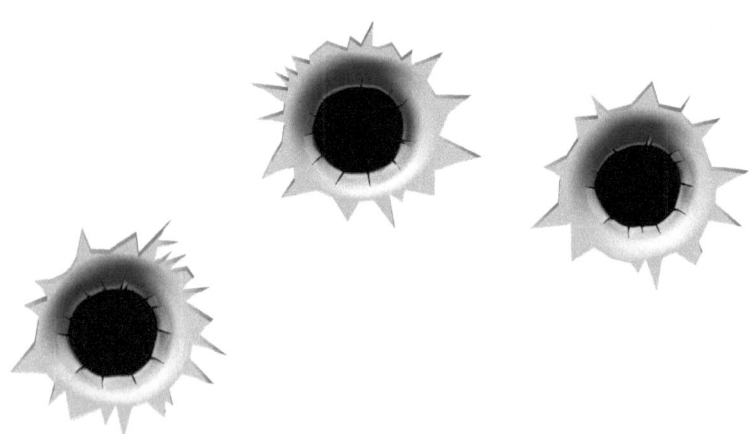

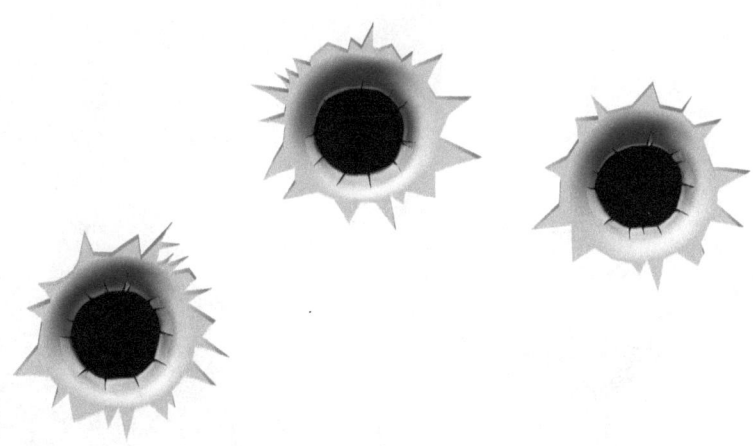

Chapter Nineteen

THE DAYS PASSED, and I didn't have any further revelations. The sessions began to decrease in frequency and duration. Connor appeared distracted. From the occasional cell phone conversations he took in front of me, I had guessed he was in the middle of dealing with some work-related crisis that took precedence over me. It must have been a doozy to be more critical to homeland security than I was, but I was grateful for the reprieve. It allowed me to recover a bit. My head cleared from the drugs, the bruises and swelling on my face and body were healing, and I wasn't bleeding anymore.

To their credit, the soldiers did their jobs well. They made sure I was always bound and my door was always locked and guarded. So, even though I was feeling stronger, I still had no hope of escape. I was able to get one of them to slip and tell me I had been in their custody for six days. I was surprised it had been such a brief time. I would have sworn a month had passed.

On the sixth night—at least I think it was night—I awoke from a restless sleep, slumped in my folding chair still chained to the floor. I strained my ears, trying to catch the noise that had awoken me. Then I heard it—the faint sound of a thump followed by a muffled groan and the gentle rattle of metal on metal. A soft click sounded from the direction of my door, and it swung open silently. A sliver of faint light from the hallway spilled in, blinding me. My eyes had seen nothing other than darkness for a week.

I blinked rapidly, trying to clear away the stinging tears. A broad figure knelt in front of me, but even at this close range, I couldn't get my eyes to focus.

"Emma, I'm going to get you out of here." I almost melted in relief at the sound of those words.

"Alex, I knew you'd come." The figure stiffened and realization dawned that it wasn't Alex's voice I had heard. I jerked sharply, trying to move away from the figure, but only accomplished tightening my chains further, cutting even more deeply into my already raw wrists.

"I know you have no reason to trust me, but I swear to you, I am here to help," Zane said, trying to sound reassuring.

"I'm not going from the frying pan into the fire," I croaked. "I would rather be tortured by the enemy I know."

"I'm not going to hurt you. I will explain everything once we're out of here, but there's no time now. We have to move."

My eyes were finally starting to focus, and I very clearly saw him pull a foot-long knife from his boot. I sucked in a breath, expecting to feel it pierce my gut at any moment; instead, he placed the blade into one of the chain links close to my wrist and wrenched. When the link snapped, he did the same for the rest of the chains. Finally, for the first time in six days, I was able to move my limbs more than a few inches.

As blood flowed back into my numb extremities, the pain was excruciating, and I bit back a whimper. Zane put a muscled arm around my waist, helping me stand then take a few steps until I felt like I could move on my own. Yet, even when I told him I was mobile, he didn't release me, and I didn't argue.

"What are you doing here, and why are you helping me?" I asked in a whisper, close to his ear.

"Alex asked for my help. Like I said, I'll explain everything when we get out of here."

"And how are we going to do that? This place is crawling with highly-trained and heavily-armed Black Ops soldiers."

"I have some … friends … that I have called in to help."

The only "friends" I had ever seen Zane with were …

"No! You can't do that. If you plan to bring in more creatures to help us fight our way out, you are putting them in danger. You don't know what the government is doing to non-humans in this place. It's horrific. I wouldn't subject even the worst of them to that kind of fate."

"It's a risk they are willing to take. You are more important." At that moment, alarms began blaring throughout the building, and the glow of flashing red security lights came from the hallway.

"We don't have time to argue. That's our signal." He pulled me toward the door, and I had no choice except to move with him. When we reached the doorway, he re-sheathed the knife and pulled his mage's staff from a sling across his back while I peered into the empty hallway.

With Zane taking the lead, we ran down the empty corridor as fast as I was able to move my weakened body. The elevators that would take us to the lobby were right ahead when, from around the corner, just past them, came a dozen soldiers with their semi-automatics pointed at us. Zane and I tried to stop our forward momentum, but the distance to the soldiers was too short. We both went down in a baseball slide, and Zane lifted his staff, throwing up a shield right as the first trigger was pulled.

"Go!" he screamed at me as we both scrambled to our feet.

I turned and ran back down the hall toward my torture room. Zane was a few feet behind me, trying to run and maintain the shield at the same time. When the soldiers advanced past the elevator, the doors slid open and three massive creatures lunged out, bowling into them.

They moved on all fours and were massive, larger than a full grown bear. Heavily corded muscles shifted under gray skin that had the hard, course look of stone. Curling horns protruded from their thick brows, and their faces were deeply lined with a mouthful of wicked teeth. Large wings were folded along their hunched backs, the tight space not allowing them to be unfurled. They were terrifying and magnificent at the same time.

Several soldiers were thrown into the opposite wall with the crack of shattered bones. Others had their throats ripped out by sharp teeth, and still others were gutted by razor claws, their entrails splayed across the now slick floors.

Gunfire stopped and screams died when the men did. One of the creatures was dead, riddled with bullet holes. The other two were wounded yet still standing. They turned their shaggy heads toward me and Zane, and I was sure we were dead, especially when Zane dropped the shield, but the creatures only stood aside, allowing us access to the elevators.

Zane grabbed my arm and pulled me toward them. I couldn't help balking as we got closer, though Zane increased his pace in response. I couldn't take my eyes off them as we moved past and into the elevator. While they kept their gazes steady on mine, instead of seeing mindless, frenzied animals, I saw something that could be described as intelligence or at least awareness in their eyes.

Before the elevator doors slid closed, I said to them softly, "Thank you." And I could have sworn one of the creatures slightly inclined its head in acknowledgment.

ZANE LEANED FORWARD to press the L button for the Lobby, but I grabbed his wrist before he depressed it.

"What are you doing?" he asked.

"Zane, I can't leave without Daniel. I have to find him and get him out of here."

He hesitated, looking torn. "Where are they keeping him?"

"Um…I don't know."

"Emma, this place is huge. We just don't have the time to search the entire building for Daniel. For all we know, he may not even be here anymore. We have to get the hell out of here."

I knew Zane was right, but I couldn't just give up on Daniel. Knowing Zane wasn't going to budge easily, I took a different tack. "We should go after Sharur. I know where it is.

After tonight, they'll move it to an even more secure location, and we may never find it again. This is our best chance to get it." I knew I was grasping at straws, but we might find Daniel as we made our way to the axe. And if we actually managed to retrieve Sharur, that would be a bonus.

Zane put his hands on his hips and took a few steps away from me, groaning in exasperation. Then he turned and came back. With a growl, he said, "Fine. Let's make this quick."

I hit the B button, and we descended to the basement.

We stood on opposite sides of the elevator doors as they slid open, which protected us from the initial barrage of bullets.

I shouted to Zane over the sounds of metal slamming into metal. "The bullets will pierce the elevator walls soon."

He nodded and held his hand palm-up in front of him. A swirling ball of orange and red flame grew in his cupped hand until it was the size of a softball. While keeping his body hidden behind the elevator wall, he pitched the ball into the soldiers. Pained wails came first, followed by a wave of suffocating heat.

The gun fire stopped, and I peered through the doors to see men engulfed in flames, trying in vain to extinguish them by rolling on the floor.

The building's fire suppression system was triggered, setting off the overhead sprinklers, but it was too late. By the time the flames were doused, there was nothing left except the charred and smoldering corpses of four soldiers.

I looked at Zane in fear and awe; however, he either didn't notice or didn't care. "Where to?" he asked.

I moved into the hallway, quickly becoming soaked with the cold water, and was soon shivering. Zane followed closely behind until we reached room B13. They had replaced the blown out retinal scanner with a keypad. I had no idea what to do with it. I could start randomly pushing buttons, but we could be here forever until I found the right combination, or I could set off some kind of security measure if I entered the wrong code a certain number of times.

I turned to Zane. "So, do you have a magic trick that can reveal a pass code?"

He frowned at the keypad. "No, but I do know who might be able to help." He reached into a pouch tied to his belt, felt around for a few seconds with a look of concentration on his face, and pulled out a stone the size and shape of a marble. It was deep black in color with a rough texture. It looked as solid as a stone, but he put the object to his lips, whispering something under his breath, and easily crushed it between two fingers. When he did, a wisp of smoke escaped and faded into the air.

I waited for something dramatic to happen, like maybe a monstrous beast would come crashing down the hallway and ram the door down, but nothing happened. I leaned against the wall and looked at Zane with a raised eyebrow.

"A few more seconds," he said.

He was good to his word. The temperature in the hallway dropped about twenty degrees, and the overhead lights dimmed to less than half their prior power. Then I felt the familiar presence of a shadow demon. Ice crept up my spine and filled my heart. The specter of death filled me until I thought I would suffocate.

Zane appeared completely unaffected. He and the creature simply looked at each other in silence before the shadow demon turned toward the door, inspecting it with a scrape of talons across metal. It found the hairline gap between the wall and the door and moved into it, it's incorporeal body slowly seeping through the crack until it disappeared behind the door.

Even in the shadow demon's absence, the cold it left behind caused my shivering to increase until I was shaking violently and turning blue. Zane moved close, wrapping his arms around me. He rubbed my arms and back briskly, trying to create friction to keep me warm. I was grateful for the contact. It not only helped to keep me warm, but it also kept me grounded. Being this close to Zane filled me with a sense of safety, as if I had nothing to fear from the shadow demon as long as Zane's arms were around me. My brain must have been as frozen as my body because, before I could stop myself, I leaned into him and rested my forehead against his chest. He placed his chin on top of my head and enfolded me in his strong embrace.

It didn't take long for me to thaw out. A few minutes later, when we heard the clicking sound of the door unlocking from the inside, I realized I was no longer shivering and was, in fact, quite comfortable. Awareness of my position washed over me in an instant, and I quickly pulled away from Zane as the lab door opened. The shadow demon was gone, but beyond the threshold were the bodies of two soldiers who had been stationed in the room to guard Sharur.

The men were curled on the floor in fetal positions. Their bodies were shrunken and their skin shriveled. It looked like they had been sucked dry, and only their wrinkled husks were left behind. Their mouths were open in a silent scream, and their fingers were curled into claws clutching at their chests, as if trying to hold on to the last of their life force. It was a gruesome sight, and the thought that I had come so close to the same fate made me sick.

Zane placed a gentle hand on the small of my back, encouraging me to enter the room. It was empty though. The display pedestal was gone along with Sharur. I ran my hands through my tangled hair, trying to hold back a scream of frustration. Why would they go through the effort to repair the security system and place guards to protect an empty room?

The answer didn't come to me right away, but when a dark shape loomed in the doorway, I figured it out. It was a trap. Connor, that son of a bitch, had expected me to escape somehow and knew I wouldn't be able to leave without trying to get Sharur. He didn't know I would make the attempt tonight, but he must have figured it would happen eventually. This was his insurance policy that I wouldn't get out.

Zane, who had his back to the doorway, saw my expression and spun on his heel, positioning himself between me and this newest threat. A giant of a man stood there. He must have been almost eight feet tall and broader than the doorway he stood in. He had to sidle into the room sideways. It looked like his muscles had muscles, with biceps and thighs as wide around as a thick tree trunk and just as solid. He had blonde hair, blue eyes, and chiseled features with a dead expression. He might have looked human, but Zane and I both knew there was something not right about this guy.

"What is it, and how do we kill it?" I asked.

"It's not one of mine," he replied. That was what I had been afraid of.

I fell into a fighting stance yet had no weapon. I felt naked and helpless without my Glock. Zane, aware of my predicament, moved to my side, lifting his glowing staff and calling forth the energy needed for his magic. Then, three hundred fifty pounds of pure muscle lunged at us.

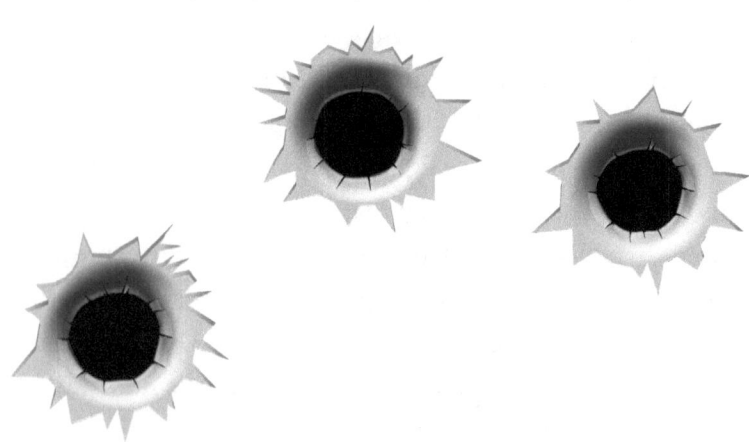

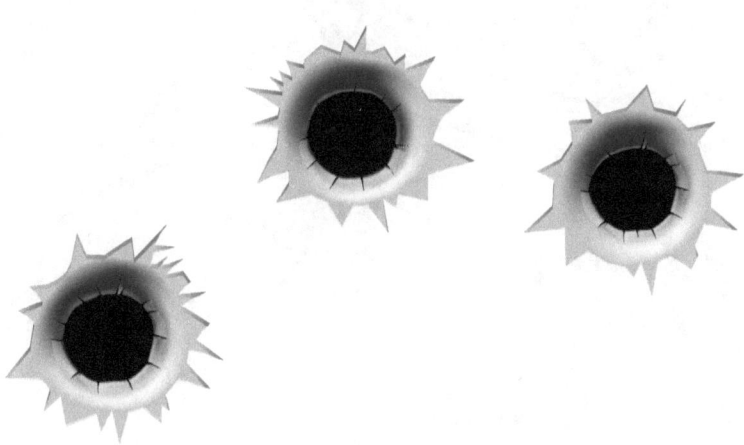

Chapter Twenty

THE CREATURE DISGUISED as a man blurred as it moved in a flash. It bypassed Zane easily and pummeled into me, the pungent odor of wet earth assaulting me along with it. I thought I was going to spit up my stomach upon the violent impact. It hit with enough force to slam me into the rear wall with a sickening thud.

As I lay on the ground, breathless and stunned, it loomed over me. I wanted to defend myself, but I couldn't unfurl my arms from around my injured stomach. Surely it was going to kill me quickly and efficiently, probably by snapping my neck. At least, that was what I would do if I had someone cornered like this who didn't have a gun.

However, before it could touch me, a fireball slammed into its back. The creature fell forward, stumbling over me as I whimpered, fearing the flames would spread to me, but he regained his balance and stood up without any of the flames licking me.

Rather than screaming and writhing in pain, it calmly and silently turned to face Zane. The smell of its cooking skin invaded my nose and made me want to wretch. It was like garbage burning in a wet swamp.

While I watched, the flames grew smaller, flickered, and then finally extinguished. A thin gel-like film coated its charred skin. The gel continued to ooze out of its pores, sloughing off the blackened skin and leaving behind shiny, pink flesh. The entire process took only seconds.

The fire had burned off its hair and melted cartilage, leaving the creature smooth, without a nose, lips, or even eyelids. It opened the hole in its face that used to be its mouth to reveal movement in the back of its throat. The creature's stomach convulsed and it gagged, the sound wet and thick. Slippery tentacles spilled out, twitching and reaching for Zane, who stood directly in their path.

One slimy arm shot out and wrapped around Zane's neck, squeezing. His hands reflexively grasped onto it, trying to pry it loose, when a second and third tentacle wrapped around both wrists, holding them wide. Zane was completely helpless and gasping for air, his face quickly turning blue. His eyes rolled toward me.

"Zane!" I screamed, surprised at hearing the pure anguish in my voice. Was that really how I felt about him? *Yes, it is*, I realized. I couldn't say why. Maybe it was a simple attraction to the bad boy, but it felt like more than that. I knew him, needed him, owed him.

Panic flowed through my veins creating adrenaline, infusing me with the strength to push myself to my feet, my stomach an agonizing knot of pain that screamed at me with every move. I had nothing to fight with other than my body. Even if I had been in top condition, which was far from the case, I didn't stand a chance against something that supernaturally large and strong. Although, that didn't stop me from closing the gap between myself and the creature, running and leaping onto its back before it knew I was coming.

It had written me off as incapacitated and hadn't expected the attack. Before it could retaliate, I slipped both arms around its neck and leaned back, using the full weight of my body to constrict its throat. I could feel the wriggling tentacles underneath the thin skin of its neck, struggling to free themselves from my grip. I pulled back harder, and one of the tentacles compressed, popping off with a gush of slime that dripped down the creature's chin and over my arms. I could feel my grip loosening as that slime coated my skin, but I didn't need to hold on for much longer.

The tentacle that had come free was the one wrapped around Zane's wrist. He shook his arm until the rubbery appendage unraveled and slipped to the floor. With his now free hand, Zane reached into one of the pouches at his waist and pulled out another small stone, this one the clear green of a Heineken bottle and all sharp edges. He pressed it into the flesh of the tentacle still wrapped around his neck, puncturing its skin and digging the object in. With one sharp punch, he shattered the stone embedded in the tentacle. The creature dropped Zane instantly, and he fell to the floor, gulping air. I couldn't maintain my grip any longer, and I slid off the creature's back, crumpling next to Zane.

The creature ignored both of us, its tentacles writhing furiously as even more rubbery appendages tried to escape their human prison. The pressure was too much, and the creature's head burst open, freeing a bulbous, gelatinous blob from the shell it had been wearing. This was the true owner of the tentacles; it had only been disguising itself as human, like the bug wearing an Edgar suit in *Men in Black*.

The tentacle that had been punctured by Zane's stone was quickly turning a mottled gray, the skin beginning to shrivel and split. The dryness spread up the tentacle until it reached the main body and branched out to all of the remaining arms. The creature's frantic movements slowed then stopped. Left behind was a pile of ash in the shape of the creature, which then collapsed, spewing forth a black cloud.

I closed my eyes, nose, and mouth, but I had been too close. I choked and gagged on the dried flesh of a slime creature. Gross!

With my eyes watering and unable to take a breath, I crawled along the floor, desperate to find the way out. Something hard and warm clamped down on my wrist. I had lifted my elbow to slam it into this new threat when the grip shifted, and I felt Zane's warm hand slide into my own, giving me a reassuring squeeze. He pulled me along behind him until we made it back out into the hallway where the air was clear.

We didn't have the luxury of time to rest and catch our breath; as a result, we coughed and panted while jogging down the hall, hand-in-hand, back to the elevator. "Zane, wait," I gasped, trying to stop his relentless forward momentum, but it was as ineffectual as halting a stamped of wild buffalo. "But Daniel"

Zane finally stopped in front of the elevator doors, pushing the button. "I'm sorry, Emma. I truly am, but even if Daniel is here, he's going to be just as heavily guarded, if not more so, than Sharur. Connor knows you would try to save him. Also, after that stunt we just pulled back there, soldiers are going to be all over us in a matter of minutes. We have to get out before they realize you're gone."

A soft *ding* signaled the arrival of the elevator, but I didn't want to get in. "Stay alive now and you'll have another chance at rescuing Daniel," Zane said, trying to coax me into the elevator. I stepped inside. When the elevator doors slid shut behind us, enveloping us in temporary safety, we slumped against the wall and exchanged a glance.

We were both covered in black ash that stuck to the slime already coating our skin. It dried into a crust that cracked and flaked when we moved. It made me think of *Ghostbusters*, when they were coated in sticky marshmallow at the end of the movie.

As the thought came to me, a crazed laugh bubbled up from my belly. It came from a combination of grief, stress and the utter insanity of this moment. I must have sounded hysterical, although Zane seemed to find my insanity quite amusing because he burst out laughing as well. We made quite a pair, but I think we both needed the cathartic moment to cut the fear and relieve the tension.

It took a few minutes before we finally quieted. When I reached up to press the button to bring us back up to the lobby, I realized Zane was still holding my hand. He caught me noticing, the smile slipped off his face, and his hand fell out my mine. Averting our eyes, I pressed the button, and we were on our way.

The lobby was dark and empty. As I suspected, Connor hadn't known this would be the night I would try to escape, and he certainly hadn't expected me to get past his pet. Therefore, no guards were on duty in the lobby, looking for an escapee.

We made it out of the building without setting off the alarms, since they didn't trigger when the door was opened from the inside. I followed Zane through the darkened woods surrounding the old hospital until we reached the water where, in a particularly dense patch of tall grasses, he had moored a black rowboat with oars and a small outboard motor.

He slid it silently into the dark waters and helped me in before carefully joining me. Picking up the oars, he rowed us down the river with only the soft sounds of the waves lapping against the hull. When we were safely away from North Brother Island, Zane started up the motor and picked his way along the coastline of the Hudson River.

I WAS STRUGGLING to stay conscious. My eye lids felt like lead weights, and I would jerk awake every few seconds when I caught myself dozing off. The excitement of the evening, the warm air blanketing me, and the lull of the motor made for a strong narcotic. However, I knew Zane was just as tired as I was, and I didn't want to leave him alone to deal with his own struggle against sleep.

"Where are we going?" I asked, wanting to know, but I also wanted to keep us awake with conversation.

He seemed grateful for the distraction. "There is an abandoned warehouse along the river in Brooklyn where I have been staying. It's safe and out of the way. You can stay there for tonight, and then we can find your friends in the morning."

"You're just going to let me go?"

"That's the plan. I'm going to do my best to stick with it."

"And if you don't?"

"Look, I'm not saying there isn't a risk in staying with me, but you're at an even greater risk if I just drop you off in the middle of Times Square when the government is looking for you. They can access street security cameras and find you in a heartbeat. Anyway, we're both injured and exhausted. Neither of us are in any shape to organize a safe transfer tonight. We'll figure it out tomorrow."

It was hard to argue with that logic, so I fell back into silence. Minutes later, Zane cut off the motor and picked up the oars.

"We're here," he said, gracefully steering us to a ladder alongside an old peer that led up to street level. He tied off the boat and helped me onto the rungs.

At the top of the ladder, a massive warehouse loomed over us. Many of the old, leaded glass windows were broken or missing, with plywood nailed over them from the inside. Colorful graffiti decorated the entire surface of the building. Trash and detritus was strewn along the street and collected against the walls.

Zane led me to the warehouse's steel doors. Although they were covered in spray paint, there was no sign of scratches, dents or rust. Clearly they were newer to the building and quite secure. Zane removed a small set of keys from his pants pocket and unlocked the door's three deadbolts. Then he pushed the heavy metal slab open and flicked on a light inside.

The light came from a single bulb on a string in the second floor loft, illuminating only one corner of the warehouse dimly. I followed Zane up a set of steel steps into his makeshift home.

I had been expecting an unmade mattress on the floor, empty pizza boxes, and a big screen television. Wasn't that how most bachelors lived? It certainly described Daniel's apartment. Instead, Zane had created a comfortable, if modest, living space for himself.

Tucked into the far corner of the room was a queen-sized bed, adorned with clean, charcoal gray sheets as well as a white feather comforter and pillows. A small black table stood next to the bed with a single, silver lamp, and next to that was a chest of drawers. The walls were unadorned. There wasn't a single painting, poster, or photograph anywhere in the room. The only object was a small, decorative box sitting on the bedside table, and I itched with curiosity to know what was inside.

Against the wall opposite the bed was a glass-topped desk covered in papers and a laptop computer connected to a large flat panel monitor. A door stood ajar next to the desk, leading to a modest bathroom with white subway tile walls and floors and a shower that was calling my name.

"Do you mind?" I asked, nodding toward the shower.

"No. Let me get you some clothes." He pulled a pair of boxer shorts along with an oversized *I Love NY* T-shirt from a drawer and handed them to me.

I took them with a grateful smile and made my way to the bathroom.

Thirty minutes later, we were both showered and dressed in boxers and tees. Zane insisted I sleep on the bed while he took the recliner, but as tired as I had been, I lay in bed wide awake. I knew Zane was awake too, since I could hear him shifting uncomfortably every minute or so. His presence was disconcerting in so many ways.

How was I supposed to fall asleep in the presence of the man who had been trying to kill me up until tonight? Could I really trust him with my life? Of course the answer was no, but I also saw tonight as a temporary cease fire. I felt like I could trust that, for the next few hours, he wouldn't try to harm me.

Then there was the matter of that ... er, vivid ... hallucination I'd had when under the influence of the serum. I couldn't figure out whether they were real memories or hallucinations brought on by the drugs. Either way, they kept intruding on my thoughts every time I looked over and saw Zane sprawled out on the chair, within touching distance.

It felt warm in the room, so I kicked off the comforter, looking to cool off a bit.

"Can't sleep either, huh?" came Zane's husky voice from the darkness.

"No. I must be wired from all of the excitement tonight," I lied.

I sat up against the pillows and turned on the bedside lamp. Zane also sat up, folding in his recliner and leaning forward with his elbows on his knees. When he ran his hands through that long, black hair, all I could think about was how much I wanted those to be my hands knotted in his hair.

"Why did you come for me tonight?" I asked instead.

"I told you, Alex asked me to."

"The last time I checked, you and Alex were enemies. Why would you do something like that for him?"

He let out a long breath and leaned back in the chair. "It's sort of a long story." I raised my eyebrows expectantly, inviting him to continue. "Alex and I weren't always enemies. In fact, there was a time when we were closer than brothers. We were raised together, apprentices to the same mage. We even joined the Council together."

"So what happened?"

"You happened," he responded softly. I flinched as if I had been struck. Was that why Alex hated me so much, because I had come between him and his best friend? "Well, that's actually an overstatement. Marduk happened, but you were directly involved."

"I'm listening."

"Emma, there is something very important that I have to tell you, and I don't know how you are going to take it." He stood and walked over to the bed, taking a seat on the edge, careful not to get too close. However, my hormones thought he was plenty close. "It was me."

I waited for a moment for clarification, but it didn't come. "It was you who did what?"

"*I* took away your memories, or blocked them, to be more accurate."

"What?" I breathed. I wasn't sure I had understood him correctly. The room was spinning, and I felt lightheaded.

"I blocked your memories and sent you through a rift to Earth to protect you. We … you and I … were together once." He looked at me from under his long lashes and our eyes met. "In love," he clarified, in the event I hadn't understood his meaning. "Marduk found out and saw our union as a threat. With our combined power, he was afraid we could have easily overthrown him. He tried to have me killed, and when you found out, you got … angry. You weren't very well-trained at the time. I had been trying, and you had made progress, but you always let your emotions control you."

It was hard to imagine that. "I've learned to control my emotions since then. I didn't have much of a choice," I responded, thinking back to my time in foster care.

"Well, back then, you weren't quite so … disciplined. You lost control, did a lot of damage. It made you the target of a lot of races that suffered from what you had done. I knew the only way to save you was to get you out, so I did."

"But didn't that weaken you?" Understanding dawned on me in that moment as I followed through the consequences. "Marduk got to you, didn't he? Because you were too weakened from saving me to defend yourself?" Zane nodded. "And that's why Alex hates me, because you let yourself become a victim for my sake." I didn't need an answer to that one; I knew it was the truth.

"What did Marduk do to you? Why do you seem so sane now when before you were … not?" Zane swallowed hard, and I noticed his hands begin to shake. He looked at the floor and merely shook his head response. His reaction scared me. Whatever had been done to him had been bad. "It's okay. You don't need to tell me."

Zane cleared his throat. "I'm not the same person I was when we were together. I can't be trusted. Right now, I can have a conversation with you because of magic. It's a spell that the Council developed years ago, hoping to find a way to fix me. It works … for a time. But, when it wears off, it takes even more of my mind, leaving me in a worse state. When they realized that, they stopped using it and left me to my fate. Alex needed me this time, though … you needed me. I agreed to the spell, even knowing the consequences. Emma, I have only a few hours left, but I want to try to fix what I've done."

Zane's eyes were bright with unshed tears. I could see the pain behind them. It made me think of that movie *Awakenings*, about the patients who had been temporarily cured of their vegetative states yet knew the cure wasn't permanent. What must Zane be going through, knowing his sanity was only fleeting, and he would once again lose his best friend and the woman he once loved? Not only that, but he would become their sworn enemy and would either kill the people he loved, or they would end up killing him. It made me want to cry for him.

"How do you plan to fix this?" I asked.

"I can bring your memories back."

I blinked in surprise. Would that fix everything? Did I want those memories back, knowing they contained a tragic love story and the destruction of good people at my hands?

I wasn't convinced I wanted to feel that kind of pain. Maybe it was a blessing that I didn't remember those things. Then again, how could I fix this mess if I didn't know what to do? How could I stay alive long enough to set things right when I didn't know how to fight these creatures that had been set against me? Most of all, the question that kept repeating itself incessantly inside of my head, demanding to be heard, was what if I had the knowledge and power buried deep inside of me to fix Zane? He said himself that we were among the most powerful in Urusilim. If I could destroy, could I also heal?

"Do it," I said. "I need to know."

"It's not that easy. I can't bring them all back at once. That amount of information crashing into your mind all at once would destroy your brain permanently. The only safe way to do it is to create cracks in the wall I erected so it gradually crumbles over time, setting free memories bit by bit. That would give your mind time to adjust to the new information at a safer pace."

"How long would it take to get all of my memories back that way?"

Zane shrugged. "It's not like I have ever done this before. I suppose it could take weeks or months, maybe even years. It depends on the capability of your mind to assimilate your memories."

I didn't see that I had much choice in the matter. I certainly didn't want to end up in a coma for the rest of my life. This was the only way to go, even if it didn't immediately give me all the answers I needed.

"Okay," I agreed. "How are you going to create these cracks in my mind?"

"The best way to do it is to reveal to you one memory. That should be enough to weaken the barrier."

"So which memory is it going to be?" I asked. My mind was churning through the possibilities—the memory of how to use magic, how to fight these creatures, how to open one of those precious rifts.

The list of possibilities was endless, though Zane knocked me for me a loop when he said, "I am going to give you back the memory of us."

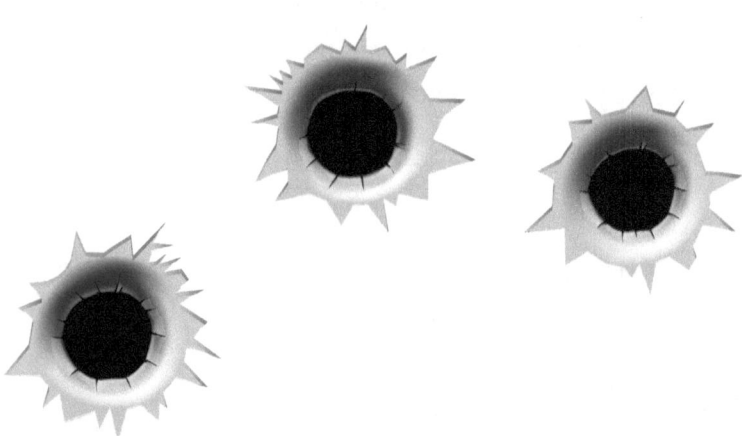

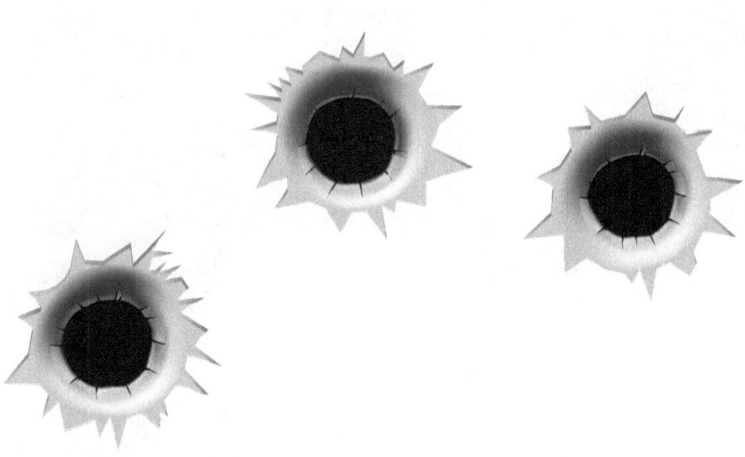

Chapter Twenty-One

"WHY US? NO offense, but aren't there more important things I should know about?" If I was being honest with myself, I was petrified to have the memories of Zane back. I didn't want the complications of feeling something more for him than I already did, knowing he was the enemy. I also didn't want to deal with the baggage of feelings in general. Too much was happening right now, and I couldn't afford to be distracted by useless emotions. I also had to consider the possibility that he was doing this on purpose to slow me down and make me weak. "No, I don't want those memories. Give me back something else."

His face fell, and he looked away for a moment to conceal his expression, but I did see his throat move in a hard swallow. If he was being sincere, and I put myself in his shoes, it must be hurtful that I didn't want to remember our time together.

"I'm sorry. I just … I'm not sure … I just don't think that information will be immediately helpful to me. I mean, I'd like to know, but now might not be the best time."

Zane turned back to me, forcing a smile on his handsome face. "I understand, Emma, I really do. I wish I could give you information that was more immediately useful, but I can't. The more useful information is also more dangerous. I don't think you're ready to handle it yet without the context of who you are … were. I need to start with us."

I searched his face, looking for traces of a lie, but all I saw was sincerity. God help me, I didn't have much of a choice other than to trust him. At this point, I was stuck. I didn't have Sharur, didn't know where it was, didn't have access to my powers, had no way of stopping the war that was coming, and my allies were dwindling as they were captured, injured, or died. I needed all of my memories back as quickly as possible; as a result, I had to man up and take this first one.

"Fine, do it."

"I just need to warn you that this won't be easy. Tampering with a person's mind is messy business, with some unpleasant side effects. The last time I did this to you, you ended up in a coma for almost a year."

"What?" I asked. That couldn't be right. I was told I had been semi-conscious for only a few weeks following my accident. Could I really have lost one year of my life? Why would everyone have lied to me about that?

"That shouldn't happen this time, though," he quickly explained. "Before, I didn't have time to be subtle or careful. I threw up the strongest wall I could conjure in seconds, and it caused significant damage to your psyche. This time,

I am only going to release a small amount of your memory. The rest will come along gradually as your mind is ready to handle it. So you won't end up in a coma, but it still won't feel pleasant."

"As long as I can recover quick enough to fight this war, I'm good to go."

"I have no way of knowing for sure, but we can only hope the effects won't last very long," Zane confirmed.

He slid up the bed closer to where I was sitting up against his pillows. His hand brushed my hip, burning my skin with the heat of his touch. "Close your eyes." He reached up with both hands and gently brushed my hair behind my ears, placing his fingers lightly on my temples. They were warm and rough, and my mind started to drift, thinking about where else I would like those calloused fingers to explore.

Then the pain hit me. I gasped at the suddenness of it. It felt like knives were being pressed through my eyeballs and into my brain before being twisted for good measure. The vertigo hit me next, spinning and tilting the world around me violently. Sparks of color and flashes of unfamiliar images bombarded my mind so quickly I couldn't make out any of details, no matter how hard I tried to focus on what I was seeing. My stomach lurched and cramped.

"Stop!" I gasped. I tried to lift my arms to bat his unmoving fingers from my temples, but I couldn't figure out where my hands were in relation to my head and only found myself flailing fruitlessly. "Please," I begged, tears springing to my eyes. If I could have chopped my own head off in that moment to end the pain and confusion, I would have done it in an instant.

Then Zane's fingers were gone, and the pain subsided enough that the nausea could take its place.

"Bathroom," I demanded, lurching off the bed.

Zane grabbed me around the waist and hauled me to the bathroom. I promptly fell to the floor, making it to the toilet just in time to lose what little was in my stomach. I sat back sweating, my skin an inferno.

"I'm sorry, Emma. Hang in there. It will pass soon." He continued cooing reassuring words at me, which my muddled brain couldn't entirely comprehend, while turning on the shower. He helped me step under the water, still dressed in his shorts and T-shirt, and followed me in to keep me upright.

The cool spray felt like heaven against my flushed skin, and the throbbing in my head subsided, as did the disorientation. I rested my head against Zane's chest, taking slow, steady breaths until I felt more like myself again.

Had it worked? Had he been able to release some of my memories?

When I focused inward in an attempt to call up anything new, images, memories, and emotions flooded my mind. I gasped and clutched tightly onto Zane's biceps, trying to stay on my feet. He wrapped his arms around me and held me closer while sobs escaped my throat and tears mingled with the water pouring down my cheeks.

"Oh, God. I remember you." I looked up at Zane. He was the same man I had spent the last few hours with, but right then he looked different to me. His hair was longer than I remembered it, and it seemed to me his sharp features were softer and more open. Those warm, deep eyes reflected concern and commitment. I couldn't stop myself from reaching up and touching his strong jaw and full lips.

As I caressed his cheek, he leaned into my palm, closing his eyes briefly. When they opened again, they were full of sadness and desire, an irresistible combination.

I stood up onto my toes, bringing my face close to his and tentatively pressing my lips to his mouth. I then drew back a few inches to measure his reaction. He looked stunned and entirely unable to move, although his heavy breathing and the tightening of his arms around my waist told me all I needed.

I closed the gap, and this time, I kissed him with more confidence. He overcame his initial hesitation and parted his lips, and when I slipped my tongue into his mouth, he lost all ability to restrain himself.

Zane spun me around, pushed me against the slippery tile, and deepened the kiss. His body pressed against mine, and I could feel his desire through the thin material of his boxer shorts. I did what I had been craving for some time and knotted my hands in his wet hair, pulling him even closer. It wasn't enough, though. I needed to *feel* him.

Lifting one leg onto his hip, I ground into him. Zane's hand moved down to my ass and held me tightly, pressing into me harder. I gasped at the sensation, heat and wetness flooding between my legs. My reaction was an invitation that he eagerly accepted, and he continued his steady rubbing of my clit through our wet clothes.

Any thought that I might be putting myself in danger flew from my mind. I could think of nothing except the weight of his strong body against mine, the feel of soft skin over hard muscle, and the tickle of his long hair on my breasts as his mouth moved over my neck.

Wet clothes stuck like glue to our bodies, blocking me from getting closer to him. I grabbed the neck of his T-shirt in both hands and, with one tug, split it down the middle, peeling it away to reveal a broad chest and abs as hard as stone and as smooth as silk.

He moaned in response. "By the gods, Ash, what are you doing to me?" Hearing the sound of my real name sounded right to my ears for the first time.

"I think you know what I'm doing," I said as my hand slid down his stomach and over his boxers, grasping his thick cock. Rubbing the length of him over and over, he thrust himself against my palm to the rhythm I had set.

His hands moved to my waist, and he lifted my T-shirt, freeing my heavy breasts. He cupped one in his large, calloused hand, rubbing his thumb over my already stiff nipple. Mind-numbing desire shot like electricity through my body, pooling in my groin, and I grew even wetter than I already had been from the spray of the shower.

Bending down, he drew one breast into his hot mouth and flicked my nipple with his tongue while pinching and rubbing the other with deft fingers.

"Oh, fuck, Zane," I moaned.

Just when I thought I would orgasm from the erotic sensations at my breasts, Zane lowered himself to his knees. I was panting in agony at the loss of him until he peeled the boxers down my wet thighs, allowing me to step out of them before tossing them away. His rough hands slid over my hips and moved behind me to cup my rear, pressing me into his waiting mouth.

I threw my head back, arching and crying out in pleasure as his tongue slid between my legs. I grabbed handfuls of his hair, encouraging him to go deeper. He obliged, slipping his tongue in and out of me, licking and sucking my clit until I couldn't hold back any longer.

"Oh, God, Zane. Don't stop, baby. Don't stop!" I exploded, screaming in pleasure.

When the wave of ecstasy had passed, leaving me flushed and panting, Zane stood and turned off the shower. Without a word, he lifted me into his arms and carried me out of the bathroom and into his bed.

THE FIRST TIME he entered me that night, it was all animalistic lust and passion, hard and fast, grunting and moaning. It was more like filling a need than satisfying a desire. We had no choice in the matter; our lives up until this point had been driving us inexorably to this moment, and we fell over the edge together.

The second time was to fulfill the need in our hearts. It was slow and deep, and we never broke eye contact, even when Zane's eyes glittered, and I thought they might well over. He kissed me everywhere—my mouth, my eyelids, my throat—as if he needed to taste and touch every inch of me.

The third time was an incredible combination of our bodies and hearts coming together. It was fun and passionate, sweet and free. We laughed when certain positions seemed a bit ridiculous or when we broke a piece of furniture in our enthusiasm. We got lost in the moments of intense pleasure when our bodies found that perfect fit, and our hands and mouths expressed the depth of our emotions.

In the small hours of the morning, we lay above the sheets in bed, wrapped tightly around each other, to cool off from the last round of love making. Our noses almost touched, one of my legs was tucked between his, and one of his hands rested on my rear end while the other was under his head as a pillow. I had one arm draped across his shoulders, twirling his soft hair around my fingers.

"I remember first meeting you when I was twelve," I said, still trying to get used to having these new memories. I felt like I needed to verify the truth of them. "You were so handsome and scary. I was terrified of you, with your long hair and black eyes, but I couldn't stop thinking about you after that. You had so much strength and confidence. But I can't remember where it was we met."

Zane smiled at the memory. "You were such a terror back then, scrappy and demanding. I think you scared me more than I scared you. What else do you remember?"

"I remember sneaking out with you on certain nights so you could teach me magic, but I don't know who we were sneaking away from. I was looking for any excuse to be alone with you."

"You were incredibly undisciplined at the time. You thought you could do anything and didn't need any training. You never thought about the consequences of your actions. I thought you hated every minute of those first lessons."

"Oh, believe me, I did. But I was willing to suffer through them to get my first kiss. Sure, it took you two and half years to finally come around, but you were worth the wait," I said, winking. "God, I was absolutely giddy and terrified at the same time, but when you kissed me that night under the twin moons, I knew you were the one for me."

"Much has changed since then," Zane said sadly. "I wish things could have ended differently for us, but we have to accept the way things are now." He rolled away from me, rising from the bed and slipping on a pair of jeans. "I'm sorry. I shouldn't have let this happen. It wasn't my intention to sleep with you when I brought you back here."

"Are you sure about that?" I challenged, but he didn't offer a rebuke.

"Regardless, I am not the same man you remember. Far from it. The person standing in front of you right now will be gone in a matter of a few short hours, maybe forever, and I'll be back to hunting you down for Marduk."

"What happened to you?"

"Don't you remember?"

I searched through my new memories, looking for the right one. I knew I had found it when fear and sadness crashed over me with the recollection. Marduk had been about to kill Zane because of me. Marduk himself was an indistinct figure, blurry and silent, but in my mind's eye, I saw my powerful warrior on his knees, begging for my life to be spared. Yet I somehow had known I wasn't in any danger. Marduk had only wanted Zane to believe he would kill me to ensure Zane didn't fight back.

As Marduk had prepared to strike Zane down with a killing blow, I had thought I would drown in the rage and desperation that flooded through me. Reaching deep inside myself, I had called upon the well of power that was curled around my soul, always looking for an escape. I had only tapped small amounts of it before, fearing to wake it fully, but this time, I had opened the dam and let it pour forth.

It had been terrifying and exhilarating, like flying. The immense power had coursed through my blood and filled me until I had felt like I would explode with both pleasure and pain. No one could have stood against me. I could have defeated my enemies in one breath and rebuilt the world as it suited me. As these thoughts had come to me, my hands had burned and blistered with the power collecting in my palms. I had needed to release it before I caught fire.

My new memories held gaps after that, though. I remembered smelling electricity along with burning flesh and tasting the iron tang of blood and ashes on my tongue. I had thought I heard my name being screamed from a long distance then had felt a wrenching and twisting sensation. A sense of vertigo had taken hold of me and everything had gone black. My next memory was awakening in a military hospital.

"I destroyed everything … everyone?" I asked, terrified that I already knew the answer.

"Not everything, but most of Urusilim between the Verde Valley and the Sandor Mountains. I threw my shield up in time, which had the unintended consequence of saving Marduk as well as myself since he was behind me holding a knife to my throat. I managed to siphon some of your power, which gave me the strength I needed to open a rift and push you through to Earth. It was the only way I could think of to both stop you and save your life."

"Why block my memory?"

"I was afraid you would try to come back. I couldn't let Marduk get his hands on you after exhibiting that kind of power. We had no idea the extent of your abilities until that moment. The only way to keep you away and safe was to take all your memories of Urusilim."

"And of you." He nodded in silent acknowledgement. "I'm sure Marduk wasn't too happy with you for that."

"I was drained from the effort, and Marduk seized the advantage. I was quite a prize—a powerful mage and member of the Council. And, after losing you, he needed me. He took great pleasure in …" Zane swallowed hard, grimacing at the memory. "I was his prisoner for years. It changed me." I didn't need him to tell me he had been tortured, both physically and psychologically—and probably magically—in horrific ways.

I thought I was going to be sick again, knowing I was responsible for what had happened to Zane, not to mention the mass murder of thousands of people. I would have given everything in that moment to lose my memory again. Perhaps Zane had given me a gift when he had erected that wall in my mind. What other atrocities were hiding in my past that remained buried? Did I really want that wall to crumble and reveal more of the real me?

"Emma, breathe." I heard Zane's voice in my ear.

Looking around, I found myself doubled over on the cement floor with what felt like an elephant sitting on my chest. I opened my mouth and drew in a gulp of air. Sobs tore from my throat. I tried to stop them, but they would not be restrained.

Zane's arms went around me, and I cried into his shoulder, repeating, "I'm sorry. I am so sorry," until I finally fell asleep.

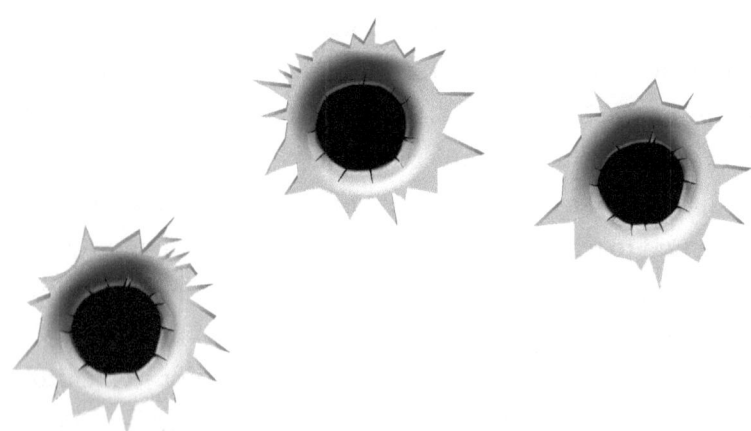

Chapter Twenty-Two

ZANE WOKE ME gently in the minutes before dawn, telling me it was time to go. I felt drained, though not completely empty of my sorrow. If I thought about all that had happened, I would break down again, and there would be plenty of time for crying after I stopped Connor from opening a rift. For now, I had to put my mask back on.

I dressed and wordlessly followed Zane into the crisp morning air. The sky was barely starting to brighten over the breathtaking New York City skyline that still glittered with millions of points of light. The city looked completely peaceful from this distance, but I knew that, even at this hour, many neighborhoods were still bustling. People getting ready for work crossed paths with people just getting home from a long night of partying.

It was the city I loved and craved, with its anonymity, lack of judgment, and sea of humanity. Yet, right then, I would have given anything to stay right where I was, in quiet isolation with the man who knew more about me than I knew about myself. However, he would be gone soon, replaced by a cruel monster, and I had that sea of humanity to save.

Zane and I walked to the dock where his little boat was gently bumping against the wooden piles in time with the lapping waves. He helped me in, and we motored our way across the East River. In minutes, we arrived on the Upper East Side of Manhattan where Zane tied up the boat near the East 90th Street Ferry Terminal. From there, we took the short walk to Carl Schurz Park where we were to meet my elven escort.

We stepped down the beautiful curving stone staircase into the park. The cherry trees and tulips surrounding the staircase were in full bloom, cloaking the area with vibrant pinks, reds, and yellows. As we neared the bottom, the East River spread out before us like a blanket of sparkling jewels. Staring across the river, my eyes landed with longing on the warehouse we had left.

Finally, I broke the heavy silence. "Zane, I don't accept that there is nothing that can be done for you. Just because a solution hasn't been found yet doesn't mean it doesn't exist out there somewhere."

"Please, Emma, don't do this to yourself. The last thing I want is for you to be haunted the rest of your life by guilt and false hope. You need to find a way to defeat Marduk and forget about trying to fix me. This is bigger than you and I. If Marduk or your government succeeds at opening that rift, think about the repercussions. Deadly creatures will come through from Urusilim that humans can't hope to defeat. The humans will go through to Urusilim and rape our world, trying to dissect and steal our magic to manipulate it for their own uses. What do you think the government would do with that kind of power? I doubt they intend to use it for world peace."

Zane painted a pretty grim picture, but he was right. Opening a rift would irreparably change both of our worlds, none of them for the better.

"Emma, I need you to promise me something," Zane continued. "When the opportunity presents itself, you have to take me out without a moment's hesitation. Believe me, I won't hesitate to kill you, capture you, or torture you, whatever I am ordered to do. I am a danger to you, and you won't get to Marduk unless you go through me. The only way to save our two worlds is to make sure I'm not standing in your way."

"I don't believe that, Zane. I don't think you would kill me. You are obviously still in there, or you wouldn't be standing here, having this conversation with me."

"Fuck, Emma!" I flinched at the threat in his voice. "You don't know what it's like. Any rational part of me that might be left is buried so deep it will never see the light of day, let alone have enough sense to drive my actions." He grabbed my arms and squeezed them to the point that I felt bruises forming. "I ought to take you back to Marduk right now while you are alone and vulnerable," he said, his lip turning up in a sneer. "Or maybe I should just kill you where you stand and tell him you attacked me and I had no choice." The crazy had crept back into Zane's black eyes.

I forced myself to stay calm and keep the fear from my voice. "Zane, please let go of my arms. My escorts will be here soon, and we don't want to give them the wrong idea. They might try to attack you."

Zane blinked rapidly, coming back to his senses. He released me so quickly you'd think I was electrified. "I'm sorry. I can't keep myself together for much longer, which is exactly what I am trying to make you understand."

"You should listen to him," Therran said as he slid like a ghost from between the park's trees. "He's not to be trusted. I would be more than happy to do the honors right now, as a matter of fact." He pulled a long dagger from his biker boot and stalked closer.

"No!" I stepped in front of Therran, gesturing for him to put down the weapon. "Zane saved my life. I think we owe him a pass for that."

Therran didn't look convinced yet grudgingly placed the dagger back in his boot. Addressing Zane, he said, "We do acknowledge what you have done to help our cause, but don't expect thanks or mercy the next time we meet."

"I didn't do it for you or your cause," Zane spat.

He turned to me, ignoring the elf, and in a softer tone said, "Go with him. I've done all I can for you. The rest is up to you."

I didn't know how to say goodbye. I wanted to run into his arms and hold him; however, I didn't want Therran to see how strongly I felt for the enemy. The last thing I needed was for anyone to question my loyalties when their trust in me was tenuous at best, given my past. Subsequently, I only nodded, turned my back on Zane, and walked away, all the while fighting the urge to look back.

Therran led me to East End Avenue where three black SUVs were waiting along the curb. He opened the rear passenger door of the center car. I peered in and found Alex sitting in the backseat looking wan and tired, but he smiled broadly when he saw me and rested his head against the seat in apparent relief.

"It worked," he said.

"Yeah, it worked," I responded, climbing into the seat next to him. I took his hand and squeezed. "Thank you."

Therran climbed into the passenger seat of the first SUV, and then the three vehicles pulled away from the curb. I assumed we were headed back to the elven compound when the quiet, tree-lined streets and historic brownstone buildings of the Upper East Side disappeared behind us as we made our way north, out of Manhattan.

"How are you feeling?" I asked.

"Not too bad. The first few days were rough, but now I'm just tired. I may not be one hundred percent, but I'm ready for a fight if needed."

"Unfortunately, I think it will be needed."

"What did they do to you? Are you okay?" he asked, concern lining his face. I still wasn't used to this softer, more sincere Alex.

"Oh, the usual—a serving of torture with a side of manipulation and a dash of terror," I tried joking. He didn't seem to appreciate my humor, though, so I sobered. "I'm okay, really. I've been trained to handle interrogations. Besides, they can work both ways. I learned some new information, but I would prefer to tell that story once. Let's wait until we get back to the compound for the full debriefing."

As if he could read my mind, Alex said, "And how about Zane?"

I hadn't intended to share anything about my time with Zane. It felt too private. However, sitting here with Alex, the words poured out me unfettered. "He's the one who blocked my memories ... and he gave them back to me."

Alex's eyes grew wide, and he sat up straighter. "You have your memories back? Do you know what this means? You can stop Marduk and save Urusilim!"

"Whoa. Slow down, cowboy. Zane said my memories will come back gradually over time. It was too dangerous to release everything at once." Alex looked crestfallen. "But he did give me back the memories of our time together," I said slowly, gauging his reaction.

"Oh," said Alex, looking away. I couldn't tell if he was disappointed that Zane hadn't given me back memories that were more useful, or if he didn't want me to remember my relationship with Zane. "So, he was ... his old self ... the whole time you were with him?"

"Yes, but he also said there was no permanent cure for him. Is it true?"

"I'm sorry, Emma," Alex responded, turning back to me with sincere regret in his eyes. "The Council has spent years trying to find a way to bring Zane back. Not only is he one of us, but he is incredibly powerful. Having him on the other side gives Marduk a significant advantage. If there was a way to bring him back, we would have found it."

I sat back in my seat, staring out the window at the black trees whizzing by as we entered the suburbs. If a highly motivated group of powerful magic users couldn't find a solution, how was I to do it? Yet, even with a high probability of failure, I couldn't give up on him.

Switching subjects, I asked Alex, "How does your magic work? I mean, you and Zane seem to use different magic, but you are both mages. And the elves have magic, too, but not like you guys."

"Elven magic is very different from mage magic. They are magical creatures, born of faery, with a close connection to nature. What they do comes less from magic and more from that connection. They can speak to the natural world, communicating their needs and desires. As long as they care for nature, nature cares for them. It's innate, something that can't be learned; it just is."

"So that's how they got the plant life to attack the soldiers at the hospital?"

"Yes. They aren't able to manipulate energy, fire, or water. They can't cast spells or create magical objects. Their abilities are limited to the living environment, but they rarely use it as a weapon. Usually, it's reserved for agriculture, building their homes, and keeping the world around them healthy and alive."

"If you can use magic, does that mean you also aren't human?"

"No, I'm human. There are some humans in Urusilim lucky enough to be born with abilities, but the strength of those abilities varies greatly. Those who have a greater degree of power typically chose to apprentice with a mage for their training. Since magic is very difficult to learn, mages are encouraged to focus on those areas that come easiest to them until mastery then move on to increasingly greater challenges.

I happen to excel at water magic. Then there are basic skills we all must learn, like shields and magical tokens."

"Do you mean the stones? I saw Zane use some."

"Yes. Each mage carries with them objects they have spelled. Given the difficulty of creating spells spontaneously, we instead create objects that hold pre-built magic that can be used at a moment's notice. The biggest drawback is that, if you don't have a needed spell at the ready at a critical moment, you're pretty much screwed."

"Zane's gift is for fire, isn't it?"

"We always were complete opposites. That's probably why we had a love-hate relationship. Sometimes, it was hard for us to see eye-to-eye, but we were always there for each other." Alex's smile faltered, and I knew he was thinking about how he hadn't been there for Zane when Zane had needed him most.

"It's not your fault, you know. It was mine. If I hadn't lost control ..." I couldn't get the words past the lump in my throat.

"You're right," he said. "I blamed you ... hated you even ... for a very long time. I had built up this image of you in my mind as an evil, soulless creature who destroyed my best friend and my world. I wanted nothing more than to avenge them, so when the Council finally located you, I volunteered to be the one to go after you. But the Council had other plans which didn't include retribution, and I wasn't very happy about it."

"I sort of noticed," I said. Although I knew he hated me, it hurt to hear him come right out and say it, all the same.

"But, now, I'm beginning to think maybe you aren't all that bad," Alex said with a smirk.

"Gee, thanks for the vote of confidence," I said, nudging his shoulder playfully.

After sharing a brief yet cathartic laugh, I rested my head on Alex's shoulder while we continued the rest of the ride in comfortable silence.

Chapter Twenty-Three

WHEN WE ARRIVED back at the compound, Jason and Lilly were waiting for us on the front porch of the farmhouse, sitting in rocking chairs and sipping steaming mugs of coffee. They looked like a fucking Maxwell House commercial.

They rose, meeting our SUVs as we pulled up to the house. Jason opened my car door, greeting me with his irresistibly charming smile. I didn't even realize what a weight I had been carrying around, worrying about his recovery, until it lifted when I laid eyes on his healthy face.

I stepped out of the car and into Jason's warm embrace. "Do you feel as good you look?" I asked.

"Almost," he responded with the comforting Texan twang I had missed hearing. "But let's face it, it's hard for anyone to feel as good as I look, especially now that I have even more character." He lifted his arm, his short-sleeved T-shirt showing the burn scars left behind from the chimera's attack. His skin was smooth and hairless, several shades lighter than the rest of his body, and lumpy, like dripping candle wax. The scars started on the back of his hand and disappeared under the sleeve of his T-shirt.

I must have had a pitying look on my face because he said, "It's all right, Em. It doesn't hurt anymore. Lilly took really good care of me. And I don't mind the way it looks. After all, chicks dig guys with scars."

"I know I do," Lilly giggled.

"Thank you, Lilly," I said. "I don't know what we would have done if you hadn't been there to help him." Lilly dipped her head trying to hide her smile, as a pretty blush bloomed on her cheeks.

Everyone moved into the house and took their customary places at the large trestle table in the kitchen. I had insisted rest could wait until after the debriefing. Lilly's grandmother was bustling about the kitchen as always, preparing some divine-smelling breakfast for the group. My mouth began to water until someone placed a hot cup of coffee in front me. Dark roast coffee with lots of cream and sugar was enough to satisfy my appetite for the time being.

"Therran, before we begin…um…do you know what happened to Lockien?" I dreaded the answer, not wanting to be the one to tell him his son tried to betray us.

"Yes," Therran responded. In a reverent tone, he said, "Alex told me of his bravery."

"He did?" My head snapped to Alex.

"Yes, I did," Alex said, fixing me with a glare that said, *I've got this covered, just play along.* "I let him know how Lockien saved our lives by standing up to those government men, buying me enough time to escape and get help. Lockien's wish was for us to recover Sharur and use it to help the Elven people."

Lilly began sobbing lightly, and Jason put his arm around her in consolation.

Therran said, "It brings me some small measure of comfort knowing he died in battle for his people." Then he pierced me with ice green eyes, his mouth tightening. "But hear this, we shall avenge him."

"This fight is as much yours as it is mine, but I would be honored to fight beside you," I replied. Therran bowed his head at my words. "Now, please, tell me what happened on the island after we went into the building."

"After you entered the building, we held out against the enemy as long as we could, but they sent out some sort of creatures—half man, half …" Therran seemed at a loss for words.

"Squid," I finished for him. "Yeah, I met one of those guys. They were pretty disgusting."

"Those monstrosities do not exist on Urusilim. Where could they have come from?" Therran asked.

"I think I know." I suspected those things were a creation of the government. Why else would they be dissecting bodies and keeping spare parts in jars? It made sense that, once the government had learned of the existence of magical creatures, they would do all in their power to understand them and exploit their capabilities for the government's benefit. The one unanswered question that I didn't want to think too hard on was whether they were experimenting on real humans or growing these things in test tubes.

I debriefed the assembled group on what had happened to me on North Brother Island and told them about the government's plans for opening the rift.

"That only gives us two days to prepare," Jason said, concerned. "How are two humans and a handful of elves supposed to stop the government with all of its resources?"

"We have resources," I said. "I have a friend who likes to collect toys."

"Do you really think you can trust Nathan Anshar?" Jason asked.

"As long as he needs me to recover Sharur, I think he'll be cooperative."

"You also have the power of the mages behind you," Alex said.

"No offense, man, but you are in no shape to be of any help to us at all," Jason said, eyeing Alex, who sat slumped in his seat, barely able to sit up straight.

"No, I'm not," Alex admitted. "But I also have friends I can call on. I have contacted the Mage Council and some have agreed to aid us."

Jason and I exchanged a glance, both questioning the trustworthiness of the Council, although we didn't have much of a choice. We needed as many allies as possible if we were to stand a chance.

"Okay, then," I said. "Let's start planning."

WE SPENT THE next several hours looking over maps while we debated strategies and tactics until we had finally reached an agreement. I then found an empty bedroom and crashed hard for several more hours, awakening only after the sun had already set. I showered and dressed in black Lucky jeans and a Yankees T-shirt. As I was pulling on my favorite black boots, a soft knock sounded at the door.

"Come in," I called.

The door opened a crack, and Lilly's bright red hair appeared as she peaked into the room. "Hey, Em. Can I come in?"

I frowned. It wasn't like Lilly to be deferential to others. I would have expected her to burst in, all effervescent and gabby. This quieter, more polite Lilly couldn't be a good sign.

"Um, yeah, sure," I said. "What's up?"

Closing the door behind her, she replied, "Oh, nothing. I just thought I would check in to see how you were feeling."

"I'm fine, thanks," I said, going back to zippering my boots.

I expected Lilly to leave then; instead, she came farther into the room and sat next to me on the bed. I sat up, giving her a questioning look.

"Sooooo," she said.

I tried to hide the twitch at the corner of my mouth. "*So?*" She clearly wanted to talk about something that she was struggling to bring up.

"You spent the night with Zane," she said without looking at me.

The half-smile fell from my face. Lilly was right to hesitate bringing up this conversation. It wasn't really something I wanted to talk about.

"Yeah, but it wasn't like that," I lied. "We were wiped and needed a place to crash for the night."

"Mm-hmm," she said with a lilt, not sounding convinced. "You expect me to believe you spent the night with a hot bad boy turned temporarily good, who saved you from the evil clutches of a torturer, and nothing happened?" I guessed, when she put it that way, I could understand why she didn't believe me.

"Look, I really don't want to talk about this."

"Ah-ha!" she yelled in triumph. "Something did happen. Come on, you can tell me. I swear I won't breathe a word."

How the hell was I going to get out of this conversation? I had already said too much. Strangely enough, however, part of me wanted to confide in her. I had never had a girlfriend, never divulged my deepest, darkest secrets to anyone. But could Lilly really be trusted? I didn't know much about her. True, her family seemed committed to helping me, yet allies didn't necessarily mean friends.

"Zane and I have a history."

"Oh? Do you still have feelings for him?"

"No. Yes. I don't know," I said sighing heavily.

"Are you confused because of Jason?" she asked, averting her eyes.

"Why? What does Jason have to do with any of this?"

"Well…I guess…I just thought. I assumed you and Jason were…"

"Wow," I said. "Lilly Alfreda is at a loss for words. I never thought I'd see the day."

She smirked, but mirth twinkled in her eyes. "So there's nothing going on between you and Jason?"

"No, not anymore. We used to be together, but it didn't last long. Don't get me wrong, he's an amazing guy and means a lot to me, but only as a friend."

"Does he feel the same way about you – just friends?"

My hesitation gave her the answer. "Why are you asking me about Jason? Are you interested in him?"

Lilly shrugged. "I've spent a lot of time with him these last few days. I think we've become good friends, but I'd like for us to be more. I can tell something...or someone...is holding him back."

"Lilly, Jason knows how I feel about him. I can promise you that I've done nothing to encourage him, but I'm not ready for him, or anyone else, to know about Zane."

"Your secret is safe with me," Lilly winked. "And what exactly is it you don't want anyone to know about? I bet it's that he's in love with you and got you alone while he had his sanity back for a few precious hours. There is no way he kept his distance from you last night."

I sighed, resigning myself to the fact that Lilly was not going to let go of this. "Okay, maybe something happened, but it doesn't matter. He's crazy again and out to get me. And I'll probably have to kill him," I finished despondently.

"Oh, shit," said Lilly, as if she only then understood the implications. "There has to be a cure."

"Apparently there isn't. The mages have been trying for years to find a way to reverse Zane's condition, but instead, they've only made it worse."

"Like they do to everyone," Lilly muttered. "Listen, I might be naive in the way of relationships, but I do believe that true love conquers all. You'll find a way; I just know it. And the two of you will live happily ever after."

I almost laughed out loud until I saw the sincerity in Lilly's eyes. She actually believed what she was saying. Unfortunately, I wasn't nearly as innocent in the ways of the world and knew happy endings didn't exist for most people. One day, someone would come along and shatter her illusions. Until then, I simply gave her a brief hug, surprising both of us at my spontaneous display of affection. I don't know where it had come from. Maybe I was grateful she had allowed me to open up, even just a little, or maybe it was the type of consolation hug an adult gives a child. Whichever it was, she gave me a broad smile in return.

"Come on, let's get downstairs. We have a long night ahead of us."

We walked into the kitchen and found Jason looking as handsome as ever in faded jeans, a blue long-sleeved tee, and worker boots.

"Are you ready?" I asked.

"Yup. I rented a U-Haul. It's out front."

We piled into the small van and set out for a self-storage facility in Easton, Pennsylvania. It was a long, boring drive through New Jersey and into Pennsylvania along Interstate 78, but at this hour, there was no traffic to slow us down.

A little less than two hours later, we were opening the door to the storage bay where I stored my weapons cache. We loaded the van with rifles, handguns, and automatics before I snagged a spare set of my military body armor.

On the way back to New York, Jason was very conscientious and obeyed the speed limit. Getting pulled over with a van full of guns would not have ended well for anyone. Thankfully, we made our way through the Holland Tunnel into Manhattan without incident.

It was almost midnight when we pulled into the garage beneath Nathan Anshar's luxury apartment building. There was no point in being sneaky about it. I was sure his security team had alerted him to our arrival the moment we had pulled onto his street. Anyway, I planned on asking nicely for his help, not taking it by force ... unless I had to.

"Mr. Smith!" I said with a broad smile. "It's good to see you again, my friend." I walked straight up to Nathan's head of security and gave him a big hug. He reflexively stepped away from me, startled, and I broke contact before he could pull a gun on me. I definitely enjoyed throwing that smug son of a bitch off his game, even if only briefly.

He cleared his throat, looking uncomfortable. "Miss Hayes, Mr. Ryker, come this way, please." He led us to the private elevator, and we ascended to the penthouse. The doors slid open to reveal the museum-like living room, and without waiting for an invitation, I strode into the back office where I knew I would find Nathan.

He was seated behind his ornate mahogany desk, speaking on the phone. I didn't wait for him to finish his conversation before striding in and taking a seat in one of the leather chairs facing his desk.

"Uh-huh. Yes, if I was a gambling man, that's where I would put my money ... I know the odds, but everyone loves an underdog ... Well, even underdogs need a champion once in a while ... Good. Talk to you soon."

"You always struck me as the type to back the obvious winner,"

"You don't know me very well, Miss Hayes. All of the greatest moments in history occurred when the little guy overcame all odds: David and Goliath, the Spartans and the Persians, the American Colonies and the British, Rocky and Apollo Creed. Need I go on?"

"So, you're a romantic at heart."

"I suppose you can call me that, which is why I am rooting for you."

"What makes you think I'm the underdog in this scenario?"

Nathan barked a short, harsh laugh. "Miss Hayes, in about twenty-four hours, you will be going up against the might of the United States government and their mutated super soldiers; the evil leader of an alternate universe and his army of supernatural creatures; and a supremely powerful mage. And what do you have? Your military skills, a handful of nature-loving elves, and a weakened magic user. Yes, I would definitely say the odds are against you."

"How the hell do you know all of that?" I asked, trying unsuccessfully to keep the shock from showing on my face.

"One does not make it to my level without the help of many, many friends. But don't trouble yourself with my extensive contact list right now. It seems you have much more important issues to deal with."

His apparent knowledge of the entire situation made me squirm with distrust. How long had he known about the government's plans? What else did he know that he wasn't telling me? However, he was also right. I would have to worry about how he had come by his information later, as long as he gave me what I needed.

"So, what can you do for me to help even out the odds?"

"Why should I do anything? Maybe I want the entertainment value of seeing whether you can get yourself out of this one on your own. If I help you, it might be evening out the odds too much, and where is the fun in that?"

"Call me crazy, but I don't think you're in this for the laughs. I'm willing to bet you stand to benefit on the outcome. And, if you intend to back me, that means you need me to come out on top. Tell me I'm wrong."

He smiled at me and leaned back in his chair. Holding his arms wide, he said, "Take what you need, that's all I can offer." He was giving me my choice from his weapons collection. "But none of these things will help you win this battle."

"I have to find a way, and heavy firepower is one of the best ways I can think of."

"This battle is to retrieve Sharur. In order to do that, you will need tools not currently at your disposal. Haven't you heard the saying that sufficiently advanced technology is indistinguishable from magic?"

Was he telling me there was some technology out there that could help me fight those who wielded magic? "How would I get access to such technology?"

"Why, from someone in a position to *procure* very well-protected secrets," he answered. "All I need to do is make a phone call."

I nodded. "Tell him to meet me at my favorite place. He'll know where it is. In the meantime, I think I'll take you up on your offer."

AFTER ADDING SOME of Nathan's more deadly collectibles to the van, we drove downtown to Raines. It served the dual purpose of keeping us safely in a public place with sufficient privacy while also allowing me to have a desperately needed drink.

We parked the van in a well-lit section of a heavily trafficked street to deter any would-be car thieves and then made our way into the bar. As always, they sat Jason and I promptly in our usual booth. It made me wonder if they actually kicked patrons out of the booth to accommodate us. I ordered a dirty martini with Grey Goose and extra olives, while Jason kept it simple with a Sam Adams.

We waited for almost two hours before Benjamin Hayes arrived. It was close to three a.m., though Raines was still bustling and would remain open for at least another hour. Benjamin slipped through the black curtain and took a seat beside me, giving me a hug that lasted a few seconds longer than usual. I gave him a squeeze of reassurance before we broke apart.

Jason left the privacy of the booth to stand sentry nearby. It was a smart move, but I also appreciated his effort to give me some privacy with Ben.

"So, you knew about me all along," I said, making it more of a statement than a question.

"Yes. I'm sorry, Emma. I never wanted to lie to you, but I did it to protect you. When you arrived, I was asked to procure a secure space and medical equipment for you. I was informed of your manner of arrival, and for the next year,

I stayed abreast of your situation because I had to approve the purchases related to your care. Those purchases included high doses of narcotics typically used for keeping people in artificially-induced comas, imaging equipment, surgical supplies, restraints, medical staff and security personnel. I finally decided to stop approving the purchases unless I knew what they were for, so the team responsible for you invited me to participate in their briefings.

"I learned that they weren't making any progress with you. When they would bring you out of the coma, you were either violent and uncooperative or not lucid enough to talk. They were getting no answers about who you were, what you wanted, or where you had come from. So discussion turned to the next steps. Options on the table ranged from harsher methods of interrogation to euthanasia and autopsy to at least learn how you might be different from us. That's when I finally stepped in."

I thought back to the lab on North Brother Island and how close I had come to being picked apart and placed piece by piece into glass jars. I shuddered.

"After everything I experienced this past week, I can't say I'm surprised at what was done to me, but I will make them regret it. How did you manage to keep me off the butcher's block?"

"I told them I would find you a foster home with someone in the inner circle, in the hopes you would grow to trust that family and reveal your secrets to them and thereby to us. It wasn't a well-received plan, but since I held the purse strings, they didn't have a lot of options. Even if they voted against me, they would need to come back to me for budgeting favors in the future, and I wouldn't be quite as willing to allocate the funding for their pet projects. So they grudgingly allowed it on two conditions. First, someone was to keep an eye on you at all times and immediately report back if anything … unusual ever happened. Second, if you didn't reveal yourself, they would go in to retrieve you to explore alternate approaches. It looks like, after ten years, they have finally run out of patience, and I have failed you."

"None of this is your fault, Ben. Believe me, if I had remembered anything, I would have told you. As it happens, my memories were forcibly walled off and remain inaccessible." As much as I cared for Benjamin, I wasn't ready to tell him the wall was crumbling. "But I have learned enough to know the government is on the wrong side on this one. They can't force open a rift between worlds. They will be allowing horrible, deadly creatures into ours, and it could mean the end of humanity. You have to see that," I said, grabbing his hands tightly.

"I do see that, which is why I have been protecting you. It's also why I brought you this." When he placed his briefcase on the seat between us, I noticed that it was made of thick steel, painted to look like a simple leather case when seen from a distance. The lock was not standard, either.

Benjamin placed his thumb to a flat plate where a lock would have normally been. The plate briefly glowed a dim green then several soft clicks indicated the locks had disengaged. "I coded the case to your fingerprint, as well, so you are the only one who will be able to access it."

He lifted the lid to reveal black foam that was cut to snuggly house the object lying inside. It was a round object, about the size of a softball and made of a metal that looked unusual. I reached out a tentative hand to touch its surface lightly. It was surprisingly very warm, as if it had a small furnace burning inside of it.

"What is it?" I breathed.

"It's called a High Density Field Generator, but the boys in R&D just call it the Blackhole. The casing is made of Tungsten Tetraboride wrapped in an atomic layer of Graphene. This makes the casing strong enough to contain a massively dense sub-atomic particle yet brittle enough to shatter upon impact. Its design is based on a theoretical concept of how to collapse a stable wormhole between worlds. It has never been tested, so I have no idea whether it will work. But, just in case they break through, this is our only hope of destroying the threat."

"I never thought about what it took to close a stable rift. All everyone keeps talking about is how to get one opened."

"That's why we have the best minds in the world on this project." He smiled at me wanly as he latched the lid closed, leaving the briefcase on the seat. "My true goal in all of this was to show you the best parts of humanity—love, friendship, day-to-day life on Earth—so when this time came, you would choose to save us, even from ourselves if need be. But that didn't happen. I was outmaneuvered, and you were placed in that sorry excuse for a foster home that only taught you violence, pain, manipulation, and distrust. However, I still have faith that you will choose to side with humanity when war comes." He leaned in and placed a soft kiss on my cheek before he slipped out of the booth and was gone.

I took a deep swallow of my martini, hoping the vodka would burn away the lump stuck in my throat. Jason moved into the booth and sat down next to me, noticing the briefcase. "Is that whatever he thinks is going to help?"

"Yes. We had better get it out of here and back to the safety of the compound. I have a feeling we're going to need it."

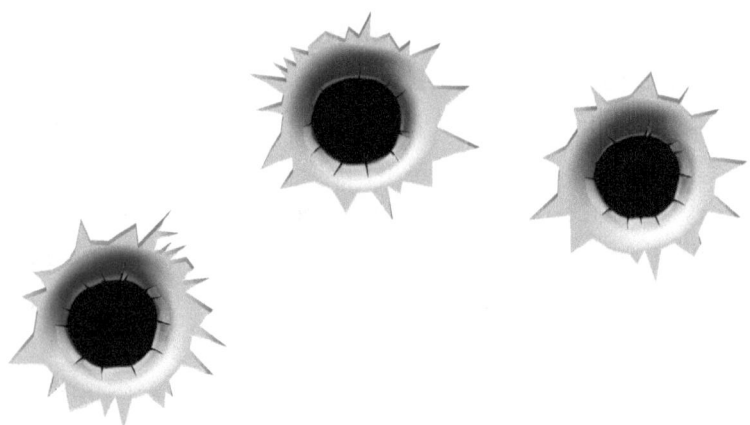

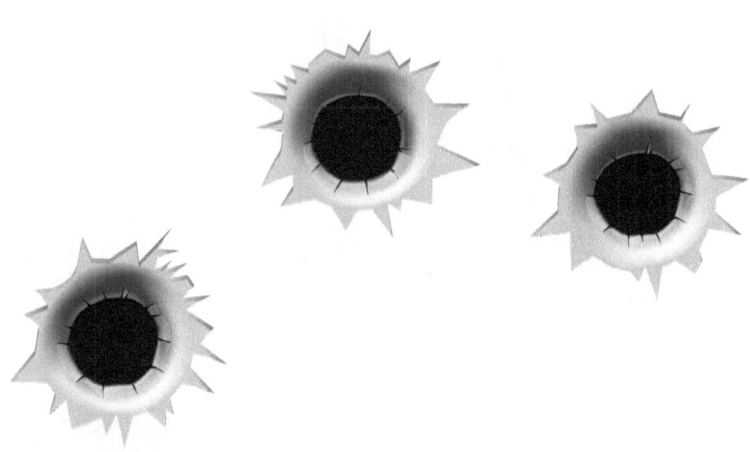

Chapter Twenty-Four

THE NEXT DAY was spent inventorying weapons and teaching the elves how to use them. They weren't natural marksmen by any means, but I figured that, if they could point and shoot, they might hit something eventually, and hopefully before someone hit them.

It was a little after noon when my stomach drove me from the make-shift shooting range back to the kitchen in search of food. I could hear the heated voices even before I stepped into the house yet was unable to make out the words.

Following those harsh tones, I made my way to the kitchen where I found Alex standing next to a grizzled old man. He had coarse, gray stubble on his chin and a wicked scar that cut down the right side of his face. It began on his forehead and ended at the jaw, running over his now blinded and white eyeball. He wore a heavy black cloak of rough spun wool and held a staff that was almost as tall as his six-foot frame.

Looking as serious as death, I could tell he was someone I didn't want to cross.

Therran was standing over the maps spread out on the table, both hands flat on the weathered wood. If he was a cartoon character, smoke would be billowing out of his ears. He glared daggers in the direction of the high-backed chair in front of me. At first, I thought it was empty; however, when I walked around the table, I saw it was in fact occupied by a little girl.

Not having spent much time around kids, I could only guess she was somewhere between six and ten years old. She was a cute little thing with blond curls, creamy skin, and a button nose. She was all sweet innocence except for her eyes. They were deep pools of ink that swallowed brightness and sunshine. This was undoubtedly one kid who didn't dream about rainbows and butterflies.

She was holding Therran's gaze steadily, looking unconcerned in the face of his rage, her arms folded across her small body.

The old man, whose voice I had heard from outside, leaned toward Lilly's father and said, "You need us, Therran, and that is our price for helping you. You know this mission will fail without the Council."

"I know no such thing," Therran said between clenched teeth. "All I can say with certainty is that the past ten years have been the same as the past one hundred. The mages are still pompous, self-important tyrants."

Fire flashed in the eyes of the old man as he screwed up his face to spew what I knew was going to be an equally vicious retort when the little girl interrupted. "And here I thought I was the only one in the room who still had temper tantrums. Ronin, sit down," she calmly commanded the old man, and to my surprise, he obeyed without hesitation. "I don't expect we have time today to settle a grudge between our people that is older than I am, so let us stay focused on the matter at hand."

She had the voice of a small child, but she certainly didn't have the language or demeanor of one. Somehow, she was far older than the age she appeared to be.

As if she could sense my thoughts, her eyes snapped up to meet mine. With a smile, she held out her hand and said, "So you are the one whom all this fuss is about. I am Minister Alcina Moretti, head of the Mage Council." I took her small hand, surprise showing on my face. "Don't take my age for inexperience," she warned. "I've been around a lot longer than it may appear."

I wanted to ask how old she really was, but I didn't believe the question would be well received. Instead, I took a seat at the table and asked, "What are you guys arguing about?"

Alcina was the first to speak up, and I got the impression she worked hard at being the first and strongest voice in a room. "We were just discussing the disposition of Sharur if it is recovered."

I sat up straighter, my hackles rising at the prospect of someone else trying to claim the weapon. "What do you mean?" I kept my tone neutral. "I was hired to recover it for Nathan Anshar." They didn't need to know that I had no intention of handing it over to him.

Alcina just barked out another harsh laugh. "No, dear, that is not going to happen." I bristled at her authoritative tone. "Sharur will be given into the safe-keeping of the Council. We are the only ones that have deep knowledge of the weapon and the strength to keep it safe. Powerful magic can only be protected by powerful magic users."

"You mean, powerful magic can only be *exploited* by powerful magic users, don't you?" Therran growled. "Let's not forget how the weapon ended up in the hands of the humans in the first place."

"That was an unfortunate accident and one I can assure you won't be repeated. We have no intention of using the axe. We will store it in a heavily warded location where no one will find it."

"Do you really expect me to believe that?" Therran asked. "There is no way the entire Council will agree to put such a powerful weapon into storage. Even if you are sincere, you cannot dictate the will of the rest of the Council. They can override your decision, and I know several members that would happily defy you just for the joy of it."

Alcina frowned at the implication. "I can assure you that I have the full support of the Council in this. If you do not agree to these terms, you will not receive our help. If you go after the humans on your own, you will fail. Then we will come in and take the weapon from the humans on our own. Either way, the end result is the same. It would simply be more convenient to work together rather than against each other."

"Or we recover it without your help and keep it safe ourselves. If you claim that your intentions are the same as mine—to never use Sharur—you know that the elves can be trusted to hide it away. Elves are true to their word. I cannot say the same for you."

"You insolent —" Ronin started to snarl and rise from his seat when I interrupted him.

"I think this entire discussion is a bit premature." I didn't want them to come to agreement, because I knew I would never comply with any decision that put Sharur in anyone's hands other than my own. It was easier to betray them if I wasn't actually defying any agreed-upon truce. "We are going up against the might of the United States military. It will take a major miracle for us to disrupt their plans of opening a rift, let alone actually snatching Sharur from them. I suggest we focus all of our energy on figuring out how to win this thing and worry later about what will happen if we are lucky enough to make it out alive. But I can guarantee you that we won't have a shot in hell of winning back Sharur unless we work together." Saying those words tasted sour in my mouth. I hated asking for help, let alone from people I knew would stab me in the back the first chance they got. Too many secret agendas were colliding in this room.

"Well spoken," said Alcina, eyeing me with suspicion. She might have agreed with my sentiment, but she didn't trust my motives. "I am happy to table this discussion until after the battle, but I do hope you are not harboring your own secret ambitions for the axe. Things would not go well for you if you attempted to take it for yourself."

Did that little brat actually just threaten me? And here I was, trying my hardest to be level-headed and diplomatic. Perhaps I needed to take a different approach with the Council. My hand curled into a fist without much conscious thought. I had never hit a child before, but Alcina was far from your typical child, and it was doubtful anyone would call Child Protective Services on me.

Alex must have seen or sensed my intentions because he leapt between Alcina and me. "Minster, I assure you, Emma has no such intentions. She is committed to the safe recovery and return of Sharur to its rightful people."

That seemed to satisfy her for the moment. I shook off my anger, prepared to address the more important issues at hand, when Therran felt the need to get in the last word. "We can speak of this later when victory is ours, but my position will not change between now and then."

"Then let's agree to disagree for the moment," I said before another argument ensued. "Now, Alcina …" Alex cleared his throat, and the child narrowed her eyes at me. "Sorry … Minister," I almost spat, but forced it to come out more politely, "let me tell you what I need you to do."

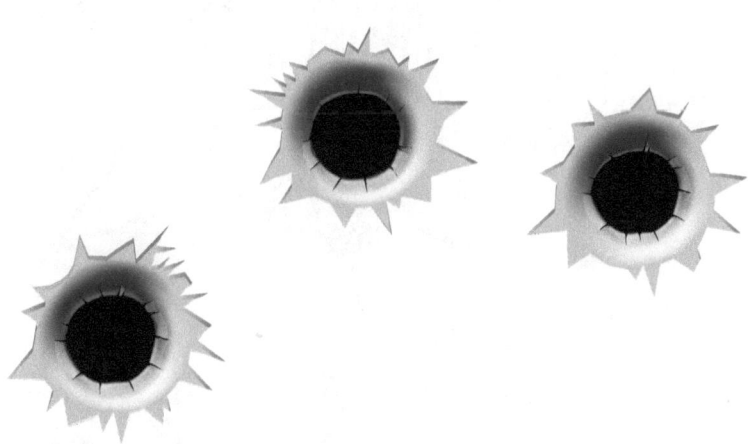

Chapter Twenty-Five

CITI FIELD WAS a bright jewel against a field of black velvet. The stadium was lit from within, casting a glow that didn't penetrate the darkened parking lot that stretched in a wide field around the building. I approached alone, dressed in my typical black military armor. The suit covered every inch of me in strong yet lightweight protection. It wouldn't stop high caliber weapons, but it would protect me against claws, teeth, and other pointy objects.

I had a Glock holstered at each hip, a knife in my boot, and a semi-automatic rifle slung across my back. I felt strong and invincible, as I usually did when I was dripping in firepower, but I knew it was likely to be short-felt.

I didn't hide my approach to the stadium, although I could have. I had already figured out that Connor wanted me to show up; otherwise, why would he have let it slip during my interrogation exactly when and where he would be? It was either a trap or he needed me to be here. I was betting on the latter; however, I was prepared for the former. I certainly didn't believe he had been stupid enough to accidentally share such critical information.

I stepped through the arched entryway and into the cavernous lobby of the stadium. Long elevators led up to the seating levels. They were not running at this late hour, though; therefore, I walked up to the next level. My heart was pumping hard by the time I reached the top, but it could have been from anxiety as much as from exertion.

Everything was riding on my success tonight. If I failed, the world would be invaded by monstrous creatures. They would hunt and kill every man, woman, and child in the entire metropolitan area and beyond. What would humans do once they found out about the existence of an alternate world that contained such deadly threats? Was Connor really so deluded and egomaniacal that he thought he could contain the threat and suck Urusilim dry of its magic? Nothing good could come of this, for either world.

I walked across the concrete promenade between shuttered food vendor stands and down a short flight of steps to the field level. It was a place where millions of people brought their hopes and dreams of victory. On some days, those dreams came true, and on others, all hopes of winning were dashed. Those walls had seen their fair share of triumphs and failures over the few short years it had been in existence. I couldn't help wondering who would walk away the victor tonight.

Soldiers holding automatic rifles were posted along the entire perimeter of the field every ten feet. As I stepped onto the field, they made no move to intercept, confirming my suspicion that Connor had wanted me to come. Speaking of the prick, there he was, standing in centerfield, surrounded by a large team of people. Some were soldiers, others were wearing white lab coats, a few were in business suits, and there was even a General dressed in full military regalia.

A dais had been erected on the grass with metal poles positioned at each corner. Wires ran from pole to pole, making the whole setup look like some sort of boxing ring. The tech guys were checking the wires and connecting them to a series of laptop computers set up on a nearby table. Two large video cameras on tripods faced the dais. It looked like Connor was planning for quite a show tonight.

As I steadily approached centerfield, one of the men sitting behind a laptop called to Connor. "Sir, it's time!"

Connor clapped his hands loudly and directed everyone to take their assigned places. Within seconds, the bustle had died down to absolute stillness as everyone found their stations and waited for their next set of instructions. I bet that half of them didn't even know what was going to happen, or they would be safely at home watching *The Big Bang Theory*.

A massive soldier, whose shoulders looked like they would have a hard time squeezing through a standard-sized door, carried over a metal box. I knew immediately from his size and the dead look in his eyes that this guy was one of those lab-grown squid creatures.

The squid held the box out to Connor who opened the lid and, with a dramatic flourish, lifted Sharur from the case. He held it high for all to see and admire. It had been cleaned and sharpened since I had last seen it. The stadium lights glinted off the polished axe head, highlighting the intricate scrollwork etched into the steel. It was stunningly beautiful.

With a deep breath, I strode purposefully toward Connor. Noticing the movement, he finally looked up and saw me. "Miss Hayes!" he shouted with enthusiasm.

It seemed as if every eye in the stadium turned toward me. I felt uncomfortable under the scrutiny yet kept my face impassive.

Stopping within a few feet of him, I said in low tones so only he could hear me, "Connor, it's not too late. You still have time to stop this. Neither of us wants to be responsible for the deaths of all of these good people." Spreading my arms wide, I continued, "I know you think you can keep this contained within the stadium, but they are waiting for you on the other side with an army."

"Let them come. I have been leading this project for a decade. Do you have any idea how much we have learned about them during that time? I have categorized and classified almost a dozen creatures, identified their weaknesses and used their strengths to create my own monster army. They are laughably primitive. There is no way they can possibly stand up to the technological might and knowledge of the U.S. government. It'll be a slaughter if they don't concede."

"Is that what you are expecting, for them to surrender?" I shook my head incredulously. "Do you really think there are only a dozen different types? Have you met the shadow demons, the ghouls, or the chimera—that guy was a pain in the ass to kill. Or what about those lizard-bear things? Did you figure out how the mages control magic?" I could see his confident smile falter momentarily.

"Connor, you can pin the blame on me," I pleaded. "Tell everyone here that I just gave you critical information that may require a change in strategy, and you need more time. They are military men; they will understand. I will go with you willingly, and together with Ben Hayes, we can convince the government to take a different course. I know we can." I wasn't actually that confident in my ability to sway the government from its plans; however, if the best I could do was to buy some more time, I would take it.

In those brief seconds while Connor seemed to contemplate my words, I shifted my eyes to subtly scan the stadium. I searched for the one face that I was interested in finding, but it wasn't there. Disappointment and relief clashed within me. I had been hoping to get Daniel back tonight, but I also didn't want him anywhere near this place, knowing what was about to go down.

I could see shadows moving inside the dugouts and prowling along the concourses yet couldn't make out any details. The soldiers stationed along the perimeter must have sensed or heard the movement above them because they fidgeted uncomfortably, their boots scuffing the earth as they shifted from foot to foot. A few furtive whispers faintly reached my ears as soldiers drifted closer to their companions, unconsciously seeking out safety in groups.

The tech guys were tapping away on computer keyboards and clicking their mouse buttons. The occasional rustle of paper and scratch of pencils sounded deafeningly loud in the oppressive silence that had descended. Time seemed to stand still as I anxiously grasped onto the slim hope that Connor would call off this folly.

I wanted to ask him about Daniel, but I didn't want to interrupt the thoughts cascading through Connor's mind at my words. I saw the moment when Connor decided to heed my advice as resignation flashed across his features, and then I saw the moment he changed his mind as a booming voice reverberated off the concrete walls.

"What the hell are you waiting for, man? Arrest her!" shouted the pudgy, red-faced General whose dress uniform looked to be two sizes too small for him. "She is a traitor and a national security threat, and you stand there, listening to her lies? Maybe we chose the wrong man for the job."

That snapped Connor back to attention, anger flashing in his eyes. "Did you really think you could change the course of tonight by trying to scare me? We are here to secure the future of this country, to protect its citizens, and to ensure we remain the undisputed superpower of this world. There is no greater cause to fight for than that."

"The only way to protect this country and all the others is to keep that rift closed," I said, even though I knew it was a fruitless argument at that point.

"Restrain her," Connor ordered the big man who had brought him the case.

I broke into a run, but I didn't get more than three steps when iron hands clasped my arms, stopping me mid-stride and pulling me back to Connor.

"We can't have you leaving us so soon," he mocked. "After all, you may still have a part to play." He reached under his tailored white dress shirt and pulled out my amulet on a chain around his neck.

"You're bat shit crazy if you think I'm going to help you do anything."

"I'm hoping you won't need to, but since this is my first time opening a portal to another world, I'm not entirely sure how it's going to work. So, just in case it requires you in some way, I am inviting you to stay. I'm actually hoping it requires a human sacrifice," he said with a wink.

Hope flared within me once again when he revealed he didn't know how to open the rift. "You'll never be able to open the rift on your own. Just walk away before you kill yourself trying."

"Oh, I know my limitations, but I also know how to make up for them, that's why I brought some help."

As if on cue, one of dark shadows broke away from the Mets' dugout and moved across the field toward us. With the field lights shining in my eyes, I couldn't make out the stranger until they came within ten feet of me, and then I realized it was no stranger at all.

"Zane," I breathed with equal parts terror and desire at his overwhelming presence. Then it hit me that Zane was working with the government. "What …? Why …?"

Connor laughed at my confusion. "This doesn't mean we're besties or anything. Zane wants that rift open as much as we do, so call it a temporary alliance based on mutual interests."

"Zane," I said urgently, straining against my captor in an attempt to get closer to the mage. "You have to listen to me. I know the man that I was with two nights ago is still in there somewhere. You have to stop this. Please." My vision blurred as I searched Zane's face, looking for some sign that he still knew me, cared for me.

His expression remained icy and contemptuous. "You are nothing but a worthless harlot, trying to seduce me into betraying my cause. Your trickery won't work on me again. I now see you for what you really are—a vile, evil liar and a murderer of innocents. You disgust me."

It felt as if my heart had stopped beating in that moment. I couldn't take a breath, my mouth opened, trying to gulp air, but my lungs wouldn't work. I felt lightheaded, and the stadium began to spin around me. I heard a distant choking and gasping. Trying to focus on where it was coming from, I realized it was me. I was still being held by the arms, but I was bent over at the waist, gulping oxygen in short breaths with wetness on my cheeks.

He is right, I thought. I was a murderer of innocents. Thousands of people on Urusilim had died because of me, because of my anger, my desperation to save Zane. And how many more had died at my hands on Earth? Even when I had been given a chance for a new life, I had chosen to be a killer. What's more, if I failed the task at hand, I could add thousands more victims to my ledger.

I forced myself to take deep breaths and looked back up at Zane. "You're right. I am evil, and I am a murderer, but I'm not a liar. I loved you once, and if you ever felt the same for me, you will help me stop this so we can save the lives of thousands of innocent people." His eyes softened almost imperceptibly, until I had to open my stupid mouth again. "We can't let those monsters through the rift."

At that, the rage came pouring forth once again. "You would call them monsters? They are my brothers and sisters, and they deserve life more than these scheming, power-hungry cowards," he spat, gesturing around the stadium. "I want these *monsters* to come forth and purge this world so we can remake Urusilim out of its ashes."

"Now, Jason," I said into the radio earpiece that was discreetly hidden under my hair. The crack of a high-powered sniper rifle echoed off every square inch of concrete. Jason was perched at the top of the stadium with a clear view of the entire field. The bullet slammed into the forehead of the giant holding me. I heard the wet *thunk* as the bullet penetrated its skull and sunk into the brain. The big guy convulsed once, then his hands went slack, and he fell hard to the ground.

In response, guns slid free of holsters, rifles were slung forward, and soon, every person on the field had a weapon drawn, trying to find the source of the shot. Zane, taking advantage of the distraction, lunged toward Connor, but instead of attacking Connor, Zane scooped up Sharur. With a graceful twist, he spun around, swinging the weapon through the air to slice open my throat.

I leaned back as I saw the axe blade coming at me, felt the swish of air rush past. Warm liquid dripped down my neck, and the biting sting of a thin cut blossomed at my throat. It wasn't deep, though it was a clear sign the negotiations were over. The battle was about to begin.

Chapter Twenty-Six

I GAVE A sharp whistle. At my signal, dozens of arrows were released into the air, arcing gracefully before raining hell down on the field. The arrows were aimed at the soldiers on the perimeter as well as Connor. A few soldiers were dropped by lucky shafts that found the soft flesh of necks or eyes, but most of the arrows bounced harmlessly off their body armor. The arrows had the desired effect, though—chaos erupted.

The workers in lab coats were running and screaming, sprinting toward exits, trying to escape the barrage. As those sharp points came flying toward me, aimed at Connor standing nearby, I held my ground, unflinching, hoping my trust hadn't been misplaced.

It wasn't. Arrows fell at my feet harmlessly, bouncing off the protective shield erected over my head like an impenetrable umbrella. I looked up at the press box and gave Alex a wave of thanks.

As expected, Zane had done the same thing. Connor tried to duck behind Zane to use him as a shield, but Zane unceremoniously shoved him away, leaving him exposed. Connor, cockroach that he was, grabbed a nearby scientist who was running past him, headed for the exit. He swung the poor man around roughly, holding the man to his chest in a vice grip. In seconds, the scientist was a pin cushion, his white coat soaked crimson. Connor then tossed him aside roughly, used and forgotten.

The soldiers turned around and opened fire into the stadium seating. Even with their rifles, they weren't able to target the elves that were scattered throughout the stadium, ducked down behind the seats and cement barriers. The General commanded them into the seating areas to flush out the enemy. *So predictable*, I thought.

As the soldiers closed in, the elves dropped the useless bows and sprung from their hiding places, opening fire with handguns and rifles. Since the elves were pretty crappy at handling high powered weapons, getting the soldiers into close range was our only hope. Jason also stayed in position to provide some extra firepower. I could see both soldiers and elves falling as the battle continued.

Suddenly, Connor screamed a command over the din of the fighting. "Attack!"

Dark shapes moved out of the shadowed dugouts and promenades, bounding into the seats and onto the field. From this distance, I could see they moved on four legs with powerfully muscled bodies and curled tails. They had a cat-like grace. I would have guessed them to be lions except for their small heads.

They moved swiftly toward the elves. One elf that had been positioned on top of the visitor's dugout didn't even see the creature coming until it was too late. It slunk out of the dugout and spread black leathery wings. One powerful down stroke lifted it silently into the air where it dropped onto the unsuspecting elf, lashing out with what I now recognized to be a scorpion tale, impaling the elf in the stomach with its venomous stinger.

The elf stopped struggling, paralyzed by poison yet gurgling in an effort to scream for help. The creature opened its jaws wide and literally bit the elf's head off. The creature proceeded to crunch and swallow the bloody skull, and then gulped down the rest of the elf's body until nothing was left—no clothes, no blood, no bones. I thought I was going to vomit as the beast moved into the seats, looking for its next meal.

An elf that had been hiding in the higher mezzanine level saw the attack and began shooting. Most of the bullets went far afield, but those that did hit home barely nicked its tough hide. Then I heard the familiar crack of a rifle, and Jason's bullet found its way through an eye socket into the creature's brain, dropping it where it stood.

"Nice shot," I said into my earpiece.

"Thank ye kindly, ma'am," Jason responded.

"Start making your way down here. I need you on the field." It was probably more beneficial to keep him where he was, but if things went bad, I wanted him to have quicker access out of the stadium. He was too far from an exit for my comfort.

"I won't have your back for a few minutes. Try to stay alive," he said, teasing me.

"I plan to. Over and out," I said.

I spun in a circle, taking in the mayhem in the stands as the beasts went after elves and soldiers alike, either not able to or not caring enough to differentiate ally from enemy. That was when I saw Zane land a right hook across Connor's face. It felt good to watch Connor impact with the ground hard. I only wished I had been the one to hit him. When Zane reached down and tore a chain from Connor's neck, a chill ran through me. He had my amulet.

I pulled my Glock and shot the entire clip at Zane. He threw up a shield the moment he heard the first shot, though. It wasn't fast enough to block that first bullet, but the rest were. The one that made it through ricocheted off the blade of the battle axe that Zane was holding and put a small hole in the nearby General's head.

I sprinted toward Zane yet wasn't fast enough to stop him from slamming the amulet into the circular depression in the center of the axe head. The amulet began to glow with that deep indigo light I had seen in Mexico and again in the alley with the shadow demons. The light poured like liquid along the scroll work etched into the double blades.

Then Alex was at my side, ice cold vapor pouring from his outstretched palms toward Zane. The fog flowed over the grass until it reached Zane. Tendrils climbed up his legs, torso, and arms. Zane struggled against it, unable to move as his body was encased in ice. He became a beautiful, glittering statue, and I had the odd desire to run my fingers across the smooth surface.

"Grab the axe," Alex said, weaving on his feet. I took his arm to steady him.

"But it's frozen."

"Not for long."

Looking back at Zane, I saw the ice weeping, droplets sliding down his chest and arms, dripping steadily to the ground. The fingers of his free hand twitched, his palm glowing orange with the beginnings of a flame.

I closed the distance, grabbing onto the axe shaft with both hands and pulling. It didn't budge.

"Look out!" Alex yelled.

A massive force slammed into my side, throwing me several feet. The soft grass cushioned my landing a bit, but I fell on the shoulder that had been dislocated only two weeks earlier, and it screamed in pain. A dark shape leapt on me. I instinctively raised my arms to protect my head and neck, stopping a vicious mouth from tearing into me. Right about then I was regretting having sent Jason away from his sniper position.

One of the beasts that Connor had called forth towered over me. I could see it clearly, and it wasn't the face of an animal. Staring back at me was Lockien, with those same green eyes, tan hair and angular face that looked so much like Lilly's. However, his mouth had been torn wide to make room for triple rows of pointed teeth. Wicked scars and stitches were apparent where he had been torn open and sewn back up. The stitches were also at his neck where his head had been attached the body of a lion-like creature. All I could think was that I had seen him die. What had they done to him, and how had they brought him back to life, if you could even call it a life?

Tail raised high over his head, he prepared to strike.

"Lockien! It's me, Emma. Your father is here. These are your people. You don't want to hurt them. Do you understand me?"

Lockien didn't strike. Instead, he looked around in confusion at the chaos in the stadium. Then he looked down at his body as if trying to remember what had happened to him. Blinking rapidly, tears sprung to his eyes as he looked at me. That hideous mouth opened and closed, keening noises bubbling up from his damaged throat until he managed two raspy words, "Kill … me."

My own vocal chords clenched as a lump formed in my throat. I pulled my gun and placed it gently against his temple. He didn't move, only continued to plead silently with his eyes. Then those eyes darkened, and Lockien was gone again. The creature recognized its predicament immediately and struck out with its tail.

The scorpion stinger scraped along the skin of my right arm. The venom initially set my skin on fire, and then the paralysis began to spread down my arm. I had to act before it reached my gun hand.

"I'm sorry," I whispered, and then pulled the trigger.

Lockien fell on top of me, his bloody head resting on my shoulder. My arm fell uselessly at my side. Then Alex was there helping to roll the body off me.

"Manticores," he said, referring to the beast, not noticing its face. "As soon as the elves run out of bullets, they're done for. These things will eat them alive."

"Then let's finish this," I responded, gritting my teeth in determination. They were brave words, though difficult to execute in our condition. Alex was weakened to the point of uselessness. I had a paralyzed right arm and an injured left shoulder. We didn't make the most threatening pair, and it looked like we might be too late anyway.

Zane was fully thawed now and had Sharur lifted over his head, rich blue light pulsing through the blades like a living thing. My breath caught as he swung the axe downward. I was anticipating some dramatic opening of a doorway between worlds; instead, the axe thunked to the ground at Zane's feet. Zane doubled over, clutching his head, struggling to stifle a scream through clenched teeth.

I made a move toward him; however, Connor got there first, snatching up the axe in a flash. "Well, it looks like Plan A is a bust. On to Plan B," he said, giving me a sly smile. "I know you want this, and I want to give it to you, but ..."

"I am not going to use it," I said. "And now that I know you can't use it, either, I don't need it after all. I think I'll just go home to get a good night's sleep and kill you another day," I said, returning his smug smile.

"I'm willing to bet I can change your mind about using the axe," he said. "Bring him out," he yelled over his shoulder.

Two soldiers stepped out of the Mets' dugout, dragging a third figure between them. Their prisoner was thin, weak. He couldn't even walk under his own power, head hanging on his chest, wrists tied behind his back.

As they dragged him into the light, I recognized his blond hair immediately, even before Connor grabbed his hair, jerking his head up so I could see the prisoner's face.

"Daniel," I choked, taking a step forward. All of my bravado evaporated, and cold terror flooded my heart.

Connor put a gun to Daniel's head, and I stopped in my tracks. "Use the axe or he dies." Daniel's eye and cheek were bruised, his lip and forehead split, face coated in dried blood. His eyelids drooped, partially hiding a glazed look, like he had been drugged.

I didn't even waste a moment to debate it. "Give it to me," I said. Connor thrust the axe into my waiting left hand as I tried to ignore the pain in my shoulder. "When the rift is open, you will hand over Daniel to me, unharmed. Understand?"

"You have my word," he replied, as if his word meant anything to me.

My fingers closed around the shaft of the battle axe. It was surprisingly warm to the touch, and I could feel that familiar thrumming against my palm. The vibration ran up my arm, soothing my wounded shoulder until the pain was nothing except a dull ache. The blue light that had dimmed when Zane had dropped the object, flared to life even brighter than before. Sharur felt good in my hands, not too much weight, only enough at the head to make for a powerful blow.

I stepped past Zane who was still kneeling with his forehead touching the cool grass, taking deep breaths. I moved onto the dais and lifted Sharur above my head like I had seen Zane do. My eyes shifted between the men who held pieces of my heart: Daniel, Zane, and even Alex. I had to help them all get out of this alive, but I didn't know what I was supposed to do.

Focus, came a faint voice from so far away I thought I had imagined it. I looked sharply at Connor, but his eager expression didn't falter. He hadn't heard it.

I closed my eyes and concentrated, shutting out the sounds of gunfire, screams of terror, moans of pain. *Focus*, the voice said again, a little louder this time. *Hold in your mind the image of what you want.*

Maybe I was going crazy, or the stress was finally getting to me, but I found myself actually doing what the voice had said. Holding the image firmly in my mind, I let the axe fall, carried by the weight of the blade. Unexpected resistance met the blade, forcing me to put my body weight behind the downward stroke. It felt like cutting through cold butter with a plastic knife—not clean and easy, though not impossible, either.

When the tip of the blade touched the ground, I opened my eyes. In front of me was the doorway I had pictured in my mind. It started as a thin tear in the air that would have been unnoticeable in the dark, but then it began to separate. I could see no lands or armies inside the tear. There was nothing other than blackness. Yet the thick stench of smoke assaulted my nose. The thunder of footsteps, crash of steel, and growls of beasts reached my ears and grew louder with each passing second. The ground shook with their impending onslaught.

I stepped back, moving away from the rift. Turning to Connor, I shouted over the din of the battle and approaching host, "It's open. Now give Daniel to me."

While Connor was assembling what remained of his troops to storm the gateway, I reached into the pouch that hung at my waist and pulled out the device Benjamin had given me. I positioned myself to toss it into the rift the moment Daniel was out of Connor's grasp to collapse the gate before anything could get out. Connor barely glanced at me, waving to his soldiers to release Daniel.

They let go of Daniel's arms, dropping him to the ground at their feet. Doing my best impersonation of Mets hall-of-fame pitcher Tom Seaver, I snapped my arm forward with all the force I could muster. It would have been a perfect throw if Zane hadn't slammed into me with his full body weight right as I released the object, sending my pitch wild.

The device landed in the seating area where it imploded. In a split second, every seat, manticore and elf that had been standing within a hundred foot radius of it got sucked into a void. The void then collapsed upon itself, leaving behind a vast section of nothing except broken concrete.

Connor and his soldiers hesitated, uncertain whether I had any more of those devices.

Hot, angry tears sprung unbidden to my eyes. That had been my only chance of closing the rift, my only chance to save Earth. My murderous gaze landed on Zane; however, he was staring rapturously at the procession stepping through the gate onto Citi Field.

A team of scouts came through first. They looked like overgrown wolves with coarse gray fur and sharp eyes. They took in the sights and smells around them, but judging from their bored look, clearly didn't feel the elves, manticores and a human army were much of a threat. The largest wolf threw his head back and gave a long, keening howl, signaling the all clear.

One black boot stepped out from the darkness then another. Zane went to his knees at the sight of the man who stood on the dais. He didn't cut a very imposing figure: average height, average build, with neatly cropped black hair. His face was pale and weathered, but it was clear he had been very handsome in his youth, and some of that attractiveness remained. He wore a black tunic with a silver belt and a gray cloak on his shoulders.

Although he wasn't physically intimidating, his cold, black eyes were those of a highly intelligent and calculating individual. They darted around rapidly, landing on every point in the stadium, taking in the entire scene within moments. And, for a reason I didn't understand, he terrified the ever-living shit out of me.

His eyes landed on me, a slow smile spreading across his face, and it was all I could do to fight the urge to run. My stomach roiled at the sight of him, and all I wanted to do was find a closet to cower in.

So, this was the infamous Gabriel Marduk. I was so distracted by the sight of him that I almost missed the figure standing behind and to his right.

The woman was tall and slender with porcelain skin and pale yellow eyes that matched the color of her golden hair hanging in long, loose curls about her shoulders. She wore a white gown that fell to her feet, clinging to every feminine curve of her body. Over her gown was a rich, red cloak. A small smile played on her full lips, and when those lips parted, I could see bright white fangs. A vampire! Was there no end to this menagerie of creatures?

Connor came scurrying out of the shadows, like a rat out of a sewer. "As an emissary of the United States government, I order you to stop. If you take one more step onto U.S. soil, it will be seen as an act of war, and we will wipe you and your people from existence."

Marduk took one very slow and deliberate step forward. I fully expected Connor to transform into a cartoon character, with steam coming out of his ears and his eyes bugging out of his head. Connor opened his mouth, most likely to spew another impotent threat, when Marduk tired of him and gave the blonde woman a quiet order.

She moved faster than my eyes could follow, nothing more than a blur in the night, and she was at Connor's throat. He managed to get out a girlish shout of surprise before her fangs plunged into his jugular. I expected blood to gush from the wound, like I had seen in *True Blood*, but it was neat and clean. The vampire drank deep, not about to waste even one drop of blood. Connor's skin turned so pale he was almost translucent. His cheekbones sank in and his breathing became erratic.

When she was done, she unceremoniously dropped him onto the ground where he lay unmoving, and returned to Marduk's side. I didn't know whether Connor was dead or just really close to it, but I didn't care either way. He got what he deserved.

Marduk lifted his arms and spread them wide as if to embrace this new world. He said in a clear, booming voice, "Earth is finally ours. Take what you have been promised!"

Stomping, braying, fluttering, and howling erupted from the gateway behind him. All fighting between the elves and manticores froze as their attention was drawn to the rift. A terrible onslaught of creatures poured forth: ghouls, shadow demons, vampires, and other creatures I had no name for. They swarmed around and past me, heading straight for the exits.

Although they had been killing each other only moments before, the elves, manticores, and soldiers now stood side by side to prevent this new threat from escaping into the city. Jason emerged onto the field and joined in the efforts to keep the creatures at bay. They fought hard, blocking the exits, but it was fruitless. The number of creatures was overwhelming.

I looked down at the battle axe in my hand. Where was all of the power I had been promised when I really needed it? How could I possibly ever hope to stop this?

Looking around in confusion, my eyes landed on Marduk, who was approaching me with a satisfied smirk, keeping his arms held wide. He stopped in front of me with an expectant look. When I didn't respond, he said, "What, no hug for your father?"

The world spun out of control. I couldn't focus, couldn't think, couldn't breathe. What had he just said to me? The destroyer of worlds was my father? If so, what did that make me? A part of me thought the revelation explained a lot about why I was the way I was. The other part of me rebelled against the idea. He was lying; he must be. He was trying to manipulate me. But, then, why did it feel like the truth?

"Wh-what are you talking about?" I asked, swallowing hard.

"Ah, yes. Zane told me you lost your memory, but I thought for sure you would remember me. Not to worry, I am certain that can be remedied when you come home with me."

That shook me out my stupor. "I'm not going anywhere with you."

"Of course you are," he laughed.

Turning to the figure in the red cloak who still shadowed him, Marduk said, "Cressida, I would like you to meet my daughter, Ashnan. Ashnan, this is Cressida Lebeau, my advisor. She will see to it that you arrive home safely while I deal with things here."

The vampire stepped toward me, and I took a step back.

"I said, I am not going anywhere with you, or your advisor." I hefted Sharur and fell into a fighting stance, making my point crystal clear. I was significantly less effective fighting with my left hand, but Marduk didn't know that.

The smile dropped from his face, his lip curling up in a menacing snarl. I noticed his hand twitch, though he didn't follow through on the move to hit me. "Cressida, if you would be so kind."

"With pleasure," the vampire drawled in a husky voice. When she came to an abrupt stop back at her designated place behind Marduk, she was cradling the semi-conscious figure of Daniel in her arms. She made it look as if he weighed no more than a feather.

"Put him down, or I'll cut your undead head off," I said, trying to keep the fear out of my voice.

The vampire merely chuckled softly. Given the speed in which she had moved, I would never get close enough to hurt her, and even if I did, I wouldn't be strong enough to beat her.

"Don't be foolish. You belong in Urusilim, and you belong with me. If you truly care for this boy and want to keep him safe, you will come with me, and I will leave him here, unharmed."

"Why do you want me so badly?"

"You're my daughter. Isn't that enough of a reason?"

The answer was a resounding no; however, this wasn't the time or the place to argue the point. It didn't really matter anyway.

I looked around me at the dwindling numbers of defenders. The bodies of elves, soldiers, and beasts were strewn about the stadium; dark pools of blood mottled what had been a neatly groomed baseball diamond. I was relieved to see that Jason was still standing and looking uninjured, but for how long? I couldn't leave Earth behind and allow it to fall into the hands of these monsters.

"I will go with you ..." Marduk looked like the cat that ate the canary. "*But* ..."—I enjoyed watching that self-satisfied smile slip off his face—"only if you recall all of your creatures back through the rift, and Sharur stays here in the keeping of the Mage Council."

His initial rage turned to angry amusement. He snorted. "Who do you think you are, making demands of me? I should have Cressida take your head and be done with you. But I think you'll learn this lesson better if I take their heads instead." He waved toward the fighting elves, soldiers, and manticores barring the exits.

As if on cue, dozens of dragon-like creatures with great, leathery wings flew out of the rift, high into the night sky above Citi Field. They were beautiful, with scales of shimmering green.

"Take her," he said to the vampire.

"With pleasure," she hissed, dropping Daniel.

I didn't see Cressida move, but I knew she was coming. I fell to my knees, barely avoiding her grasp. Swinging Sharur, I buried the axe in the vampire's thigh. It certainly wasn't a fatal blow, although I hoped it might at least slow her down. She barely seemed to notice, painfully pulling me up by my long braid. I kept my grip on Sharur, yanking it free from the bone.

Bearing her fangs, Cressida pulled my head back and sunk her teeth into my flesh. I cried out at the initial bite, but then the pain subsided. Soothing warmth flooded through my body, calling on me to stop struggling and simply give in to that peaceful sensation. My fingers started to loosen on the axe handle when I heard that strange voice push its way clear of my muddled thoughts. *Kill her!*

I struggled to focus, but looking skyward, all I could think was how beautiful those dragons were, breathing arcs of orange flame. Everything moved in slow motion. Then I was falling. The ground rushed up to meet me and jarred me back to my senses.

Zane and the vampire were nose to nose, Zane breathing heavily and the vampire not breathing at all. "He said to take her home, not to drain her dry," Zane snarled.

"I had no intention of draining her," Cressida said calmly. "I was simply making her more docile for transport. Although, I now see why you find her so irresistible," she goaded.

I staggered to my feet, using the axe as a crutch. With a light toss, I spun it in the air, catching it so the handle was facing forward. I pulled back and threw it like a javelin straight at Cressida. The spike at the end of the axe handle pierced her rib cage and sunk deep into the vampire's heart. Momentary shock crossed her face before she exploded in a spray of blood and gore, all over Zane, but he didn't look too upset about it.

Before Zane could take up the call to drag me home, he was hit from behind by a barrage of icy blasts that came in rapid succession, preventing him from doing much more than try to protect himself. The ice was coating his skin faster than he could melt it off. Alex was buying me the time I needed to end this thing. I knew by looking at him that he had rallied all of his strength for this one last act.

Marduk was walking purposefully toward the exit from the stadium, trailed by a menagerie of his devoted followers. Although some creatures had immediately made a run for the exit when they had come through the rift, the majority had stayed within the stadium, following Marduk's commands. At this point, they were ready to march on New York City by his side.

I hesitated, not wanting to leave Alex, knowing he didn't stand a chance against Zane. But Marduk was making his way toward Jason, and the small group of defenders. Would Zane kill Alex or remember their old friendship and spare his life? I didn't want to take that chance; however, I couldn't let Marduk go. My mission wasn't yet finished.

Chapter Twenty-Seven

WITH VAMPIRE AND manticore venom still flowing through my veins, it felt like I was moving through molasses. Though, the vampire venom must have somehow counteracted the manticore venom because the feeling returned to my right arm.

I snatched up the now slippery axe from the puddle of vampire goo and took off after Marduk at a sprint, pressing through the inertia and throwing my body into overdrive.

Creatures threw themselves in my path, and I cut them down easily with Sharur, the axe blade slicing through flesh like Jell-O. Yet, even as the bodies piled up behind me, I knew the odds weren't in my favor. Only a handful of elves were left fighting. The rest were either dead or wounded. Alex would be incapacitated soon, and dragons were descending from the sky.

One well-placed blast of dragon fire would end me well before I could hope to reach Marduk. In the openness of the baseball field, there was nowhere to hide. I was a perfect target. Firing a gun into the sky at moving targets while running was no way to actually hit anything; therefore, I simply kept sprinting and hoped the dragons would ignore me, since I had no other options.

I closed in on Marduk's rear guard, chopping and hacking at them from behind. I took the first few creatures by surprise and was able to slice off heads and limbs without much of a fight. Blood and brains flew through the night air, splattering my face as I pushed through the throng. When the creatures finally took notice of me, they parted like the Red Sea at the sight of Sharur.

Marduk stopped walking and turned to see what was disrupting the group. I stood between the parted rows of creatures, covered from head to toe in gore, holding the axe at the ready and breathing heavily.

"We're not done here yet," I said.

"On the contrary, I believe we are. If you hadn't noticed, you are defeated. All of your elven and human friends are dead or will be very soon. Have some sense, girl, and join me."

"Actually, I invited some other friends to the party. They were just fashionably late." I removed a small stone from the pouch at my waist. Alex had given me the pink oblong crystal for exactly this moment. I dropped it at my feet and ground my heel into the object, crushing it. When it cracked open, a spark of light was released high into the night sky. It only lasted for a moment, but it illuminated the stadium as if it were daylight.

When the light faded and nothing more happened, Marduk laughed. "My dear child, you are going to have to do better than that."

"Oh, I did."

Just then, a blast of energy slammed into the crowd of creatures immediately surrounding Marduk, scattering them like so many bowling pins. Alcina, Ronin, and two other mages, all in flowing white robes, were blocking the exits from the stadium, holding glowing staffs.

Marduk spun to face this newest threat, and when he saw who it was, screamed into the sky in anger. "Alcina, you little bitch!"

The little girl merely smiled sweetly. "Don't tell me the big, bad Lord Marduk is afraid of little girls."

"Kill them!" he commanded his army.

Half of the monsters hesitated, not wanting to go up against the Mage Council, though some of the more confident or maybe more stupid creatures rushed forward.

I took advantage of the distraction and headed for Marduk. His back was to me, and I had a clear path right to him. I wouldn't get a better chance than this.

When I came within three leaps of Marduk, a brick wall slammed into my side, sending me reeling away from my target. Arms wrapped around me like a vice as we hit the ground, tumbling. I slammed my head back and heard the satisfying crack of a nose breaking. My captor grunted and loosened his grip enough to allow me to break the hold. I found my footing and spun around, swinging Sharur, but pulled back at the last instant when I saw my opponent was Zane.

"What did you do to Alex?"

"I didn't realize you cared about him so much. Are you trying to make me jealous?" he mocked, wiping blood from his nose with the back of his hand.

"Did you kill him?"

"And what if I did?"

"I would have to return the favor."

He gave a sharp, humorless laugh. "I don't think you would or could. After all, you still *love* me. Fortunately, I don't have such emotional weaknesses and plan to kill you without any remorse whatsoever." He lifted his hand, gathering that familiar orange glow I knew meant a fireball was on its way.

Before he could fully form it, I swung Sharur and smashed him in the temple with the flat of the axe blade. He fell to his knees, stunned, blood running down his temple.

I threw a roundhouse kick and knocked him fully to the ground. He tried to get his hands under him and push himself up; however, I sat on his back and put the shaft of the axe to his neck, pressing it into his throat. "Doesn't feel so good to have your air supply cut off, does it? Consider this payback for our meeting in the alley," I snarled close to his ear.

He tried rocking from side to side to throw me off, but I only pulled back harder on the shaft. His face turned red then blue. He gasped and gurgled, making weak wheezing sounds, before his eyes fluttered closed.

As soon as he lost consciousness, I released my hold. He took a shallow, rattling breath yet didn't awake. I could have killed him, but he had been right. I was still in love with him, and I had promised him I would try to find a cure to bring him back to me.

I stood and looked toward Marduk. A chaotic mass of writhing bodies blocked my view. I turned back toward centerfield, searching for Alex, but there were corpses everywhere, and I couldn't pick him out. I hoped that meant he wasn't among the dead or dying, but if he wasn't with me, where else would he be?

Alex might be past saving, and stopping Marduk was my priority; as a result, I decided my best course was to fight alongside the mages. I started to move in that direction when pain exploded across my back, causing me to stumble forward.

"Hurts, doesn't it?" came Zane's growl.

I turned and saw him wielding his staff like a baseball bat. He took another swing, aiming for my knees, and swept my legs out from under me. I fell hard on my ass, agony shooting through my hips. Zane stood over me and lifted the staff for the final blow to my head. He brought it down as I brought up Sharur, and the two weapons collided, sending a shocking jolt through my hands, though I managed to maintain a grip.

Zane stomped a foot down on my stomach, and I doubled over with a breathless "oomph." He began raining kicks on my sides, cracking a rib in the process, while looking for an opening to swing the staff again. I was in a terrible position, prone on my back with my hands full, trying to block his staff, unable to protect my vulnerable body from the vicious blows of his heavy boots.

"You were too weak to kill me; now I'm going to make you regret that decision," Zane said with a hint of glee in his voice.

Maybe he was right. It wasn't like me to show mercy. Maybe I should have just finished him, but the point was moot. I would die at his hands.

The pain wracking my body was unbearable. I couldn't take a breath without searing torment in my chest from the cracked rib. I was taking fast, shallow breaths to avoid the rib pain, but dizziness overcame me from the lack of oxygen.

I couldn't focus through the haze in my brain. I felt a great distance arise between the fighting and me. Even the pain was starting to feel farther away. Blackness crowded the edges of my vision. All I had to do was let it in, and I would be free from this agony, from this battle, from Zane, Marduk, and the Mage Council. Maybe it was time to lay down the axe.

Then Zane was gone, and the blows stopped. I blinked into the night sky, and hovering above me was a dragon. Zane was sprawled on the ground a few dozen feet away after being body slammed by the great beast. The creature let loose a stream of fire in Zane's direction, but Zane threw up a shield. Then another dragon flew in low and plucked Zane from the ground, carrying him off into the night sky.

The dragon that stood next to me began to transform, shrinking. It's bright green scales turned to smooth pale skin until a naked man was on all fours, leaning over me with concern.

"Hey, love. Don't give up on me now. I haven't even had a chance to shag you yet."

"Eddie?" I managed to squeak. His unremarkable features came into focus. I had never been so happy to see anyone in my life. Tears sprung unbidden to my eyes.

"Yeah, love, it's me. I always could make the girls cry," he teased.

"But Alex killed you."

"Nah. Shifters are damn hard to kill. Your bloke and I had planned the whole thing. He needed to know whether you were telling the truth about your memory loss and which side you were really on. Me and my shifters have been wanting to get free of Marduk without raising suspicion, and Alex needed to know whether I could be trusted. The whole thing on the train was a good, all-around test, and we all passed."

I was struggling to follow his words. I was unbelievably freaking tired. "What's happening? Marduk?"

"Let's get you on your feet." Eddie gently put his arms around me and helped me up. I leaned heavily on him, barely able to stand under my own power. We looked at the crowd of battling creatures and mages. It had thinned out quite a bit. Bodies littered the ground, but many more of the creatures were retreating. The group was steadily being driven back toward the rift.

Then the dozen dragons that had been flying in circles above the field swooped down and turned against their former allies. They dove into the masses of monsters, biting, clawing, and burning. The shrieks and wails grew louder, and many turned tail and rushed headlong back through the rift.

"All of the dragons are shifters?"

"Indeed they are," Eddie said with pride.

As Marduk's army broke and ran, only a small handful of defenders remained by his side—a few ghouls, another vampire, three of those gargoyle creatures that had helped

Zane and I escape from North Brother Island— but it wasn't enough.

The elves and manticores, along with Jason, had regrouped and joined the mages, and the shifters were now on our side. While we didn't have the numbers, the elves had human weapons; the manticores had poison; and not only did the mages have powerful magic, but holding them back until the end had ensured they were fresh and strong when we needed them the most.

With the rift close at our backs, dragons landed on all sides of Marduk's party. The fighting was over when Marduk realized they were defeated.

I shrugged Eddie off, wanting to approach my father under my own power. I tried to walk with confidence and a straight back, but my injuries wouldn't allow it. I probably looked and shuffled along more like a zombie from *The Walking Dead*.

"I should have them kill you where you stand," I said.

"You would murder your own father, the only flesh and blood left to you? I think not. You don't even have a clue as to what's going on here. You think you're fighting for good, for justice, for freedom. Well, think again. You, my child, are on the wrong side of this war, and you will learn that soon enough. These traitorous mages will take off their masks eventually. The only question is whether it will be too late for you when they do."

That was not at all the speech I was expecting from him. I expected the ranting and ravings of a lunatic monarch calling for world domination or even groveling and begging for mercy. This information gave me pause. I knew for sure I couldn't trust Marduk, yet I also didn't trust the mages. Sure, they had come to my aid tonight, but the price they had asked was to take possession of Sharur. They had claimed they would seal it away; however, the elves certainly hadn't believed them, so why should I? I had never had any intention of handing it over anyway.

Marduk was right, though, that I still didn't fully understand the politics of this situation. I was in the battle only to save earth from being overrun by monsters. I had been mostly successful, although a number of creatures had slipped out of the stadium and into the city during the chaos of the battle. Short of that objective, I didn't really know why Marduk wanted to come through to Earth, why the mages wanted Sharur, or even why the elves had decided to get involved rather than hunker down in their quiet corner of the world like they had been doing for years.

"He is our prisoner now," came Alcina's small voice. "He will be brought before the Council and given a trial before his execution."

"That doesn't sound like a very fair trial if you've already determined he will be executed," I said. It's not that I cared much about what happened to Marduk, but the statement gave me some insight into the workings of the Council.

"I doubt he can say much that will save his life, but he will be granted the opportunity," she said, looking none too pleased at being challenged by me.

"You are too kind, Alcina, as usual," Marduk sneered. "But a trial will not be necessary." From behind Marduk, another vampire that had been in his party stepped forward. He looked like Cressida's twin brother, with golden curls and yellow eyes. He could have been a model for any of Michelangelo's statues, including David.

The vampire was holding a now unconscious Daniel in his arms. "This is one of yours, is he not?" Marduk asked me, like he was offering me a cup of tea.

I tensed, my muscles bunching painfully in my neck and shoulders. "Hand him over," I said between clenched teeth.

"But of course, as long as you allow me free passage through the rift."

"No!" barked Alcina.

Turning to me, she said, "We cannot sacrifice all we have done for the sake of one human boy. This is war, and in war, there are casualties. It is the Council's decision, and we will not allow Marduk to walk away from this. I'm sorry."

She didn't really sound like she was sorry. Although, it did seem almost absurd that we would have fought for so long and hard tonight against this enemy only to allow him to walk away in the end when we had him dead to rights. However, Daniel was my family, more so than Marduk, and I wasn't about to lose him.

"Release him and go," I said to Marduk.

A satisfied smile crept across his face, right before a high-pitched scream pierced the air. I spun to face Alcina, who was in the throes of a tantrum. Her face turned bright red, and her small fists were clenched at her sides. It would have been amusing if not for the knowledge that the little brat could raise serious hell on Earth.

She lifted her glowing staff and threw out a bolt of white hot electricity aimed for Marduk. I dove out of its path, the fine hairs all over my body standing on end from the static electricity.

The bolt hit the ground where Marduk had been standing only a split second earlier. The vampire had moved faster than lightning to pull Marduk out of the way. The creatures in his army were forming a wall around him, and they were all moving him quickly toward the rift.

"Stop!" I screamed at Alcina. "They are going to take Daniel with them if you don't stop." She was beyond hearing though.

She threw another bolt, blasting one of the gargoyles into rubble.

"Marduk, leave him," I screamed at my father.

The vampire was still holding Daniel and looked to Marduk for orders. Marduk paused long enough to give me a wolfish grin and said, "Under the circumstances, I think I would be better off with a hostage, my dear. I'm sure you understand." Then they were gone, stepping through the rift and into the void beyond.

With all of her fury fueling her magic, Alcina threw one last bolt at Marduk as he retreated through the rift, barely missing him. Instead, the blast caught the edge of the gateway, creating instability. The doorway shuddered, throwing off sparks, its edges contracting and expanding wildly. Everyone in the vicinity backed away to a safer distance. The portal collapsed with a searing flash of light and an invisible concussive wave that slammed into us, knocking us all off our feet. Then the night was quiet and dark once again.

I had just gotten unsteadily back to my feet, leaning on Sharur for assistance, when Alcina came at me like a feral kitten. "This is all your fault!" she raged. "Because of you, he escaped. Do you have any idea how long I've been waiting to get him in a position where he could be arrested?"

Ronin stepped up behind her, placing a restraining and comforting hand on her shoulder. It made her pause, and I could see her forcibly trying to regain her composure.

"At least we can salvage some of this mess. Give me the axe, as we agreed."

"I didn't agree to that," I reminded her. "We agreed to discuss the disposition of Sharur after we won the battle."

"Fine. Sharur belongs under the protection of the Mage Council. You have no right to claim it. Consider the matter discussed. Now, hand it over," she retorted with her staff glowing again. The threat was clear.

I clutched the axe tighter, knuckles whitening, frantically trying to think of a way out of this where I got to keep Sharur. However, Alcina would never allow it, not under any circumstances. Eddie came up close beside me in dragon form. He must have shifted unnoticed while Alcina had been throwing her tantrum. Our eyes met in a wordless exchange.

I slid an arm across his scaly neck, grabbed onto one of the horns adorning his head, and vaulted myself onto his back right as Eddie spread his wings and made a powerful leap into the air. When a bolt of electricity chased us into the sky, Eddie banked sharply to the left to avoid being hit. I almost fell from his back, scrambling to gain a better hand hold.

The other dozen dragons lifted into the sky, as well, in a flurry of wings and fire. They spit streams of flames in the direction of the small group, forcing them to scatter. The elves, with Jason, regrouped and retreated from the stadium, having no interest in lending the mages their support. The manticores fumbled about confused and without a master until Alcina took out her rage on them, slaughtering every last one with lightning.

Before the mages retreated, I saw them pull a body from the carnage and carry it out of the stadium. Based on size and build, I was pretty certain it was Alex. Was he still alive, or were they recovering his corpse to give him an appropriate burial? I tried to follow them, but they were quickly swallowed by the darkness surrounding the stadium. I refused to believe that the strong, steadfast, determined man who had just started to become a friend could be gone forever. I decided in that moment to believe he was still alive, and to find him.

Eddie and his clan climbed on air currents until we were high above the city, unseen. The cool air rushing past my face and through my hair felt exhilarating and cleansing. The soft beating of dragon wings was comforting, and all I wanted to do was sleep for days or maybe weeks. I rested my head on Eddie's warm neck and gazed at the sparkling splendor of Manhattan below us.

My beautiful, crazy, uncaring, soulful, hard, and loving city. It was a city of contradictions, and I supposed I was too. Born of an evil man, loved by an insane man, defined by my job as a killer, and yet, the unlikely savior of humanity. I laughed quietly until I remembered this had only been the beginning.

Some creatures had escaped the stadium and would be roaming the city, looking for places to hide and people to eat. The mages would not let Sharur go so easily. I would be hunted relentlessly by the Council as well as the U.S.

government. I had to find Alex, and hope I could convince him to take my side over the Council's.

I had also made a promise to Nathan and I fully expected he would hold me to it. I didn't know Nathan's true purpose in all of this, nor did I know how Vincent Darko fit into the picture — the two men were mysteries I was determined to solve. Most importantly, I needed to find a way to rescue Daniel from Marduk. And, the hardest of all, I had to fulfill my vow to Zane. Though, for now, I needed sleep.

I closed my eyes and allowed myself to drift into a dreamless slumber while Eddie carried me to safety. I didn't know where that was; however, for some reason, I trusted him. I would figure out the rest later.

To be continued…